D1345480

CUBAN PASSAGE

A teenage boy left in Cuba during his father's absence on a business trip rebels against the domination of his mother's powerful, sinister Cuban lover, and determines on a violent solution. Tutored in toughness by an American dropout scarcely older than he is, who introduces him to life on Havana's waterfront, Dick Frazer trains for his mission with revolutionary fervour, and just as David slew Goliath, so he triumphs over Juan Stilson. Or seems to.

From then on Dick is in the hands of Cuban justice, and Fate, which Stilson still seems able to manipulate, decrees that every circumstance of his life, past and present, shall tell against him. His mother, his American friend, the British Embassy staff, an English lawyer, are powerless to help, as the boy is swept into the vortex of inefficiency, corruption and confusion which marks the death-throes of the Cuban state.

For Dick's is not the only rebellion. From the hills of the interior the insurrection that has been brewing for months and has for months been dismissed as a little local uprising, now sweeps down on Cuba's capital, led by Fidel Castro and his young revolutionaries. Ignorant though they are of Dick's existence, these young men are to become the real arbiters of his fate.

In this powerful, brilliantly characterized novel, Norman Lewis, whom V. S. Pritchett describes as 'one of our very few capable experts in the novel of the exotic and revolutionary setting', portrays with sardonic sympathy and insight the last days of a tottering regime and the rites of passage by which a boy becomes a man.

CUBAN PASSAGE

NORMAN LEWIS

COLLINS
14 St James's Place, London

William Collins Sons & Co. Ltd
London · Glasgow · Sydney · Auckland
Toronto · Johannesburg

British Library Cataloguing in Publication Data

Lewis, Norman
Cuban Passage.
I. Title
823'.914[F]   PR6062.E95

ISBN 0 00 222620 0

First published 1982
© Norman Lewis 1982

Photoset in Times Roman
Made and Printed in Great Britain by
William Collins Sons & Co. Ltd, Glasgow

PART ONE

Chapter One

Visiting the harbour café in the first cool of the evening had become a social habit of the city. People sat there to calm and steady their vision with a pacific vista of ships, and to catch a little of the emotions of travel, the gaiety of arriving and the melancholy of departure. Women believed that tar and brine in the breeze benefited their complexions, while the men who brought them here clung to the legend that the shellfish for which the café was famous improved their virility. So they chewed prawns, threw scraps to test the unerring swoop of the terns circling overhead, listened to the sweet, rootless music of the house-musicians' flutes, and sniffed at the odour of fine cigars mingled with those of the ocean, and thus the hours slipped by.

There was no better place in Havana, Hollingdale believed, to introduce a newcomer to the rich and complex flavours of local life. For this reason he had brought here the new junior man at the Embassy, Sanger, who was being shown the ropes. They were discussing the national character.

'You'll find them easy to like,' Hollingdale said, 'amiable, shallow and profoundly superstitious. This must be the only capital city in the world where Woolworth's have a counter stacked with charms and voodoo paraphernalia. One of the ministers in the present government is said to belong to an African cult practising human sacrifice. Presidents start off as starry-eyed idealists and finish as monsters. They still have a law on the statute book giving a woman the right to be present when her husband is tortured.'

Sanger made a face. 'And most people speak English, you say?'

'In the city, anyway. This is virtually an American colony. Ah yes, one thing I ought to tell you. Should you have intercourse with a local woman you must remember to thank her profusely after the act. She will do the same.'

'Useful to know,' Sanger said. Hollingdale did not join his brief laughter. A side-glance at his superior assured Sanger that he was quite serious. The information, conveyed in the driest and most matter-of-fact tone, had been made to sound like a statistic. It was something about Hollingdale that Sanger much admired; part of the professional approach – an attitude that went with the crispness of the ill-fitting tropical suit bought off the peg at Lillywhite's. Sanger, observing him, was conscious and ashamed of the sweat-stain spreading from the armpits of his jacket.

'What about this rebellion?' Sanger asked.

'Eighty-two zealots bent on changing the face and destiny of this incorrigible land started it off in Oriente eighteen months ago. They were ready and willing to throw away their lives and most of them did.'

'But the thing still keeps going?'

'It's dead,' Hollingdale said, 'but it won't lie down.'

'Cameron called it an invention of the press.'

'That's not quite true, but it's been blown up by the newspapers out of all proportion to its significance. After all, it sells papers.'

'But you think it will come to nothing?' Sanger asked.

'It *has* come to nothing. Quite shortly now it will either be suffocated – or even more probably it will simply peter out. What can you expect? A couple of hundred crack-brained university dropouts and middle-class unemployables led by a bearded and bespectacled lawyer taking on the best equipment and best-trained army in Latin America, with the US at its back? In one year from now it will have been forgotten.'

'That's a comfort.'

'Leave me to worry about the rebellion. It's my job. If

6

there's anything turns up I feel you should know I'll be the first to tell you. Otherwise don't let it bother you.'

'I won't.'

There was a lapse in their conversation as the eddies of excitement reached them from the quayside where a spruce white ship of the Grace banana fleet was about to leave for New York. Several hundred streamers stretched and snapped. The enforced outcry of farewells, the routine jollities passing between the passengers lining the ship's stern and the friends and relatives who had come to see them off, quietened, then were silenced. An exceedingly beautiful woman accompanied by a boy who had been among the quayside crowd came towards them, turned to wave for the last time in the direction of the departing ship, then sat down at a nearby table.

'Don't see too many blondes in this part of the world, I imagine,' Sanger remarked.

'The ones you do are foreigners,' Hollingdale said, 'British, Americans, a German once in a while.' He dropped his voice. 'The lady in question is Mrs Frazer. Her husband has just gone off on that ship, leaving his most attractive wife alone and unprotected. My fear is that sooner or later she may provide us with a headache.'

'Why do you say that?'

'Because professionally we're bound to keep an eye on her.'

'You mean she attracts the attention of predatory males?'

'It's something that can't be avoided in a place like this. A man called Juan Stilson is about to move in. He's a friend of her husband, and a frightful thug.'

'Pity,' Sanger said. 'Looks such a nice quiet girl. Still, that's the way it so often is. Bad men seem to have something that good men like you and me lack.'

Hollingdale withheld amusement. 'Caryl Frazer's a lively, intelligent woman. Illustrates children's books in her spare time, *Guardian* reader, interested in Third World problems. Stilson's a wide boy; subtle, persuasive and corrupt. He has a finger in every pie. What's unusual is he used to do a mind-

7

reading act in a cabaret. Not for the money. Just for the fun of it.'

'All the same, we don't really have to worry about people having a bit on the side, do we?' Sanger asked.

He was disciplined with a slight frown.

'We could find ourselves involved. Love-affairs in this country can be dangerous. We have a responsibility towards any of our nationals who get into trouble. There is a personal involvement, too, as I happen to know the family. To be frank, this has the makings of a disaster, and I'm worried.'

'I'm sorry,' Sanger said. 'And the boy's the son, is he?'

'The boy's the son, Dick.'

'Hard to believe she could have a son of that age.'

'She's in her mid-thirties, although I agree you'd never guess. The boy's our second potential headache. He was tried for arson under the Children and Young Persons' Act and did a year in Stoneyfields. You could call him disturbed. Possibly very disturbed.'

'Nothing should surprise me, but that does. He looks as if butter wouldn't melt in his mouth. What actually happened?'

'I don't know all the details. Set fire to a number of cars, as I understand.'

'He looks so quiet, so placid.'

'That particular brand usually does.'

Sanger was fascinated by the discretion shown by the males in their vicinity as they subjected Mrs Frazer to their appraisal; the long earnest contemplation screened by raised newspapers, the side-movement of eyes, like that of Indian dancers, in heads that remained pointed to the front. Mrs Frazer's face was seen in profile, and all he could see of it proclaimed candour and innocence. It was the face of an early Italian painting of a child that was still part angel. The sunshine and a stirring of breeze moved softly among the fair ringlets of hair, and when Mrs Frazer took a white carnation from a vase standing amid the squalor of prawn husks on the table to hold it to her cheek, Sanger saw Filippo Lippi's irreproachable Lucrezia, recreated for him in this

8

tender light. She had turned her face from the direction of the departing ship, now a quarter of a mile away, dragging a creamed wake like a comet's tail towards the pearly distances of the bay.

The boy – fifteen years old, Sanger would have said – showed interest in the terns. He picked up the remains of a demolished prawn and bent to place it on the ground within reach of his foot. As he straightened two squealing birds hovered above him. Folding their wings, they swooped in perfectly matched flashing curves, and one, snatching up the prawn in full flight, shot up fifty feet into the air with it, chased by the loser, screaming its frustration. The boy tugged at his mother's arm, laughing to draw her attention.

'So that's Dick,' Sanger said.

'That's Dick, and now here comes Stilson. Just watch what happens.'

A black Cadillac which had nosed stealthily through the harbour gates crept towards them.

'Enter the Black Knight,' Hollingdale said. 'Let me explain. There's a pecking order here in the way you park your car. You're not supposed to bring your car into the port area at all, but if you do and you get away with it, that means you're already someone to contend with.' All the unofficial car-parking space round the café was already taken. The Cadillac stopped. There was a soft bleat from its horn.

'Ugly beast, isn't it?' Hollingdale said. 'Sinister with those fishtails. Just like a shark.'

'What's going to happen?'

'Somebody's going to have to make room for him.'

In fact two men sitting at different tables had got up at the same moment and were hurrying down towards the Cadillac. One of the men, seeing himself outdistanced, went back and sat down, seeming to Sanger to have suffered a small defeat. The other reached the car; the electric window slid down, and he bent his head to talk to the driver, of whom only a shoulder and an arm were to be seen. After a moment he straightened, raised his hand in something between a wave and a salute, went to one of the parked cars, got in, started up and drove it some fifty yards to an opening among a number of upturned boats.

'Stilson is one of the six top car-parkers in this town,' Hollingdale said. 'Most people think it pays to stay on the right side of him.'

Stilson climbed out of the car and straightened himself. He threw back his head, showing the café assemblage a two-thirds profile in the manner of General MacArthur, and Sanger catalogued the sparkle of sun-bleached greying hair, the clipped moustache, the loud Madison Avenue shirt, the Bermuda tan, and the eyes clenched in the style of a Man of Achievement in an old *Esquire* advertisement. Only the Hathaway patch was missing. Making towards Caryl Frazer's table, he reached for outstretched hands like an American presidential candidate.

'More dangerous than he looks,' Hollingdale commented. 'He was involved in an unpleasant case over a teenage girl he was alleged to have imprisoned in a farmhouse somewhere and seduced by the administration of drugs. They also say he ran one of those private armies you hear about used to keep the peasants in their place. I once saw him hypnotize a chicken at a party. Not an edifying sight.'

'Whatever makes women fall for them?'

'Something we shall never know.'

Stirring eddies of interest in the vicinity, Stilson had reached Caryl's table. He raised her fingers to his lips, clasped Dick's shoulders, and settled in a chair. Two waiters had sprung from the earth at his back to compete good-naturedly for his order.

'So despite all our pleadings dear old Andrew decided to leave us,' Stilson said.

'There wasn't any option,' Caryl told him. 'The Far Eastern trip couldn't be put off any longer. He stayed a week longer than planned as it was.'

'It's been too short,' Stilson said. 'We shall all miss him. Tell him that when you write.'

'I will,' she said. 'I know he enormously enjoyed his stay.'

'And how long can we hope to have you with us?'

'Two months,' she said. 'If the money holds out.'

They both laughed. 'And tell me, Dick,' Stilson said, 'how are you faring today? Tell me, how is life with you?'

Dick, who had been called to attention by an urgent nudge from his mother, mumbled something into his hands.

Stilson nodded affably, pretending to have heard. 'Enjoying life in Cuba, I hope?'

'You've been having a wonderful time, haven't you, Dick?' his mother said.

Dick hated having his mind made up for him. 'No,' he said. 'I haven't really, Mum.'

'I'm very sorry to hear it, Dick,' Stilson said. 'How's that? What do you put it down to?'

'Dick's not quite himself today,' Caryl said.

'He's sorry to see his father go. That is to be expected.'

'I didn't like it here even before he went,' Dick said. 'There's nothing to do.'

'Well, that does surprise me,' Stilson said. 'That's a situation we shall have to do something about. What do you like to do, Dick?'

'I like to make things,' Dick told him. He had turned his face away in the hope that this would be interpreted as a sign that he had no wish to continue the discussion. Picking up the last langoustine's claw, he threw it towards a tern hovering hopefully near by.

Stilson insisted. 'So you make things. Well, that's what I call creative. I like that. What do you make?'

'The last thing I made was a two-stage rocket, but I never got it right.'

Stilson and Caryl exchanged quick surreptitious glances. 'We don't have much in the way of facilities for that kind of thing here,' Stilson said. 'We go in more for sporting activities. Do you like cars, for instance? I'll bet you do. I'll bet you go for them in a big way.'

The tern had taken the claw in full flight, changing direction with infinitesimal adjustments of its pinions to soar with it to a mast-top.

'Do you know what a Stutz Bearcat is?'

'Dick, Mr Stilson is asking you a question,' Caryl said.

11

'I'm sorry, Mr Stilson. No, I don't.'

'It's one of the classic cars of the past,' Stilson said. He rolled his lips together, eyes withdrawn, as if trying to identify an elusive flavour. 'I have a souped-up version in my stable that can do nought to eighty in eleven seconds. How would you like to drive a car like that? I also own one of those new Dodge beach-buggies. Would that be of interest? Any time you want to try it out, all you have to do is to speak up.'

'I'm too young to drive,' Dick said.

'Not in this country you aren't. If you want to drive one of my cars and if I say it's OK, all you have to do is get in behind the wheel and drive and nobody will say you nay.'

Caryl's laugh failed to conceal misgivings. 'Well, I don't know that I'm altogether happy about that. Much as I don't think I'm an over-protective mother, beach-buggies and Bearcats for a boy who can't drive do sound a trifle risky.'

'Another suggestion then. Horse-riding. We have the latest in dude ranches just out of town. You dress up in Western style and they teach you to rope steers and use a six-shooter. It's possible even to qualify as guest-sheriff, but it can take a few months to win your way through to that particular badge.'

'I don't – ' Dick began.

'I assume you don't, Dick, and I was ready for it,' Stilson said. 'If you don't ride you can drive a stage-coach, or you can just sit in one. All tastes and degrees of ability are catered for.' He explained to Caryl, 'There's a waiting list to join as long as my arm, but I think we could slip round that one.'

Hollingdale and Sanger looked on. 'I hate to use the word "Greaser",' Hollingdale said, 'but there are times when it can be peculiarly descriptive. I'm told our friend went to an American university, which probably did little to change him. The strategy appears to be to cultivate the boy as part of the plan for ingratiating himself with the mother.'

'He's not getting very far with him by the look of it,' Sanger said. 'He looks terribly bored.'

'Probably resentful too. I would be if I were in his shoes.'

12

'Young people seem to have an instinct in things like this, don't they?' Sanger said.

Dick appealed silently to his mother, who was unreceptive to his SOS. From Stilson's description it was clear to him that dude-ranching came under the heading of having nothing to do. He felt uncomfortable at Stilson's over-insistent interest.

'But why didn't I think of it before?' Stilson asked. 'Sea-fishing for big fish. That's the answer.'

'Isn't it very expensive, besides requiring a lot of skill?' Caryl said.

'In Dick's case expense wouldn't come into it, because I've just bought myself a new toy – a deep-sea fishing-boat. As for skill, a couple of hours' tuition, that's all. You'll go a long way to find anything to equal game fishing for involvement and challenge, and it's the ultimate in excitement. Ever done any fishing, Dick?'

'In a river.'

'With a hook baited with a worm, am I right?'

'Yes.'

'Well, you'd find this somewhat different. It doesn't happen all the time, but you could get into a tussle lasting several hours with a fish weighing up to two hundred pounds. You wouldn't be bored.'

'Who could be?' Caryl said. 'He loves the sea.'

'And there's no better way of getting to know it,' Stilson said. His eyes were half closed and a slight drone had entered his voice. 'In all its moods. Game fishing calls for dedication and stamina of a special kind. Really, Dick – and I mean this – it's something you have to try. Would you have any objection to Dick coming out with me in the boat, Caryl?'

'I? Certainly not. There's nothing dangerous about it, is there?'

'The most that's going to happen to him is that he's going to give his muscles a bit of a work-out. Tell you what, we're going out on Sunday. Just a short trip over the reef. Nothing to set the pulse racing in the way of fish. Grab ourselves a few jack-snappers and maybe stake out our claim to any marlin that happens to come swimming by. But apart from that, strictly a pleasure trip, and I'd be very glad to have Dick come along. I think he'd be interested even if he doesn't want to fish himself. It would be a nice introduction to the sport.'

'It's a wonderful opportunity,' Caryl said. 'He's a lucky boy.'

As if Caryl's agreement were all he had been waiting for, Stilson glanced down at his watch, muttered his surprise at the passage of time and jumped to his feet. 'A poor fellow whose existence I'd quite forgotten, waiting patiently for me in my office. Caryl, I'm sorry . . .' He took her hand and bent over it. 'Dick – be seeing you, huh?'

Dick scuffled back in his chair to avoid Stilson's embrace as he reached out to him. Stilson's expression tightened for an instant, then he backed away, smiling and waving, and three men got up to bow as he passed. A moment later his Cadillac shot away from the kerbside, its horn bleated twice to clear the traffic from its path, and he was gone.

'That's a relief,' Dick said.

'I simply can't understand why you should have been so rude,' his mother told him. 'You wouldn't even put yourself out to say goodbye.'

'Why should I, if I didn't feel like it? And Mum, why do *you* have to decide what I want to do and what I don't want to do?'

'Because you'd never do anything if I didn't give you a push.'

'This is different. You could see I didn't want to go out with that man, couldn't you? I don't want to have anything to do with him at all, so it's useless for you to tell him I'll go fishing with him on Sunday when I won't.'

She gave him the soft but invincible smile that clinched all their arguments. 'But you will, dear. You're going on the fishing trip with Mr Stilson, as arranged. And what's more you're going to enjoy yourself like you always do when I push you into doing something you say you don't want to do.'

'Well, we'll see about that,' he said.

Chapter Two

When Dick looked in one direction at the sea it was black, but in the other, against the light, it was powdered and whitened as if under hoar-frost, and the far horizon was creamed by a Norther coming in on the limits of vision, which, said Stilson, would take three hours to arrive. They were over the reef now, the water moving in great shining folds over the pink stains spreading from the coral heads. Seagulls settled nearby in a white chaplet on the surface and were suddenly snatched from sight as they dived. Dick could see the fish flickering like shadows over the coral. Stilson had come up behind him and Dick flinched when he laid his hand on his shoulder.

'Want me to fix up a line for you, Dick?'

'No, thanks, Mr Stilson.'

'Just so long as you're not bored. You're not bored, huh?'

'I'm not bored, Mr Stilson, I'm just looking at the fish.'

'They're pretty intelligent. More than you'd think. They come in here where the boats can't reach them with their nets. They're safe. Or so they think.' There was a faint metallic resonance in Stilson's laughter. 'We play our little tricks on them,' he said.

He went to take over the wheel, and Dick moved behind the deck-house where he would be out of Stilson's view, and he could watch without being watched. A crew member passed, carrying a large spanner. He looked through Dick, giving no indication that he was aware of his presence. There was something strange about this boat. The crew could have been deaf-mutes, because none of them ever appeared to speak, and Stilson transmitted his orders in a kind of sign language, by a crook of the finger or a nod of the head.

A youth came into sight carrying a rod. He had a

bleached-out look; blisters over the cheekbones, white eyelashes, sun-scaled ears and a dazed and ragged smile.

'I'm Jerry Carmichael. Who are you?'

'I'm Dick Frazer.'

'What are you fishing for, Frazer?'

'Nothing. I don't fish.'

'What are you doing here, then?'

'I got talked into coming on the trip.'

'By who?'

'Mr Stilson. I couldn't get out of it.'

Carmichael spat on the deck. 'How do you come to know the guy?'

'My father's firm sells him plant for his sugar mills. We were over here for a holiday and they got friendly.'

'He's an asshole,' Carmichael said. 'I go out with him to catch a shark or two. He likes to do a favour for my old man. They have something going together. I left home.'

'You don't live with your father?'

'Not any more, since he went off with a broad. I catch sharks and sell the fins to the Chinese. When the shark-fishing season is over, I work the boxes.'

'What's that?'

'I shine shoes. Make up to ten dollars on a good day. That way I can drink whisky and buy myself a piece of tail when I want.'

'A piece of tail?'

'A piece of ass. A broad. A hooker.'

'You mean a whore.'

'Right, a whore. That's what I mean.'

'Where do you live?'

'On the wharf. I sleep under a boat. Anywhere. I'm down at the Anchor Poolroom when I'm not fishing or out with the box. Stop by some time. I'll show you round. Ask anyone for Mr Carmichael. They all know me.'

Stilson jerked back his head in the direction of the crew member with the spanner, who was tightening a bolt, and the man took the wheel from him. He found Dick with Carmichael behind the deck-house. 'So you two guys got together, huh? Sorry I couldn't introduce you, Dick. Jerry

16

was throwing up in the can when you came aboard. You all right now, Jerry? What tackle are you using today?'

'Light plug gear with a wire lead.'

'Well, maybe you won't need it. We've got a warm current and the big fish are moving into deep water. If you get anything it won't be for the book. You want to change your mind about taking a hand in the sport, Dick?'

'Thanks, Mr Stilson. I'd rather look on.'

'Anyway, it's a wonderful day, huh? And a nice change, I'd have said, to get out here and fill your lungs with fresh air after being cooped up in that hotel. Mother happen to say anything to you about the possible move to the country by any chance?'

'No, she didn't,' Dick said.

'Well, in that case I'd better not go into details. There was some talk of a change of scene, that's all. I thought she might have mentioned it.'

Dick shook his head.

'Well, I expect she will in her own good time.'

Stilson turned to scan the horizon from which tiny puffs of cloud were going up like cannon smoke. 'Blowing up over there,' he said. 'We have about a couple of hours left to fish. I guess I'll go get my rod.'

They watched him go aft.

'That your mother you were with on the quay?' Carmichael asked.

'That's right.'

'D'ya see the way he was looking at her?'

'Who, Stilson?'

'Sure, Stilson.'

'How was he looking at her?'

'The way a guy like that looks at any doll. He supposed to be a friend of your old man's?'

'Yes.'

'Somebody should have warned him.'

'What do you think I can do?'

'Christ, Frazer. You're his son, aren't you? Lemme tell you. If I had an old lady, I wouldn't sit around with my hands under my ass and let Stilson lay her.'

17

The boat slowed down, swung round and began to feel its way up a tight lane in the coral. Stilson was back and he and Jerry Carmichael went back to the taffrail to fish. Following them, Dick heard the hiss of Stilson's reel, then the splash as his lure struck the water, bounced once and sank. Seconds later the line went taut and Stilson began to reel in. He lifted a five-pound jack-snapper over the rail, unhooked it with the faintest sound of tearing cartilage, and dropped it on the deck. Dick watched the fish arch and straighten its back, watched its shuddering leaps as it tried to escape from its waterless prison, and the brusque change of its colours – glowing here, fading there, as its blood starved of oxygen.

Stilson made his second cast, and conjured another fish instantly from the water. The process, repeated several times in as many minutes was effortless, mysterious, almost magical. He seemed to Dick to exercise power over the fish in the same calm, almost absent-minded way he controlled his crew.

Jerry caught a shark. 'Big sonofabitch,' he whooped. A half-hour's fight had been enough to convert a ferocious steel-muscled predator whose forebears had dominated the seas for ten million years to limp submission. The gaff went in deep, its point stirred to inflict what final damage was possible to muscle, before the fish was hauled up by a rope looped round its tail, and suspended with its snout three feet from the deck. A wooden spike was used to wedge open the jaw while a crew member cut out the hook. Small drops of thick, brilliant blood spattered the deck, and a man knelt to wipe one of these from Stilson's shoe. The hook removed, the man with the knife turned his attention to the fins, which were the only part of the carcase that had a marketable value, and these he sliced away, leaving gleaming white flesh with beads of blood oozing through. The man dropped the fins into a canvas bag Jerry held out for them.

Dick bent down to stare into the fish's small, indifferent eyes. He smelt Stilson's cigar, and heard his voice close behind. 'Ugly beasts, aren't they?' Stilson said. 'They have very little feeling.'

'Is it a man-eater?' Dick asked.

18

'I wouldn't think so. Very few are. We can see what it had for breakfast if you like.'

'No, thank you.'

Stilson laughed. He raised his hand, and just as if he had pressed an electric switch the spar from which the shark hung swung away over the water. The man who had cut off the fins had reappeared, carrying a cutlass. Stilson nodded, and then there was a flash of steel and a chop as the blade sliced through the base of the tail. With a great splash the big fish went into the sea.

They all went to the rail as the shark, belly upwards at first, its mouth still wedged open, rolled over and began to sink, diluting the green water briefly with its silver before disappearing from sight.

'It wasn't dead, was it?' Dick asked.

'No, it wasn't dead,' Stilson said. 'Sharks are very difficult to kill. That's the way we punish them. They are our natural enemies and we are theirs. Some fishermen put themselves to the trouble of cramming broken glass down their gullets before they cut them loose.'

Dick made a face.

'You don't seem to like the idea. Why?'

'I don't know. Because it's cruel.'

'Life is cruel. It's cruel everywhere. Even in England. Here the cruelty's less concealed, that's all. It's brought out into the open. You have to come to terms with it if you live here. In other words you have to toughen up. I don't mean to seem over-critical, Dick, but it's something to think about.'

'I'm not going to live here. I'm going home soon.'

Stilson patted his shoulder. 'You never know, Dick, you can never be sure.'

The fishing was at an end. They ran for port with the horizon of white water coming closer, and docked in the drowsy calm of the early afternoon.

Dick and Jerry went ashore together after Stilson had shaken them both by the hand and told Dick that he hoped to be passing the hotel later that day, and might look in. A Chinese was waiting and Jerry opened the bag to show him

19

the fins. The man took one out and held it up to the light. 'Small,' he said.

A boy accompanied the man, carrying a laundry basket, and the Chinese took the fins one by one out of Jerry's bag, wiped their bloody edges with a piece of cloth and placed them in the basket under several layers of clean linen. He counted out four dollars and fifty cents, and gave it to Jerry. Then he and the boy went off.

'Sells them to the restaurants,' Jerry explained. 'They turn them into soup at two dollars a throw.'

'Soup from sharks' fins, eh?'

'The rich Chinese eat it all the time. Sometimes they put snake's gall in it. Know why? To get their backs up. Knock back a bowlful of shark's fin and snake's gall and you can set up three or four women in a row. Guys like Stilson live on stuff like that.'

They set out together down the wharf road.

'Planning on any more fishing trips with Stilson?' Jerry asked.

'No.'

'You didn't go for it all that much, huh?'

Dick hesitated. 'I don't like cruelty to animals.'

'You mean about the shark? What's a shark?'

'A man was cruel to a dog I had once. He hit it with a stick and broke one of its toes. I was upset.'

'But you couldn't do anything about it, huh?'

'I fired a rocket at his house.'

'You did what?'

'Just what I said. I made up a big rocket from a lot of small ones and I fired it at his house.'

'You hit it?'

'No.'

'So what was the point?'

'It was intended to be a warning.'

'He take it that way?'

'I think he did. The propulsion charge was wrong for the weight so it came down short, but I wrote him a letter to make sure he knew about it.'

'He know who it was from?'

20

'I didn't sign it, but he found out.'

'Jeeze. A rocket, huh? How did you find out about making rockets? Not something anybody can do.'

'It's easy enough. All you do is to get any rocket and copy it, except as it gets heavier, the charge has to be a lot bigger in proportion to the weight.'

'Seems like a big hassle to get into for a dog,' Jerry said. 'And a shark isn't a dog. Nobody can get steamed up over a shark.'

'I suppose you can't. Not in the same way. Stilson said I ought to toughen up.'

'Let's face it: right now, you're a bit of a wimp.'

'What can I do about it?'

'About toughening up, ya mean? Frankly, in your case, I don't know, Frazer. You live in a hotel. You eat three meals a day. You're an only kid with an old man who's well-heeled and a mother who probably worries about what time you go to bed. I don't see much hope for you.'

'What about you? How did you do it?'

'I wasn't given much choice. The broad my old man shacked up with wanted me out of the place. The way I see it now, she did me a favour. My pad's only a coupla hundred yards from here. Why don't you come and look the place over? See how it grabs you. Maybe you'll want to move in.'

They turned in through the gate on to the wharf. 'Here it is, Frazer. This is the nearest you're ever going to get to Kingdom Come in this world. How about it?'

Dick found himself in a wide space backed with decaying sheds. Beyond them rose the masts and rigging of fishing schooners at anchor, and behind these the great, wide, sloping funnel of a cruise ship was being drawn slowly by. The wharf was strewn with the litter of the sea, with ruined engines, broken fishing lamps, piled-up nets, and old anchors beautified with rust. Among this abandoned gear he saw a number of upturned boats, five or six mooching cats, two blind men with sticks, another man sprawled face downwards in a corner of shade, and a mulatto girl with pink hair and a mouth like a wound standing in the doorway of a shack, from which issued vociferous gramophone music.

21

They walked together towards the sea lapping softly at the piers. 'What sort of room you have in that hotel, Frazer?'

'Oh, just a room. A place where you can sit and a balcony.'

'Well, I guess this is just about the biggest room there is. And you don't pay for it. See all those boats over there? Guys sleep under them. I sleep under one. I can fix one up for you any time you want. Only problem is the rats. If they smell the caña on you when you're asleep they think you're gone and they start in to eat you. You gotta make friends with one of the cats, persuade it to stick around at night and take care of you, buy it a can of milk once in a while.'

'What's caña?' Dick asked.

'Wharf rum,' Jerry said. 'Half the guys on the wharf are hooked on it. It sends them blind in the end, but it takes so long they don't notice it happening. The poolroom's over there, where that broad's standing. They sell caña for two cents a mug. A mugful of caña and your problem is not to spread your wings and fly away. Like it, Frazer? Pretty nice scene, isn't it? Artists come down here to paint the place.'

'I like any place by the sea,' Dick said.

'This isn't just a place by the sea. Guys come here to get rid of their problems. When you're on the wharf you stop worrying. Nobody starves. You can go down to the fish-canning plant and they give you the heads and tails of the fish. You need dough, you can sell a half-litre of blood for two bucks at the hospital right across the road. You can peddle your ass to one of the tourists who come around, or you can pick up a little cash by hauling bodies out of the water. A lot of guys in this country end up in the sea, and if you find a corpse, the police pay you five dollars for it.'

'Have you ever found one?'

'Once, but the guy turned out to be some student the police knocked on the head and threw in themselves, so they wouldn't pay over. Anyway I don't need that kind of money. I get all I need with the boxes.'

Dick looked at his watch. 'I'd better be going,' he said.

'You hungry? You can get a hamburger at the shack.'

'I have to go. My mother is going to be waiting for me at the hotel.'

22

'If you hafta. Know your way back from here?'

'I've got a map.'

'Be seeing you sometime, huh?' Jerry said.

'I expect so. One of these days.'

'Any time you feel like battin' the breeze a while, you know where to find me. Just come on down.'

'I will.'

Chapter Three

Dick and his mother went straight down to lunch after he had washed up and changed his shirt.

'Tell me about the trip,' Caryl said.

'Tell you what?'

'You're very surly today,' she said.

'Am I?'

'Yes, very. And I don't understand why.'

'I can't stand fishing, and I can't stand Mr Stilson either.'

'I don't see why you should dislike Mr Stilson in any way. He put himself out to be nice to you.'

'To please you. That's the only reason.'

'Nothing of the kind.'

'I hate the way he looks at you.'

'And I hate it when you say things like that.' For one of the few times in his life Dick saw his mother really angry. She had drawn her lips tight, and a sharp little bone showed at the bridge of her nose. A moment of unnatural calm followed before she spoke again. 'Remember I'm your mother.'

'I know that.'

'Nobody could possibly be more considerate and more polite in every way than Mr Stilson is. I object most strongly to remarks of the kind you've just made.'

'An American boy came out with us. He said he's an animal. He runs after any woman.'

A wizened couple at the next table had been distracted from their Chicken à la King, and Caryl suffered the scrutiny of watery and reproachful eyes.

She hissed to silence him. 'Don't speak so loudly,' she said.

'He said that everybody detests him.'

'I suppose your informant was the Carmichael boy,' she said. 'I thought I saw him on the boat.'

'Jerry Carmichael,' he said.

'They call his kind layabouts,' she said. 'The last person whose opinion I'd ever consider.'

'He's not a layabout,' Dick said. 'He lives on the wharf and sleeps rough, that's all. He works like anybody else.'

'All I know of him is he's caused his parents a lot of trouble. They had the police bring him back home, and he went off again, so now they've washed their hands of him in despair.'

Dick glanced sideways at a waiter who had slowed in passing them to stare at his mother in a way he was sure Stilson had stared at her. Suddenly the man's expression had changed from servility to impudence. Dick made an angry face at him and he hurried away.

She had been watching him, and when she spoke her voice had become gentle and coaxing. 'You didn't have a nightmare last night, did you?'

'No.'

'What about that funny noise?'

'It's still there. Not bad, though.'

'All the time?' she asked anxiously.

'No, only when I think about it. I think it's getting better. If I don't think about it, it goes.'

'What does it sound like?'

'Just the same. Like an engine starting up. It gets faster and faster and then it slows down and stops.'

She put her hand over his. 'I do wish you wouldn't take those violent dislikes to people. People who wish you nothing but well. That's what brings it on.'

'I can't help disliking some people. Everybody does.'

'Not in the way you do. You promised me you'd do something about it.'

'I'm trying to. Mum, why didn't you say anything about a house in the country?'

The set of her mouth altered and her eyes lost focus. He knew that she was pressed for an excuse. 'Nothing was decided,' she said. 'There didn't seem any point in mentioning it.'

'Has anything been decided now?'

'Well, I think so, yes,' she said. 'Mr Stilson has been looking round for us, and I think he's found something.'

He had bitten into a fruit that turned sour in his mouth. He pushed it away.

'Why couldn't we go on staying where we are? What's wrong with the hotel?'

'Living in hotels is uncomfortable, besides being very expensive. The arrangement with Dad was we should rent an apartment or a house as soon as we could find one. You know you don't sleep well here with all the noise that goes on.'

'Don't think about me. I'll put up with the noise. I want to stay here.'

'If we have a house I'll do the cooking. You'll at least have the food you're used to.'

'It doesn't matter. I don't care what I eat. The country's boring. There's nothing to do in the country and I don't want to live in a house Mr Stilson's had anything to do with. That's what I'm trying to tell you. That's what I'm trying to make you understand.'

He was beginning to twist his hands together in a way she feared. 'You see, Mother, I can't bear the sight of Mr Stilson. I don't want to be anywhere where he's around. So naturally I'm not interested in any house Mr Stilson finds for us. Can't you see that, Mum? That's the way I feel about him. This is someone I never want to see again.'

Next day Stilson sent a car to take them to the house he had found for them. It was in a village of tattered grey houses and streets full of horse manure. The house had no windows

25

overlooking the street, and it was surrounded by a high wall with a gate kept locked by a witchlike old woman who carried the key in her pocket, who was always there tailing a few paces in the rear, wherever they went. There was no electricity or running water, no telephone, no place of entertainment of any kind in the neighbourhood, and no form of transport but a bus which left for the city at dawn, crammed with peasants, and returned after dark. The house stank of animals in neighbouring byres.

It turned out that this house actually belonged to Stilson. Dick carried out a moody exploration of dim passages, and dishevelled, mould-smelling rooms. He came back. 'Do you really mean we're going to live in this dump, Mother?'

'I do,' she said gaily. 'And I can't tell you how lucky we are to have been given the opportunity. It's charming. You won't recognize it when it's been thoroughly cleaned out.'

'Dad would never have let us stay in a place like this.'

'You're quite wrong there. He'd have been wild about it. He always said that when you live in a foreign country you ought to try to live as the people do, because you learn so much more that way. Don't you *understand*? This is an adventure.'

'But you said it's Mr Stilson's house.'

'One of his houses.'

'That means he'll be coming here.'

'It doesn't mean anything of the kind. He'll come if and when he's invited, as he would wherever we happened to be staying.'

'I don't want to see him.'

'So you've said, but I'm afraid you may have to put up with it. Mr Stilson is a friend of your father's. He's gone out of his way to be helpful and kind to us, and the least we can do is to show our appreciation for what he's done in any way we can.'

Chapter Four

Mr Stilson made three jaunty appearances during the first six days of their tenancy. On the third occasion he managed to detach Dick from his mother and steer him into a corner.

'Well, Dick, settling down to enjoy the good life in Cuba these days?'

'No, I'm not, Mr Stilson.'

'Surely you like Villa Maria? I quite understand how boring life must have been in the hotel, but there's plenty of interest for anyone in a village like this.'

'I don't like it. I didn't want to come here. It was Mother's idea. I'd much sooner be back in the hotel.'

Stilson's laugh contained a metallic echo like a bad connection on the telephone. 'You're not afraid to speak your own mind, are you, Dick? And I like that. Still, I'm surprised. They're friendly people in this part of the world.'

'I know they're friendly but I don't speak the language, so what's the point?'

'And I'd have said the village itself was a good place to explore.'

'It's dirty,' Dick said.

Stilson nodded. 'Yes, I suppose it is. The people are poor. Perhaps I don't notice any more. Anyway, stick with it, eh? Its charm may grow on you.'

'I don't think so, Mr Stilson. I don't think we'll be here long enough.'

'Well, you never know in this world. You never know,' Stilson said. 'And by the by, how about calling me Juan?'

'I'd prefer not to do that.'

Stilson laughed again with an even stronger metallic echo. 'Well, as you will. I'm beginning to have a sneaking suspicion you don't like me all that much. Could that be true?'

Dick looked away. He said nothing.

'Well, I guess that's confirmed my suspicion,' Stilson said. He laid an arm on Dick's shoulder. 'Listen, Dick, this situation could work out to be impossible. Tell me sincerely, what would you really like to do?'

'Go home,' Dick said.

'You really mean that? You're quite sure that's what you want?'

'Yes, that's what I want. I want to get away from here and go home.'

Stilson gave him a quick, penetrating stare. 'Well, there seems to be nothing for it, does there, eh? No use trying to keep you here against your will. We'll have to see if something can't be done about it.'

To Dick's horror Stilson had been invited to stay for supper. His mother went to dress and he followed her to her room.

He sauntered on the threshold, doing his best to appear casual. 'I just let him know how I felt about him,' he said.

'You did *what*?'

'I didn't actually say so. He said something about thinking I hadn't got much time for him, and I didn't say anything, so he knew what I meant.'

'You horrify me,' she said. 'And after all he's done. You've put me in a dreadful position.'

'Don't worry about him, Mother. He isn't going to be upset. He doesn't care one way or another what I think about him. It's only you he thinks about.'

'For the last time, Dick, I won't tolerate that kind of remark.'

'I want to write to Dad,' Dick said.

'I'm glad to hear it. You should have written to him long ago. I've been begging you to, almost every day since he left.'

'First of all, I'd like to know when we're going home.'

'I've told you, your father and I haven't decided. We're seeing how things go.'

28

'Do you mind if I tell Dad I've had enough of this awful place?'

'Well, I certainly can't stop you, but try not to upset him. He spent quite a lot of money on giving us what he thinks is a happy holiday.'

'Dad always thinks about us, doesn't he?'

'He always puts his family first. He's a good man.'

'You do love him, don't you, Mother?'

'Of course I do.'

The supper that followed was an unhappy experience for Dick. His mother wore a long white dress he had never seen before. It reminded him of the kind of dresses he had seen little girls in the country wearing on their way to their first communion. There was something terribly wrong to him that his mother should be wearing it, and the sight filled him with a kind of nausea.

He next became aware that in talking to Stilson her voice had changed, that it was more high-pitched than usual and a little childish. There was a change, too, in Stilson's tone. He had dropped his habitually breezy manner and now spoke to Caryl with an unnatural gentleness, reminding Dick of the soft-voiced government spokesman who had frequently interrupted items at peak viewing times on the hotel's television to urge support for the policies of the moment.

Stilson spent some time describing the beauties of the simple life as lived in a Cuban village and his mother was anxious to agree. Dick found himself excluded from the conversation. 'Many women in this country become so attached to their homes that they never leave them once they are married,' Stilson said.

'I'm sure that could happen.'

'They feel no need to do so. A devoted servant like Anna attends to the domestic problems, leaving them free for creative activities in the house.'

'I think there's a swing of the pendulum back to the old idea of a woman's place being in the home,' she said.

Dick made a desperate effort to include himself. 'When you get used to living in a town the country's boring,' he said. 'In London we go out two or three nights a week. Dad takes us out to a restaurant, or we see a film, or something like that. Mother and Dad are fond of dancing. They go out quite a bit dancing together.'

Neither of them showed any sign of having heard him.

The servant, who was ugly and scowling and wall-eyed, came to set the table.

'And Anna,' Stilson said. 'Has my devoted Anna been behaving herself?'

'She's been very kind to us,' Caryl said, in her obedient, slightly squeaking voice. 'She's hardly left my side.'

'Anna's been with my family since she was a young girl. I'm glad you get on so well.'

'Could you ask her if we can have the key to the gate, Mr Stilson?' Dick said. 'Every time anybody wants to go out or come in she has to be called.'

They both turned to him. Stilson clearly in surprise, his mother with a kind of dreamy reproach. 'I think she might be very hurt if we took her keys away,' Stilson said. 'It's something like a badge of office. The word for housekeeper in Spanish is key-carrier. If we asked her to hand over her keys she'd assume she was being dismissed from the job.'

'Of course she must keep the keys,' Caryl said.

Anna appeared again, carrying a tray laden with glasses and plates. She put it down, and Stilson picked up a glass. He held it up to the light for inspection. Then he spoke to her in a low voice and she scurried off.

'I'm sorry,' he said. 'The glasses are not clean, and I shall have to speak to the person responsible to make sure that it doesn't happen again.'

A moment later an old man showed in the doorway between the two patios and came towards them. Dick and his mother had seen him several times before, moving slowly and stealthily about the house, brushing away the cobwebs that formed continuously in the corners, removing dead leaves, and stamping flat the cones of earth raised by ants wherever they set out to establish a nest. He had stopped a few yards away, hunched a little, one eye bulging and one almost closed above small muscular convulsions in his face.

30

His big hands made of bark scrabbled together over the pit of his stomach.

Stilson had turned to Dick and the familiar breezy, bantering voice was back. 'This man is Simon. As you see, he is rather stupid and negligent and will have to be put in his place, so I'm going to try a little experiment that may interest you. It's based on fear and heightened sensitivity. He knows he's been lazy and is afraid of what may happen to him, so he wants to put things right between us and in an effort to do this he'll appear to read my thoughts. I shall talk to him in English, which he does not speak, but he will understand.'

He held up the glass. 'Dirty,' he said to the old man. 'Understand, dirty?'

The old man grunted and nodded. 'Good, you admit it,' Stilson said. 'Come closer.'

Simon shuffled a step nearer. His lower lip sagged to release a dribble.

'Wipe it,' Stilson ordered.

Simon unlocked his hands and drew the back of his right hand across his mouth.

'Animal,' Stilson said.

The old man nodded again in eager acceptance of the insult. His mouth began to twist in the beginnings of a fawning grin.

'You are employed by me to keep this house clean. It is filthy,' Stilson said. 'From where I sit I can see a cigar-end left in a pot. Do you understand, Simon?'

The old man nodded and whimpered, his expression burdened with guilt.

'Go and find it,' Stilson said.

Simon began a shambling walk, making a wide detour to avoid them on the way to the large pot housing a bedraggled cactus, in addition to the chewed end of a cigar. Stilson, watching him, swivelled slowly in his chair. 'Look at the way his arms hang down,' he said. 'More like a monkey than a man.'

Having reached the pot Simon peered into it, nodding his head sorrowfully, then shuffled round to face them again. He moved his feet like a man treading deep snow.

31

'So you've found it?' Stilson said.

Simon gibbered a sound that might have meant assent.

'Pick it up, then. Show it to us.'

Simon held up the cigar-end.

'What should I do with him?' Stilson asked Caryl.

She seemed to Dick to come to with a start when he spoke to her. 'I asked what I should do with him?' Stilson said. Dick noticed once again that he became ugly when he smiled.

'Please send him away. Just send him away,' Caryl said.

'I could have made him eat it, but I won't,' Stilson said, 'I'll let him off with a caution this time.'

He waved the old man away out of sight, then got up. 'I've got something to show you.' He crossed the courtyard, unlocked a door, went into a room and came back holding a yellowed photograph in a cheap frame. It was of a young officer in a showy uniform, mounted on a white horse. He was holding a sabre, arm outstretched as if to lead a charge, against an absurd background made up from what was clearly a separate photograph of a fuzzy group of soldiers and a cannon belonging to a much earlier period.

'Recognize that man?' Stilson asked.

They both shook their heads.

'Simon in his heyday,' Stilson said. 'When he was the dashing Captain Simon Veragua of the Hussars.'

Caryl was troubled and bewildered. 'You mean to say they're really one and the same man?'

'Right. One and the same man.'

'How very terrible. What happened to him?'

'He did things he shouldn't have done, and got into trouble. Dropped out of sight for quite a while. When he showed up again he was like you see him now. I took pity on him and let him live here.'

Stilson seemed to be waiting, a little anxiously, for further comments, but neither of them could find anything to say, so that after a few wordless moments he put the picture under his arm and went off with it again.

Supper was served and eaten largely in silence. Dick suspected that his mother had found the Simon incident in some way frightening, as he had himself. There were unusual signs of preoccupation in Stilson's manner, too, and some evidence of impatience. He glanced several times at his watch, and presently Dick, outwardly preoccupied with the remnant of a mango on his plate, intercepted a signal passing between Stilson and his mother, and understood that with the slightest possible movement of his head, Stilson had ordered his dismissal.

Stilson got up as if to go, and almost immediately Anna was there carrying Dick's lighted lamp. Despite his protests, he now found himself banished to an area known as the second patio, isolated from the main body of the house. He pretended not to see Stilson's outstretched hand, kissed his mother goodnight, then followed Anna into the shadows of the second patio. Anna went off to her own room. Dick heard Stilson's car start and accelerate away. He waited a few minutes, then opened his door cautiously and went out on to the verandah. He tiptoed to the steps in the corner, and climbed them to reach the roof. He looked out at the village houses, as flat as cardboard under the hard impact of the moonlight. Sharp-edged white squares and oblongs representing buildings in their simplest form, plumed here and there by the shadow of palms, had been fixed in position one behind the other, like the stage properties of a child's theatre. The narrow main street, pinched between the houses, appeared as if carpeted with snow.

He waited and listened and searched among the flat shapes of houses and trees, and presently he heard the faint drumming of a car engine, saw a yellow patch as of a car's headlights jumping and dodging from wall to wall, lighting up a corner here and stretch of roadway there, and then Stilson's Cadillac came out of the houses into the open, swung round in a squelch of dust, and came to a stop outside the gate.

Dick heard the rattle of the lock and the soft creak of the gate on its hinges. There was the faintest murmur of voices, a soft scuffle of footsteps, then silence. He waited again, finding himself breathless like a runner at the end of a sprint, and listening through the gasp of his breathing to the other

33

sound, not quite a sound, that had started in his head, an intimate pulsating rhythm that slowly built to its crescendo, faded, then began again.

He went down the steps, unbolted the courtyard door through which he passed along a crooked passage into the first patio, then began to walk slowly, softly, one foot exactly in front of the next, balancing like a tightrope-walker on the balls of his feet to reach the door of his mother's room. He took hold of the door-handle, tugged gently, turned gently, and pushed, but the door did not budge, and he knew it was bolted. Half way up in the wood close to the doorpost a small hole had been left by the removal of a lock. He put his ear to this and listened. He heard a sound that he would have taken for a snore, but which shortly changed, took on a more urgent tempo and became recognizable as a moaning. Underlying this moaning he heard a man's voice, a soft bass commentary to the high-pitched sharpness of anguish.

'Ah, aha, ah,' moaned the woman in her distress, and in the pauses taken to recover her strength, Dick heard the matter-of-fact reassuring rumble of a man's bass. The cries were coming faster, and Dick understood that his mother was being made to undergo something that passed all endurance, and now in the intervals of outcry there were desperate pleadings that went unheard until these were drawn out wordlessly into a terrible scream.

Dick rattled and kicked at the door, and then, noticing a heavy stone ornament propped against the wall, he picked this up and began to smash it into the door panels. He splintered one panel, raised the stone above his head and was about to bring it down when the door opened about a foot, and he saw Stilson in pyjamas bending to release it from a chain. Dick hit out again through the gap, tearing a six-inch splinter from the edge of the door. The door opened. Stilson's arm went up to protect himself, the stone ornament was knocked from Dick's hands, and Stilson, straightening himself, opened the door wide and came out on to the verandah. Dick saw the beginnings of a smile on his moonlit face; he was as bland as an idol, but blood was running from his cheek. Stilson laid his two hands on Dick's shoulders, and Dick felt himself being carried back, pushed away, weightless, lifted almost from his feet. He tried to dodge round Stilson to get to the door, but the two hands laid lightly on his shoulders steered him wherever Stilson wanted him to go.

Dick screamed out. He was full of raging incoherence, but Stilson took one hand off his shoulder, still holding him effortlessly under control, and placed a finger on his lips, and the stream of unspoken protest dried up. Two trickles of blood had reached the corner of Stilson's mouth, and darkened the greying fringe of his moustache.

'Let's go, Dick, shall we?' Stilson said softly. He took Dick by the arm and began to walk him away, and then, as their bodies came closer, Dick smelt his mother's perfume on Stilson's flesh, and he tried to tear himself away. Stilson's grip tightened on his arm and he began to laugh, and Dick, bending suddenly, caught the hand and bit into it, feeling as he did so the crunch of gristle trapped between teeth and bone.

Stilson pulled his hand away and struck Dick a light blow with his fist over the solar-plexus which carried him back with a rush. He tripped over the bricked edge of a flower-bed and, falling, struck the back of his head on the brick kerb.

Dick lay still, stunned but quite conscious, eyes closed and head thrown back, and Stilson picked him up and carried him back to his room. He laid him on the bed, forced water between his lips and swabbed his face with a wet cloth.

'OK, Dick, I know you're kidding. Do you want to have a sensible man-to-man chat about this now? Or do you want to wait until the morning?'

Dick opened his eyes and turned away from him.

'So far, Dick, you're proving to be one of my few failures,' Stilson said. 'You're going to throw all those complexes away and stop hanging on to your mother's skirt and be a man. I had to hit you, and I'm sorry for that, but what else could I do? Have you seen what you did to my face? Say something, for Christ's sake.'

'I don't want to talk to you. In any case I'm not staying

35

here any longer. I'm going away. You can tell my mother that.'

He threw Stilson's consoling hand off, got up brusquely, found his shoes and began to put them on.

'You're not taking off right now? Surely not now? Be sensible, the farm dogs will eat you up if you start walking round the streets this time of night. If you want to go, OK. Nobody's going to stop you. But at least leave it until morning, eh? So you can see where you're putting your feet.'

At that moment in fact a great distant baying of dogs had started. Dick sat down.

Stilson said, 'I regard you as a rational adult, Dick, let's talk, eh?'

Dick shook his head.

'We could thrash this thing out right away. No holds barred. Get it settled.'

'I just want to get away from here.'

'Well, in that case I guess there's not much point in me hanging around any longer.' He got up. 'Get a night's sleep, Dick, that's my advice. Tomorrow is another day. Things are going to look a lot different in the morning. I'll come through to see how you feel.' Stilson went out, closing the door very gently behind him.

Chapter Five

Dick found Jerry in the poolroom down on the wharf. It was seven-thirty, with fishermen who had been out fishing with the lights playing the pin-tables, and two drunks already on the floor.

'For Chrissake, Frazer, you look terrible,' Jerry said. 'Where'd you spring from at this hour?'

'I just got in on the bus from Villa Maria,' Dick said. 'I've been up all night.'

'What happened, man?'

'Stilson. I found him with my mother last night.'

'Let's walk a little,' Jerry said. 'Get a little of God's fresh air.'

Dick followed him out on to the wharf and they sat on one of the bales just unloaded from a freighter. Jerry spat out the rags of a cigar he had been chewing at. 'So what's it about, Frazer? Your old lady got layed by Stilson. It's not the end of the world.'

'It's not the end of the world. I'm thinking about my father.'

'You can't say I didn't tell you what to expect. He was humping her, was he?'

'It sounded as if he was hurting her.'

'He probably was. Everyone knows he's sick. There was a case with some schoolkid he got his grips on a coupla years ago. He was up before a grand jury and he fixed it to get an indefinite postponement.'

'I think he's mad. He has a mad old man for a servant, and he treats him like an animal. Worse than an animal. Like a pig.'

'I heard of him. Simon Veragua. My old man used to have him around the house once. *He* gave him a rough ride, too.'

'I've left for good. I'm not going back,' Dick said.

'You mean, let him get away with it?'

'What can I do about it?'

'Well, if I was living at home like you, and my old man was away and Stilson was laying my old lady, I'd kill him.'

'How?'

'Any number of ways,' Jerry said. 'You can buy nigger poison here for a dollar. A dollar's worth in his coffee would kill him as sure as if he stepped in front of a high-speed train. Trouble is, people do it all the time, so it's kind of easy to recognize the symptoms. You could go fishing with him on that yacht and push him into the sea, some place like Punta Negra where all the sharks come around.'

'What about the crew? What are they going to say about it?'

'It's only a suggestion. There are hundreds of ways of

knocking someone off. You could pay a professional to put him to sleep. Leg-breakers around here will whack anybody out for a hundred bucks. If you can find one.'

'And the money.'

'And the money, sure. Another way would be to go hunting with him. They hunt hogs every year down in Santa Clara, and the guys shoot each other.'

'You mean on purpose?'

'No, they just shoot at everything that moves, and it ends up a massacre. The churchyard down there is full of hunters. They have deer in the woods round Escambray and the same thing happens. A guy gets shot once a week. They think nothing of it.'

'Sounds easy, doesn't it?'

'Easier than firing a rocket at him, huh, Frazer? The thing is that if you've pulled out for good there's no point in discussing it further, because believe me, friend, there's no way you're going to persuade Stilson to take his hooks out of your old lady by correspondence.'

'You think I ought to go back?'

'You'll have to, sooner or later. If you're going to fix Stilson you have to be close to him, and you've got to stop showing him just how much you hate his guts. Think about it, Frazer. You any good at planning?'

'I don't know. I'm supposed to go in for fantasies. I make a lot of plans, but it always turns out they wouldn't work.'

'If I were you, I'd ask myself just how much this whole thing meant to me, and if it meant as much as it probably means to you, I'd begin to think about how I could get rid of this guy without risking my own skin. Follow me, Frazer?'

'But you're tough.'

'I had to learn to look after myself. You'd be the same if you were in my shoes. Right now you have to do something about yourself. Remember the way you got upset about that shark?'

'Stilson sickened me, that's all.'

'Bet you never killed anything in your life.'

'No,' Dick said. He felt a kind of shyness, almost a sense of shame in making the admission.

Jerry shook his head pityingly. 'Supposing somebody told you you had to kill a dog, maybe a cat. Let's say they were sick, or run over or something, and somebody had to do the job. Could you do it?'

'It wouldn't be easy.'

'How about a chicken, huh? You're on a farm, say, and everyone has to eat, and you happen to be the only man around, and they ask you to knock off a chicken. How about that?'

'I'd get out of it if I could.'

'OK, let's forget the chicken and pass on to a rat. You going to tell me the same thing applies?'

'Probably.'

'Well, I happen to know better. Anybody can kill a rat, Frazer. There's an Indian temple down the road, and the Indian guys there have cockroaches running round all over the place because their religion stops them from knocking them off. I seen an Indian with a mosquito on his arm sucking his blood, and he wouldn't flatten it because that's the way their religion is. But even those Indians will kill a rat. Know why?'

'No.'

'Because it's the embodiment of evil. A rat *is* evil. That's why even you could kill one. They have mean eyes. When you see a rat come out of its hole and look up at you with those mean eyes, know what you want to do? You want to crush it. Listen, want me to prove to you you can kill a rat?'

'How are you going to do that?'

'Come on,' Jerry said, 'let's discuss this over a drink.'

They walked back to the poolroom together. 'Your old man in England know about Stilson and your mother?' Jerry asked.

'Not yet.'

'You going to tell him?'

'I don't even know his address. He was leaving on a business trip as soon as he got back. To China or somewhere like that.'

'You gotta find out his address and do something. That's

39

another reason you have to get back to Villa Maria pretty fast.'

They stood at the counter together and Dick smelt the sour vapours of the liquor splashed and smeared over its zinc surface. Intoxicated flies that had sucked at the spirit sprang into the air spinning and buzzing, then fell back to gyrate noisily on the counter. Dick found himself surrounded by laughter, the sound of it sometimes indistinguishable from that of grief.

'We're drinking caña,' Jerry said. 'It's kind of raw, but as they say here, it makes your mind up for you. Drink it in Coke and you won't notice the taste.'

Jerry ordered two Coca-Colas. Small blue cups holding cane spirit were lined up along the counter, and he picked up two cups and tipped their contents into Dick's glass and his own.

Dick tasted his drink. 'No difference, huh?' Jerry asked. 'You wouldn't know there was anything in it. Give it a coupla minutes and it hits you. Things don't seem so bad.'

Dick sipped the Coca-Cola, testing its sweet, shallow flavour on his palate and tongue, then not quite taken by surprise by an oily fuming deep in his throat, and a taste that reminded him of the smell of the alcohol-wetted zinc. He sneezed into his hands. Someone laughed as the door was opened and the wind from the sea blew out the laughter. The girl at the counter's smile flashed on and off like an electric sign, and a fisherman with the face of a preacher standing at Dick's side moved away to vomit into a spittoon at the end of the counter, and came back smiling an apology.

Dick's body had lightened and his hands floated up from his side. He funnelled his lips to blow out a spiritous belch. A bubble of anger in him exploded in laughter.

Jerry was watching him. 'Kind of takes over, doesn't it? How do you feel about those rats now?'

'The same, I suppose. Why shouldn't I?'

'They give you every known disease, including syphilis. Know what that does to you? It sends you blind and your jock falls off. Knock that back. I want to show you something.'

Jerry went round the counter and through to the kitchen and came back. He was holding a piece of fat the size of his fist. 'Chinese cook in there,' he said. 'Guy never cooks anything but pork sweet and sour. How are you feeling, Frazer? That grog made your mind up yet?'

'I feel all right.' Dick tried to pull down the corners of his mouth that had slid out of control into a vapid smile.

'Well, let's go take another look at that wharf, shall we?'

Following him through the door, Dick found he was holding the piece of fat in his left hand, and carrying a short length of iron piping in his right.

Dick followed Jerry to the end of the wharf. It was a yellow morning that would soon turn white as the sun rose into the sky behind the derricks and the masts, to set fire to and burn out all the colours. The nomads of the sea had tied up their boats and left their watery blue desert for the day. Dick saw them like clowns in the shirts they had put on, of chocolate, of magenta, of purple and of chrome yellow to protest against the colourlessness and monotony of the sea, and heard them shout for the pure pleasure of having their voices thrown back at them in the hard echoes of the earth.

The short yellow waves were flogging at the pier timbers below, and Dick went after Jerry down the slimed steps leading to the water, which sucked and slapped at the wood under its skin of flotsam. Down at the water's edge the wharf was seen to be supported by a forest of beams rising from massive wooden platforms. It was a place resounding with the splash and the rinse-back of the tide. Black crabs darted in and out of crevices in the wood, hunting just above the reach of the water, and were themselves pursued by swooping gulls, and here and there something grey and lumpy at the edge of a platform, taken at first to be part of the structure, shifted a little, and in doing so became a rat. 'Look at them,' Jerry said. 'Hundreds of the ugly bastards. They're filthy. Diseased. Eat each other. Half of them blind. They don't see you coming. That's why when you go after one you get it every time.'

He took the lump of fat from Dick and wedged it into a cavity in the wood, where the lowest platform projected just

41

above the level of the falling water, and had hardly straightened when a big rat jerked into sight, as if released from the darkness by a spring. It was a bigger rat than Dick had ever seen before, mouldy grey, with the glisten of bare skin in its eroded fur, pink feet like clutching hands of a young baby, a blue-ringed, fleshy tail, and the mean eyes that so disgusted Jerry, each in a setting of scabs. The rat jumped on the meat, clung to it, and pressed its haunches against it in a copulating posture. 'That's what they do,' Jerry whispered. 'Just look at that bastard. Put out a lump of fat for them and they try to screw it before they eat it. Hit it, for Chrissake. Lemme see you knock its brains out.'

Dick lifted the iron pipe and brought it down with all its force on the rat's body. Through the iron, he felt its instant shuddering ruin, the rupture and the explosion of its organs, and the splintering of tiny bones mashed into the sinews and flesh. Once again Dick struck down, splashing blood through the rat's eye-sockets, nostrils and anus. He heard Jerry laugh his pleasure and approval.

'One more for luck,' Jerry said. Dick hit the rat again; a blow that found no resistance in the mangled tissues, and Jerry, making a squeamish face and using the side of his shoe, scooped its remains off the platform and into the water, leaving a most brilliant and sticky smear on the wood where it had been. Jerry clapped Dick on the shoulder. 'I bet you were thinking about Stilson when you hit that rat.'

'I was.'

'Well, don't admit it even to me,' Jerry said. 'Never admit a thing like that. Tell you another thing,' Jerry said. 'You're hungry, aren't you?'

'How did you know that?'

'Get worked up like that and you always are. Let's go grab a bite to eat, and talk about where we go from here.'

There was a hot dog and hamburger stand outside the wharf gates where they bought a ten-cent burger apiece.

Dick bit into the burger and swallowed a mouthful. The last back-rinse of the fizzing alcoholic tide had drained from his head.

'Sobered up?' Jerry asked.

Dick nodded.

'I figure you have plans to make. What are you aiming to do now?'

'I don't know.'

'You hafta eat twice a day. How much money you got?'

'Nearly ten dollars.'

'You can stretch it out. Three days, four days maybe. It costs you nothing to sleep here. If you feel like a piece of ass on Saturday night you hafta pay a coupla bucks for the whorehouse. You gotta fit into the way things are in a place like this, and make allowances for the climate. Having a broad once a week is like drinking fresh lemon. It's good for the blood.'

They finished their hamburgers and strolled together outside the wharf fence but still in an area where the sea laid strong claims to the land, where beachcombers put up shacks overnight, and where the air smelt of sailcloth, stockfish, and, so far as salt had a smell, of salt.

There was something hesitant in Jerry's manner. He started to speak and stopped in mid-sentence before plunging in.

'Happen to notice that guy standing by the gate when we went out?'

'No.'

'Little guy. Yellow straw hat, glasses. Reading a newspaper.'

'I didn't see anyone.'

'You gotta use your eyes, Frazer. That clown belongs to the wharf police. He's there to watch everything that goes in and comes out. Everything that comes ashore on this section of the harbour has to go through those gates. That's why he's there.'

They turned back and in a few moments reached the wharf gates. The small man was there, propped against the fence, sagging a little as if about to slide to the ground, his face in a comic supplement. He gave no sign of being aware of their presence as they passed.

'Listen, Frazer,' Jerry said. 'I have a problem, and maybe you can do me a favour. I hope so. We got a guy back there hidden in one of the sheds and he has to go through these gates under this clown's nose. Maybe you could help.'

He led the way into a slum of old warehouses and sheds, many of them empty and abandoned. They found one with a door hanging from a single hinge. Wood screeched on the hard ground as Jerry tugged the door open wide enough for them to squeeze through. The shed was stacked to the roof with bales, several of which had burst open to release little landslides of mouldering, no longer recognizable contents. Dick followed as Jerry pushed his way through lanes among the forgotten merchandise, until they were halted by a dead end in the near darkness.

'Gimme a hand,' Jerry said. Between them they removed a low wall of bales to open a small enclosure. Dick could make out the form of a man squatting there. He got up with difficulty.

Jerry spoke in a short incomprehensible burst and the man replied, speaking very slowly in Spanish, each word seeming to require its own quota of premeditation and effort.

'Well, here it is,' Jerry said. 'This is the trouble we have on our hands. Remember those guys I told you about who pick up five bucks once in a while pulling bodies out of the water? They were out this morning before it got light, and they found this guy swimming in the Entrance Canal.'

Dick's eyes, getting accustomed to the gloom, began to fill in the details of the scene. He saw a young, anxious face, one eye half closed, a damaged mouth, a hand raised in what might have been greeting or a wary gesture of self-defence, sweat that had gathered whatever it could from the light to glisten like yellow grease on forehead and cheeks. A bloody bandage was tied round the young man's neck.

'This guy is a rebel,' Jerry said. 'Anybody ever tell you there was a rebellion going on?'

'Stilson said something about it. I read something in the English paper. I thought it was all happening up the other end of the island.'

'It was, but not any more. This man is a rebel captain. Take a look at him, Frazer. He's nineteen, which is to say

44

he's about a year older than I am, and he commands a company in the rebel army.'

Dick stared in wonder into the smooth-skinned, sweat-smudged face that was if anything younger than Jerry's. 'What happened to him?' he asked.

'He was sent up here on a mission, and he says everything would have been OK but for one thing. All these guys grow beards, and since he was still a bit of a kid it took about a year to grow what he had. It was only about a half-inch long, but he didn't want to cut it off. So he got himself picked up. The police around here are kind of allergic to guys with beards.'

Jerry turned to explain to the young man. '*La barba*,' he said. He caressed his chin with his thumb and fingers, grinning, and the young man returned a painful smile.

'Where's the beard?' Dick asked.

'We cut it off. This guy had a bullet shot through his neck. They didn't have anything on him, but they weren't taking any chances so they shot him in the neck and pushed him into the water. He has a hole in his neck you could put your finger through. Got that, Frazer? He could die, for Chrissake. He feels like he's got a red-hot poker stuck into his throat, but you don't hear a peep out of him. Shit, why don't you say something?'

'You're doing all the talking, Jerry.'

'You sorry for him?'

'Of course I'm sorry for him.' Dick was sure he detected gratitude in the anxious eyes.

'Well, I am, too, but being sorry isn't enough. We gotta stop him from dying. He lost a lotta blood and he's picked up some motherfucking infection, so he's running a high fever.'

'I can see that. What are we going to do?'

'Get him to a doctor fast. It's the only hope. This is where you come in, Frazer. I want you to change clothes with him. If we dress him up to look like a tourist, we can walk him past that clown on the gate. We were planning on keeping him here until tonight, and then moving him out, but the way he looks to me now he won't last till then.'

'I'll change clothes with him,' Dick said. 'What happens to me?'

'Nothing. You're English. You can prove your identity. You gotta right to wear what you want to wear. We dress this guy in that fancy shirt of yours, and those nice pants with the crease up the front, and those black shoes, nobody's going to take a second look at him. He'll be some guy off a cruise ship taking a look at the picturesque view, maybe on the prowl for waterside ass.'

'Can he walk?'

'A coupla steps maybe. You and I have got to get on each side of him and hold him up by the arms, and walk him that way. If the dick at the gate stops us, we tell him we have a drunk on our hands.'

'How about the wound?' The bloody bandage had slipped up to reveal what looked like part of the lip of a tiny black mouth that had opened in the neck about an inch to the right of the man's windpipe. Dick cringed.

'I got one of those spotted handkerchiefs tourists wear. It won't show.'

'What happens if we're caught?' Dick insisted.

'We don't think about that, Frazer. We got other things to think about.'

Dick helped Jerry with the slow and delicate process of undressing the wounded rebel. Naked, he was like a lanky child, with protruding hip bones, and a flat belly drawn back into the cavity of his ribcage. The muscles, devoid of any covering of fat, were displayed in sharp separation under the skin, like those of a plaster anatomical model. Something like a tiny silver barrel hung on a chain from his neck.

Dick stripped. He took the wounded man's stained and grimy shirt and held it up. 'What am I going to do about the blood on the collar?'

'Tear it off, for Chrissake. You don't need a collar when you live on the wharf.'

Jerry took the shirt, ripped the collar off and handed it back.

Dick put on the ragged shirt, the frayed trousers and the loose peasant shoes made of strips of leather sewn together.

46

Jerry looked him over. 'It's OK,' he said. 'You'll get by. You just give the impression of a guy who's been sleeping rough for a week or two. Our friend here is going to look great in your things. I guess he's the first rebel captain ever put his feet into a pair of black city shoes.'

They finished dressing the wounded man, then, taking him by the arms, one on each side, they began to manœuvre him along the lanes through the bales of goods towards the door. Jerry pushed it a foot open, and squeezed through. 'OK,' he said. 'Bring him out, and let's take a look at him.'

Dick pushed the man gently through the door, and he stood swaying a little and smiling into the sun. The sweat had formed tiny pools in the hollows behind the collarbone, which were beginning to spill over. Jerry had tied the spotted handkerchief with a knot under the ear.

'Hold him there a minute,' Jerry said. 'I'll be right back.'

He went off and a moment later was back carrying a camera in its case. He slung this by its strap from the wounded man's shoulder.

'Know something?' Jerry said to Dick. 'Right now he looks more like a Limey tourist than you did. *Pareces bien*,' he said to the wounded man. 'You look great.'

The man tried to laugh, then coughed. '*Si. Bien*,' he said, and Dick caught at him as he lurched to one side.

'OK,' Jerry said. 'I guess it looks like the great moment has come.'

They began the slow, wary march towards the gate, Dick and Jerry holding the wounded man between them, half lifting him by the elbows. 'He's not there,' Dick said, as the gate came into view. But then they saw the man in the yellow straw hat across the wharf road lurking under a dust-silvered wall where he was peeling an orange and throwing the peel at the pigeons. Alerted as if by some mysterious telepathic signal, he looked up, appeared to see them, and began to cross over to the gate.

'Don't look at him,' Jerry said. 'Try to act like you haven't noticed him. We're just three guys looking for a good time, and hitting the caña. Hold it, I've got an idea.'

He took the camera from the wounded man's neck,

unbuttoned the flap front of the case, gestured to Dick to stand at his side, then, holding the camera to his eye, he clicked the shutter. 'This is the way people act,' he said. 'You gotta be normal.'

They moved on, and the man at the gate watched them as he broke the orange into segments and then put one in his mouth.

'This poor guy can hardly walk,' Jerry said, 'so we gotta look like we're not going any place in a hurry. We gotta walk a while, then stop and maybe horse around a bit, then walk some more. So it comes across natural.' He suddenly broke into laughter, put himself into a boxer's stance, and jabbed several quick, playful blows into Dick's ribs. The wounded man, looking on, forced his mouth into an agonized smile, scooped the sweat from his face, then shook it from his fingers.

Jerry turned to him, still capering. '*Bien?*' he asked.

'*Si. Bien,*' the man said, swaying like a pendulum.

'That motherfucker over there got his eye on us all the time,' Jerry said. 'For Chrissake, we look normal, don't we? What's eating him? Our friend's gonna have to walk a bit if he can, otherwise it's going to look wrong. *Puedes caminar?*' he whispered to the wounded man.

'*Creo que si.*'

'Let him go, Frazer. Let him walk a coupla yards on his own. And keep talking, huh? Say something. Laugh. Recite a poem. That guy's gotta hear us talking English.'

The only thing that came to Dick's mind was a verse of a Scottish ballad. They were within fifteen paces of the man at the gate now. He watched intently as they came closer.

'The king sat in Dunfermline toun,' Dick said. 'Drinking the blude-red wine.'

'He did, did he? Dunfermline toun, huh? And where's that? D'ya happen to know?'

'In Scotland. It's not much of a place.'

'Dunfermline toun, shit. Tell you something, Frazer. I'll bet you'd like to be there, wherever it is, right now.'

'I would,' Dick said. 'You never said anything truer.'

They had come to within ten yards of the gate. The wharf

48

policeman pushed the last segment of orange into his mouth. He wiped his hands together, and took a pace forward.

'Listen, Frazer, grab this guy again before he falls over,' Jerry said, 'and keep walking right through that gate. Just keep going. Don't stop for anything. I'm going to try to head the dick off.'

Jerry left them, beginning a jaunty, hip-swinging advance on the wharf policeman, then greeting him in a loud and confidential voice. Dick panicked at the boldness of the manœuvre. Never get away with it. We're done for, he thought. He listened to the thump of his heart as he hurried the wounded man along, and they trudged unseeing into a patch of road that had been broken up, then left. The wounded man stumbled over an outcrop of old railway line, and gasped as their bodies collided. Dick stopped to balance him. The man groaned through a smile that had gone a little insane. Five yards from the gate, then three. Now they were level with Jerry and the wharf policeman, whose body was momentarily overlapped and screened from them by Jerry's larger frame. Jerry seemed to have engaged him in some topic illustrated by lively movements of hands and shoulders.

They were through the gate, almost out of range of the wharf policeman's instinctive doubt. Encircling the man, bewildering him with unrelated questions and facts, Jerry had finally succeeded in extracting a cigarette and sticking it between his teeth. He laughed like a rainbird signalling a change in the weather, and Dick, hearing the sound at his back, felt a collapse of tension that left him weak and breathless like a sprinter at the end of his race.

For a moment he clung to the wounded man who, buckling a little, smiled back at him terribly, unable now to close his lips over his teeth, and Dick's skin picked up the heat of his fever through their two shirts. They began to fumble their way down the street which, serving only to feed the docks and having no life of its own, was devoid of curiosity and offered no threat. The waterfront had at last given up its claim on them. Symbolically a dry, saw-edged wind had sprung up from the land to separate them from the

49

oily wharf odours and the screech of derricks, sweeping them back into the sea where they belonged. Taxis that had dropped off their passengers in the port went past, for the most part empty, wallowing on broken springs, but presently one made a sudden stop with a yelp of brakes, and a kettledrum rattle of loose fenders, and Jerry sprang from its open door.

'Gimme a hand to get him in.'

Jerry caught the wounded man under the arms from behind. Dick took him by the legs and they lifted him in. The driver watched what was happening in his mirror, without moving his head. He crossed himself with a quick discreet movement, as if buttoning his jacket.

'Where are we taking him?'

'To a doctor I know. I can handle this on my own.'

'Don't you want me to help?'

'Sorry, Frazer, I have to leave you out of this. There's a one in a hundred chance you could be picked up for this. If they asked you a few questions and twisted your balls a few times, you'd sing. You'd hafta. This way you can't tell anybody any more than I went off with this guy in a taxi, because that's all you know.'

Dick got out. Jerry slammed the door and wound down the window. 'What do I do now?' Dick asked.

'Go back to the wharf and wait for me. See you in a coupla hours.'

'What about the man at the gate?'

'Pay no attention. He won't bother you. If he says anything, just talk back to him. Say anything you like. He won't understand. Give him that poem of yours, huh, Frazer? The king sat in Dunfermline toun.'

The driver crashed into bottom gear and they went off. Dick stood watching until it was out of sight, then he turned and began to walk back towards the wharf.

Chapter Six

Dick stood at the water's edge for three hours, watching the ships go by, until Jerry tiptoed up from behind to clap him on the back. 'OK, Frazer. You can relax. It's all over. We're in the clear.'

'You found a doctor all right?'

'Sure I found a doctor. Guy who specializes in gonorrhœa and syphilis, but he'll fix him up. Coupla days on his back and he'll be OK.'

'What happened with the fellow on the gate?'

'No problem. I said I was looking for a dame, and he wanted to fix me up with one.'

'Do you think the wounded man will go back? What I mean is to the fighting, wherever it is.'

'You can bet your sweet life he will.'

'Does he have to cross any lines?'

'They don't have any lines in this war. The fighting can break out any place. Say a bunch of these guys happen to be up in the hills and they happen to hear of government troops in the neighbourhood. What they do is come down, shoot them up, then get the hell out of it back where they're out of reach. That's the way they play it in this war.'

'What's the war about?'

'I guess you'd have to ask someone who studies politics. A buddy of mine from Paris, Missouri, came down here to join up with the rebels. I figured he didn't know too much about what he was going to fight for, either. Wanted me to go along with him, but I chickened out. Wonder where he is now?'

'You're still on the rebel side, though?'

'I suppose you could say that. I like the one or two I see. Like this guy we had on our hands.'

'One thing I can't understand. How many of the people who live on the wharf knew he was there?'

'All of them. That kind of news gets round fast. All those teaheads, those winos and those guys who sell their blood to the hospital. They all knew he was there.'

'And nobody gave him away?'

'They're Cubans.'

'So's Stilson.'

'Yeah, but Stilson is special. You'd never run into an asshole like Stilson on the wharf. Listen, I got something to show you. That guy gave me a memento.' He opened his hand to show the little silver barrel Dick had seen hanging on a chain from the wounded man's neck.

'This comes apart,' Jerry said. 'There's a bullet inside.'

He unscrewed the two halves of the barrel, took out the bullet and Dick reached out for it. 'Is this silver?' he asked.

'The nose is. If these guys are cut off somewhere, surrounded maybe, and they see there's no hope, they use a bullet like this to blow their brains out with. It's got his name on it.'

Dick rotated the small, shining bullet to find the engraving. He read, 'Abel.'

'That's not his real name. The name he's known by in the rebel army. He said he wished he'd had something to give you, too. The guy was very appreciative of what you did for him. He said to tell you he hoped he'd have a chance to hand back that clothing of yours one of these days.'

'Not much chance of running into him again,' Dick said.

'Well, who knows? Maybe we will.'

They turned back towards the shack.

'So you want to stay on here, Frazer?' Jerry asked.

'For a few days anyway.'

'What are you going to use for bread?'

'I've got ten dollars.'

'That won't last long. We have to find you something to do. You could shine shoes if you want, like I do. There's plenty of money in it but it's tough. Liable to run into competition and if you don't know all the angles you get your face busted in.'

52

'I'll have a go at it.'

'It'd be good for you. If you can work on the boxes and survive you'll be getting some place. Give you time to think things over, too. Let's face it, sooner or later you're going back, but when you do you've got to be ready to take Stilson on. That's if you're planning not to let him get away with this. You can't beat Stilson in a straight fight. You have to play it so as to put him off his guard. You gotta shake his hand and explain you understand his point of view and you want to let bygones be bygones. Otherwise you don't have a prayer.'

'I know I don't.'

'OK, that's settled. That's the way it's going to be. Tomorrow we'll go out and make a start with the shoes. Right now we'd better find a boat for you to sleep under tonight.'

Chapter Seven

The first day went well. They hired two shade boxes from the shoeshine contractor entitling them to choice pitches in the Prado where bourgeois citizens promenaded by the thousand. Dick soon learned the knack of selecting and pouncing upon an unsuspecting victim deep in conversation with a friend, seizing a foot and daubing polish on the shoe before he could raise a protest. By the end of the day he had earned nearly four dollars. 'It's too easy,' Jerry Carmichael said. 'You're never going to learn anything this way. Tomorrow we take sun boxes down Animas Street where the brothels are. The quicker you toughen up, the better it's going to be for you.'

Dick slept under the boat again, disturbed by the noises of the night and by his fear of rats, and next day he and Jerry worked in the red-light area. They defended themselves against competitors and juvenile gangs with knives, collecting a few minor bruises, cuts and abrasions. When it was time to hand in the boxes Jerry seemed pleased with the way the day had gone. 'You're coming along, Frazer. Keep this up and nobody's going to call you a wimp any more.'

Later he asked, 'Thought any more about what you're going to do about Stilson and your old lady?'

'No, but I'm thinking all the time,' Dick said.

'Give it another day or two,' Jerry said. 'Whatever you do, you got to do it right. Got to be able to cover your tracks.'

The final challenge was the National Hotel, forbidden territory to the freelance shoeshine boy, where the concession was held by the hotel's head porter.

Dick and Jerry smuggled themselves into the gardens, where Jerry resisted the overtures of a homosexual guest, and then was half strangled by him until Dick beat the man over the head with his box. They made their escape hotly pursued by members of the hotel staff. They rested in a soft-drinks kiosk.

'I'm beginning to change my opinion about you,' Jerry said. 'I didn't think you could do that.'

'I didn't either.'

'You hit him hard. Lucky for me, too. I was just about passing out. Christ, Frazer, to look at you anyone would think you hadn't got any muscles at all, but you must have some.'

'I thought I heard the bones crunch.'

'Well, let's hope it was only your imagination, because I have a hunch that guy's a politician. I seem to remember his picture some place. If you busted in his skull we're in bad trouble. Anyway thanks, Frazer, you saved my life.'

The toughening-up process continued next day with a foray to the slaughterhouse. After living on the poolroom's inferior hamburgers, Jerry craved fresh meat, had in exchange for helping out with the killing. This slaughter-house was not equipped with electric stunners, and for several hours they worked 'pulling on the ropes' by which steers were dragged by their horns down to a ring set in the floor to be pole-axed by one of the team of Negro slaughterers.

When they were leaving with the five pounds of fillet steak they had earned, they were stopped by a watchman, who had to be satisfied that they had not stolen the meat.

'That clown troubles me,' Jerry said. 'I seen him before, and I know all about him. He's applied to be a detective, and he can't quite figure why white guys like us should come down here to pull on a rope. He's gotta figure if he can pin anything on us it'll help him get into the force.'

Chapter Eight

They were relaxing on the wharf on the evening of the fourth day with the boxes.

'Come to any decision yet?' Jerry asked.

'Not entirely. I've got an idea, though.'

'Great.'

'First of all I have to write to my father and tell him to come over here quickly.'

'What about his address?'

'That's the trouble. We only heard from him once, from New York. He always writes twice a week when he's away.'

'Where was he supposed to write to?' Jerry asked. 'That hotel you were in?'

'No, the Poste Restante. Stilson was going to pick up the mail for us.'

'Well, that's probably just what he did.'

'You mean he collected the letters and hung on to them?'

'Well, knowing Stilson, I'd say that's a good bet. The Post Office closes at seven,' Jerry said. 'It's right on the San Francisco wharf, a coupla hundred yards from here. Why don't you go up there and see if anything's come in. You can just about make it.'

Dick got to the Post Office five minutes before it closed. The woman at the Poste Restante counter took a pile of letters from the pigeon hole marked 'F', and began to go through them slowly. Some of the envelopes were discoloured as if they had been there for years, and these old letters had somehow found their way to the top while the cleaner and fresher-looking letters were at the bottom of the pile, and they were closing the Post Office doors by the time the woman had discovered the letter that came from Dick's father. The letter was addressed to his mother. She had once collected postage stamps, and his father had not recovered from the habit of plastering stamps all over the envelopes of letters sent from foreign parts, and this one bore a row of showy Hong Kong commemorative special issues. Dick turned the letter over, staring at its front and its back, trying to bring himself to open it. It was something, he felt, that would have to be done in secret. He had noticed a row of telephone kiosks outside the office, and finally he went into one of these and tore open the envelope, and began to read.

He deciphered his father's confused and almost childish handwriting with difficulty, and there were words here and there which he had to puzzle over to decipher. What he read revealed perplexity, but he detected a coolness in the tone that surprised him.

Still no news. A little worrying, especially as I'm just off to Hong Kong. No point in writing here as I shall most likely have left by the time you get this letter, but you might cable me at the Cathay Singapore. In the circumstances I can't expect to be bombarded with letters but it would be nice to know you're both well. Rang the Embassy yesterday but caught Cameron on duty and found him as unforthcoming as a hospital consultant. You were both in good health, he understood, but had moved to the country without leaving an address with them. No more than that. Money, before I forget, has been sent to the Chase Manhattan, but don't hesitate to go to Juan in an emergency. Keep dear old

Dick out and about and well occupied. I hope to have good news of you both.

Dick put the letter away. He was overtaken by weakness and his mouth had filled with water. There was a metal rubbish bin at the edge of the pavement and he went and sat down on it in the sun, but the heat of the metal seared through his cotton trousers, so he got up, unsteady on his feet for a moment, and set off down the road.

'What happened?' Jerry asked.

'I picked up a letter Dad wrote from Hong Kong. He hasn't been hearing from us any more than we have from him.'

'Well, you aren't surprised, are you? Where is he?'

'In Singapore. He had to go down there on business after he left Hong Kong.'

'Did he give an address?'

'The hotel he's staying at.'

'You going to write to him, then?'

'I'll probably send a cable.'

'Saying what?' Jerry asked.

'About what's happened.'

'It would be a mistake. I'll tell you why. Whatever you put in a cable about fifty people are going to see it. It could get back to Stilson. Probably would. He has his own network.'

'How long does a letter take?'

'From New York four or five days maybe. To anywhere in the world. From this asshole I don't know. Lemme see the letter.'

Jerry examined the date stamp, and the arrival date stamped on the back by the Poste Restante.

'You're lucky. This only got here yesterday. It took twelve days to come from Hong Kong, so you can figure it's going to take at least another twelve to get back to Singapore. And he's on the move. What happens if your letter doesn't get there in time? Where's he heading after Singapore?'

'Back home.'

'You gotta write two letters, Frazer, so whatever happens one of them gets to him. And you gotta move fast. Post

Office is closed now, so why don't you write those letters right now and we'll bum a ride over to the airport to mail them. A plane goes to New York every night about ten. They could be there tomorrow and on the plane to Singapore the day after. All you hafta do is to pay ten cents extra and put a special label on the envelope. Save yourself days.'

'Good idea. Let's do that.'

They went over to the poolroom and the Chinese owner gave Dick paper and envelopes. Dick wrote:

Dear Dad,

Glad you got back all right. We got a letter from you from Hong Kong, but I expect you will be in Singapore by now, and I am also sending another letter home in case this misses you. The weather has been good since you left. It rained once, that's all. We left the hotel as soon as you left, and went to live in a village called Villa Maria, which is about 15 miles from town, and we are living in a farmhouse owned by Mr Stilson. I don't like it here. Dad, I don't want to worry you and I know that everything will be all right, but I would like you to come and get us as soon as you can. What I am worried about is you will think this is the kind of thing I used to make up, but it is not. Mum does not know I am writing this letter to you, and the other letters you sent before the one from Hong Kong have not reached us. You say you have not heard, but Mum had written three or four letters so all I can say is something has happened to them. I want Mum to go back to the hotel where we were before, because it is pretty dreadful for everybody at Villa Maria, but Mr Stilson doesn't want to let her go. I think you should come over here as soon as you get this.

He made a copy of the letter, and sealed both letters in their envelopes addressing one to his father care of the Cathay Hotel and the other to their home address in London, and they went off to hitch a lift to the airport.

'Can you see there's any hope of me being able to get back to Villa Maria tonight?' Dick asked.

'Not unless you walk. What's the hurry anyway? Wait till

the morning. Bus leaves at about five, takes you most of the way. And this is the one time in your life when you have to play something very cool.'

'I'm going to. You're right. I'll go out there on the bus.'

Chapter Nine

Sanger tapped on the door of Hollingdale's office, opened it and went in.

Hollingdale looked up. 'Your collar button,' he said.

Sanger, who had hoped to conceal the fact that he had not done up his collar button by knotting his tie well up in his neck, groped guiltily to make the adjustment. 'It's hot in the office,' he said. 'Don't you think we ought to go in for air-conditioning?'

'I don't,' Hollingdale said. 'You can have an additional desk-fan if you like. When one works in the tropics, it's better to accept the fact. The body makes its adjustments more rapidly.'

'The trouble is I perspire so terribly.'

'Will yourself not to,' Hollingdale said.

'I'll have to try that,' Sanger said. 'There's a letter here I thought you might want to see. It's from a man called Bates. Runs the Ganaderia Bates down in Camaguey.'

'What does he want?' Hollingdale asked.

'He wants to know if we have any official policy regarding evacuation.'

'Do *you* know what he means? Don't read the letter. Give me the gist of it.'

'He seems to be worried because a group of rebels have established themselves in some hills near his ranch.'

'There are no rebels in Camaguey,' Hollingdale said.

'Would you care to draft a reply?' Sanger asked him.

'No, I wouldn't,' Hollingdale said. 'Simply write and say

the nearest rebels are about 175 miles from his ranch, in the Sierra Maestra, where they are surrounded and completely cut off. Tell him he may continue to go about his business with absolute peace of mind.'

'Am I to say that we have no plans for any evacuation of our nationals?' Sanger said.

'Say nothing about it at all,' Hollingdale told him.

'I suppose he's been listening to rumours.'

'I imagine he has, and if you do that you will end by believing anything. The letter can be quite short. Three lines should suffice.'

Sanger shot his chief an admiring glance. 'Right. I'll do that.'

'While you're here,' Hollingdale said, 'Andrew Frazer was on the phone yesterday. Cameron spoke to him. I believe he was ringing from Hong Kong. Remember we saw his wife down at the harbour with that fellow Stilson?'

'The beautiful blonde. I remember her very well.'

'He said he'd had no news of any kind from his family since he left, and naturally he's worried, and I would be too. I believe I told you we could probably expect trouble in that direction.'

'You did.'

'It's started sooner, and it looks worse than I expected. I thought it prudent to take out an extended status report and it's just come through. Caryl's gone to live in one of Stilson's houses. Whether or not she's living with him they don't say. The boy's run off and he's on the Missing Persons list. He's said to have been seen working as a bootblack, and there's a possibility that he may have been already involved in a crime of violence. Quite a can of worms, in fact.'

Sanger whistled. 'Yes indeed,' he said.

'You'll see why I can't really bring myself to be bothered by reports of phantom rebels hiding in the hills.'

Sanger nodded his agreement. 'What's the attraction as far as Mrs Frazer's concerned? As I understand it, she's an intelligent woman. Is it a purely sexual thing?'

'In the first instance, probably yes. Thereafter I'm terribly afraid something more unpleasant may come into it. The status report people sent an agent down to the village where they're living to make a few enquiries. She's never seen out except in the company of a servant who has a somewhat sinister reputation. Nor's she ever heard to speak, and has consequently been nicknamed La Muda. One can't help thinking of such things as narcotics and whatever else Stilson may keep in his witch-doctor's bag of tricks. They all say he's mixed up with the Santeros, or the Ñañigos, which is even worse. You'd never imagine it to look at the man, but he's of mixed ancestry. At one level this is a very African scene.'

'Have you spoken about it to H.E.?'

'Not yet. What I propose to do is to go over there myself, force my way in if necessary, talk to her and find out what's going on, after which, if it appears that something nasty's happening, H.E. will have to be brought into it. We may have to devise some means, if it can be found, either as it were of taking the pair of them into care, or getting them out of the country.'

'We're going to be up against Stilson, aren't we?' Sanger said. 'And from what you say he's going to be a tough nut to crack.'

'I'm afraid he is. A very tough nut indeed. He's capable of anything.'

Chapter Ten

The conductor stopped the bus in San Francisco at the Villa Maria crossroads, and Dick walked five miles before a lorry carrying fruit-pickers through the weak morning sunshine to their work in the plantations stopped to pick him up. It was not quite six when he pulled the bell-handle on Stilson's gate.

Within seconds Stilson opened it. He was dressed in

Chinese silk pyjamas, freshly shaved and alert. He took Dick firmly by the hand and a shoulder, steered him through into the courtyard and closed the gate. 'Dick,' he said. 'Great to see you. You're earlier than I expected.'

'Did you expect me today, Mr Stilson?' Dick asked.

'Yes, I expected you. But a little later. In an hour or two's time when there's more traffic on the road. Did you walk?'

'Part of the way. Then I got a lift.'

'You seem surprised,' Stilson said.

'I didn't know I was coming myself until a few hours ago,' Dick said.

'Well, I did, and there's nothing extraordinary about that. It's a question of understanding the workings of the human mind. Never mind, the thing is how are you? It's been five days, hasn't it, and needless to say you've been missed. Your mother's been in a somewhat agitated state. As you can imagine.'

'I'm sorry about that. I'd have phoned or sent a message if I could have.'

'I've been a little concerned about her. She's not been sleeping well, and the doctor's put her on pills. I don't want to wake her if I can help it. She'll come on the scene before long, but in the meantime why don't you and I have some coffee and talk about a couple of things that need to be discussed?'

Dick found himself in an unfamiliar room in the first patio; one that had been closed up when they first moved into the house. Stilson, bustling between cupboard and pressure stove, seemed to have shrunk a little, and Dick found more cunning and less contempt in his smile. For the first time he noticed that Stilson had short legs; when he passed Dick a coffee cup he did so with a strange flourish of the free hand, as if about to make it disappear.

'Well, tell me all about your adventures while you've been away, Dick.'

'I went to stay with Jerry Carmichael.'

'So I heard. You were on the wharf, weren't you? And I'll bet you were having a good time. I told your mother there was nothing to worry about. I hear you boys were seen on

62

Animas Street together. They tell me that's where all the best whorehouses are located. Well, I guess the time comes when a guy your age has to start flexing his muscles.'

'We went down Animas Street shining shoes.'

'Shining shoes, were you? Great. Wonderful. That's what I call enterprise, Dick. And if there's any better introduction to what life is all about than shining shoes, I'd like to know what it is. Well anyway, Dick, whatever you've been up to you look in great shape. Physically, I mean. Otherwise, as is to be expected, you're a terrible mess. My God, wherever did you find those things you're wearing? I'm going to get you a clean pair of pants and a shirt to put on before your mother sets eyes on you.'

Stilson went off and came back with the clean clothes and turned his back while Dick changed into them. He poured more coffee. 'Listen, Dick, something about your manner, your attitude, I don't know what it is – maybe the way you look at me – suggests to me you've had a change of heart since our last meeting. Would I be right?'

'I think I have, Mr Stilson,' Dick said. 'I've had the chance to think things over and I don't feel the same as I did.'

'Well, that's great news. That's really music to my ears. I'm beginning to feel optimistic. Does that signify you might be ready for that little man-to-man discussion I suggested? Is this the right moment? If so, why don't we make a start right now?'

'I'm quite ready to talk about anything, Mr Stilson,' Dick said. 'I think we ought to talk.'

Stilson had put down his cup with a flourish of dismissal. He groped in the opening of his shirt to bring a religious medal into sight and dangled it at the end of its chain.

'In this country we treat a kid one way and a man another. You're going to be sixteen next week. For me you're a man. So why should I fool you? Why should I insult your intelligence? I guess you know all about the relationship that exists between your mother and myself. The only thing is, how are we going to handle this situation? This is something you can either go along with or reject. Do you want to come in at this point? Do you want to ask me anything?'

'Is my mother going on living in this house?'

'That is her intention.'

'What's going to happen about my father?'

'We have a problem there. Don't expect me to feed you any crap. No one holds your father in greater respect than I do, but there's no point in shutting our eyes to one important fact. He's a good many years older than your mother. Why don't we come straight to the point and say that this was a marriage in name only? And has been for many years by my information. The way I figure it, he knew this only too well. Maybe that's the reason he took off the way he did and left you two over here. And it could also explain the fact that there's been no news of him. He could have felt he owed your mother the opportunity to start a fresh life, and if this was the way he decided to play it, I personally feel nothing for him but admiration.'

'He wrote us from New York and he said he was going to write again as soon as he got to London.'

'Your mother has shown me the only letter she received, and reading between the lines you can see what's coming. As I see it, your father's pursuing a deliberate policy of silence. He must have seen that your mother and I were attracted to each other. He could be a generous man.'

'Are you and my mother going to get married?'

'That is our hope. Yes. As soon as all the problems are ironed out.'

'You mean like getting a divorce.'

'Like getting a divorce among others.'

'It takes a long time, doesn't it?'

'Less here than in most places. Weeks rather than months. The question is, what's going to happen about you, Dick? You could live with us here, and we'd be happy if you decided you would like to do that. The alternative would be to go back to England. It's for you to choose.'

'Would I see my mother again if I did that?'

'Of course you would. There'd be nothing to stop you coming here on your school holidays.'

'It's a long way.'

'Less than a day's journey by air these times.'

'I don't know how my father could look after me. He's always away travelling.'

'You'd go to boarding-school again. You'd be no worse off than any boy born here. Every family that can afford it sends their boys to Europe or the States to be educated.'

Stilson set the religious medal spinning on the end of its chain. Dick remembered now that he had done this before on the few occasions when they had been alone together. Stilson was watching him closely, his eyes narrowed and their pupils very small. His expression was smiling and sympathetic. The medal had become a little glistening sphere. Dick forced himself to look away from it, suffering a mind-wandering moment of forgetfulness in which Stilson's face was that of a total stranger, then hearing Stilson say, 'You have a natural feeling of loyalty towards your father, Dick. Something I admire. Your presence would be a great consolation to him.'

'Would it, Mr Stilson? Do you think so?'

'I'm quite sure of that. No normal affectionate father wants to feel he's lost touch with his son.'

'We used to spend a lot of time together. I'm sure Dad would be very sad.'

'He would, Dick. Any father would. So what's the decision to be?' Dick felt Stilson's will press down on him, an intolerable, almost irresistible weight.

'What does my mother want me to do?'

'She wants you to do whatever's best for you.'

Dick's nod was full of understanding. 'I better see her. I'll do whatever she thinks I ought to. I don't want to spoil things for her.'

'She's very tired,' Stilson said softly. 'I want to let her sleep on if possible. This is a decision that has to be yours.'

Concentrating, mustering all his strength in a last effort to thrust back the pressure, Dick heard his voice break through like a thin shriek in a nightmare. 'I want to stay here with my mother. I don't want to go.'

'Well, that's great, Dick. That's all I was hoping to find out. Your real feelings in the matter.' Suddenly the firm smile had become conciliatory. 'I ask for nothing better,

Dick. And I'm sure we're going to have a great time together.'

He jumped to his feet. 'Listen, Dick, I'm going to wake your mother and break the good news. I can't wait to see her face when I tell her her wandering boy is back. She's never going to forgive me if I let her sleep on.' Dick got up to go with him and then suddenly realized that he was debarred from his mother's bedroom from now on, and that the intimate territory of night and morning that they had shared with his father had now been invaded and fenced off by this stranger.

Stilson, indeed, had held up his hand, palm outwards, in a gesture that meant wait. Dick sat down again and waited, and a long time passed, and then the door opened and his mother came in and they were in each other's arms.

'Where have you been? Where *have* you been?' There was something close to passion in her voice.

'Jerry Carmichael wanted me to stay with him, so I thought I might as well for a few days. I'm sorry I didn't let you know, Mum. I honestly am. I couldn't think of any way of getting in touch with you and letting you know where I was. If I could have phoned I would have. You know that, don't you?'

Holding her, he found her in some way smaller than he had expected her to be, and when they let go of each other and he could study her again, he saw how total the change in her was. There was something muddled and muffled and timid in her expression, and for a moment the clearly defined boundaries of the relationship between mother and son had become blurred, reducing them to a kind of false equality which neither of them would have wished for.

'You're really going to stay with us, aren't you?' she said. 'You said you were going away.'

'I soon had enough of it. I changed my mind.'

'I don't know what I'd do without you.'

'And I don't know what I'd do without *you*.'

'It's wonderful. I can hardly believe you're back after all.'

'And for good,' he said. 'I'm not going away again. Where's Mr Stilson?'

'He's gone already. He wanted to give us a chance to be by

66

ourselves and talk . . . And you don't mind staying on in this country? You always said you hated it.'

'I don't hate it any more. I suppose I'm getting used to it. Jerry and I had a pretty good time. It was like camping.'

'I'm glad of that,' she said. 'And you wouldn't really hate living in this house?'

'Not if you were here, Mum. If you're here I don't mind. Is Anna just the same as she was?'

'I suppose she is. I'm probably getting used to her, too. She's never far away.'

In fact at that moment Anna came into view through the glass panel in the door. She slowed in passing and screwed up her eyes to peer at them through the glass.

'Mr Stilson said that you and he were probably getting married,' Dick said.

She made a small, finicky gesture as if wiping a stickiness from her fingers. 'Nothing's been settled yet,' she said. 'Don't let's talk about it now.'

'Are you and Dad getting a divorce?'

'I don't know. Please don't press me, dear. It depends on so many things that haven't been settled yet.'

'Mr Stilson says you are.'

'He shouldn't have said that because nothing's been decided. We're not even sure whether a divorce here would be recognized in England. Countries have different rules. Besides which, I don't want to be hurried into anything until I'm quite certain in my own mind.'

Dick's fingers were on the letter in his pocket. She'd be sure to give it to Stilson, and he'd ask questions, he thought. Find some way of making me tell him what I wrote. Put him on his guard. He decided to flush the letter down the lavatory.

'How much does Dad know about this?' he asked.

'Very little really, apart from what he probably guesses. It's something it's very hard to write about. It has to be discussed. I wanted to see him again and try to explain to him. I think he wouldn't feel so badly. The last thing I want to do is hurt him if there's any way of avoiding it.'

'I know that,' Dick said.

Chapter Eleven

They spent the rest of the morning happily together. Little was said. Dick watched his mother as she did nothing in particular, shuffling from one small task to the next. She wore a shapeless white cotton dress; the near-purdah adopted by local married women before going into permanent black in early middle age.

'Painted anything lately, Mum?'

'Not very much since you left.'

'Have you been out at all?'

'I don't think I have. I've found quite enough to keep me going in the house.'

At midday, to their surprise, Hollingdale arrived in an Embassy Austin Princess. Sanger, who had accompanied him, remained in the car while Hollingdale hammered on the gate. He had some difficulty in persuading Anna to let him in. 'Bit of a character, your servant, isn't she?' he said to Caryl. It was his only reference to his astonishment at her attempts to shoo him away, as if he had been some beggar at the gate.

He made it clear by a concealed gesture in Dick's direction that he wanted him out of the way and Dick was dismissed with the suggestion that he get on with his efforts to reassemble his radio set. Once in the second patio, he took off his shoes and ran up the stairs leading to the roof. Here he hid himself out of their sight behind the foliage of a vine, where he was best placed to eavesdrop.

Caryl was only able to offer Hollingdale a soft drink. 'We live a very simple life,' she explained. 'One soon learns to do without so many things.'

'But you like it?' he said. 'That's all that matters.'

She brought the orange squash. 'Sorry we don't run to ice, either.'

'It couldn't matter less,' he assured her, smiling thinly. 'I usually leave out the ice until sundowner time. Better for the digestion.'

He glanced round warily, noticing the half-finished picture propped against the wall. 'Still busily painting, I see.' He got up, glass in hand, and went to inspect it. 'Charming,' he said.

'Do you like it?'

'Very much. I didn't know you'd finally given in to the abstract.'

'I haven't,' she said.

'Sorry. I'm an illiterate in these matters. It's a street scene, isn't it?'

'Actually, the scene outside the church. It's only half-finished.'

'Of course,' he said. 'How stupid of me not to realize that.'

He came back and sat down again. The situation, he thought, was worse than he had feared. That slowed-down, drawling voice. The vague painting, hardly better to him than a scribble. The total absence of make-up in daunting combination with the incredible garment she wore. Stilson, he decided, must have dressed her up like this to ensure that other men kept their eyes off her. They were all Arabs at heart. As for Caryl, he was reminded of a convert to some hare-brained cult – in this case the most idiotic of all – machismo, and all that went with it.

'I imagine you can guess why I'm here,' Hollingdale said.

'I have a pretty good idea,' Caryl told him. The slight shock of his visit had cleared her head, and she watched him warily. Paul Hollingdale made her nervous. She found him a little inhuman. He had played the part of the diplomat for so long that in the end the real man had merged with the disguise, beyond reach of separate identification.

Hollingdale sipped the warm, weak, orange squash, detecting through the synthetic fruit flavouring the flat, iron taste of the well-water.

'It's a trifle embarrassing,' he said, 'particularly when friends are involved, but part of my job is to keep an eye on our nationals and see to it that all is well with them.'

'I know,' she said. 'I expect you have a file on me.'

He ignored the attempt at a joke. 'Charming old house, this,' he said. 'You see fewer and fewer of them. It belongs to Juan Stilson, doesn't it?'

'Yes, do you know him?'

'I know *of* him.'

'When you say it like that, Paul, you make it sound like a judgement.'

'Do I, Caryl? Please forgive me. I assure you nothing of the kind was intended. I've never met him personally, but I know of him because he's received a good deal of publicity.'

'Go on, say it. He was mixed up in a scandal.'

'Nothing extraordinary about that. He's rich and successful, and rich and successful men make enemies.'

'Of course they do,' she said eagerly. 'That girl who made charges against him was bribed to say what she said.'

'It's conceivable. I know nothing of the details. It's the kind of thing that happens all the time.' He broke off. 'I say, do you think you could ask your servant to go away? I don't suppose for a moment she understands English, but one never knows.'

Anna, having brought the drinks, stood there glowering at them.

'Could *you* persuade her to go?' Caryl asked. 'She doesn't pay any attention to me.'

Anna was dismissed, local style with a flip of the finger, and went off grumbling loudly. Hollingdale said, 'Andrew's been twice on the telephone to the Embassy, asking for news of you and Dick. The last time was from Hong Kong. I spoke to him.'

'Oh dear, what a sad, sad business it all is. What did you tell him?'

'I told him no more than Cameron did when he phoned from London. I said that as far as I knew you were both in excellent health, and that as I understood you were still staying with friends in the country. H.E. thought I ought to call on you so as to keep up to date with the situation.' He gave her another of his solemn smiles. 'We should naturally have preferred to be left out of this,' he said.

70

'What should I do?'

'That must be your decision, Caryl. It would help us, though, if you established direct communication.'

'I've heard nothing from him. Not a single letter has come since he left.'

'Which is far from meaning that he hasn't written.'

'Do letters go astray here?'

'Frequently.'

'I'd better cable his hotel. He should be in Singapore now.'

'I think you should do that. Are you planning to stay in this country much longer?'

'When you ask me that, I get the impression you'd be glad to see the back of me. Yes, I am.'

'Can I tell H.E. whether it's likely to be a matter of weeks or months? Believe me, nobody wants to see the back of you, but to a certain extent you *are* our responsibility.'

'It could be more than months. I'm planning to settle here.'

'Oh,' he said, 'I see.'

'I'm glad you came,' she said. 'I want to ask your advice. Juan Stilson and I are living together, and he's very anxious that I should get a Mexican divorce, so that we can get married. Can you tell me if they're recognized in England?'

'That,' said Hollingdale, 'is something quite out of my field, so I can't advise you. I would be prepared to take a hefty bet that they are not. What you're contemplating is a totally one-sided affair in which a person is deprived of his right to defend himself. It doesn't make sense.' He mastered his indignation, feeling only the familiar tightness of his lips that warned him of lurking anger. The most effective brainwashing, he thought, if nothing worse. Stilson had left her with hardly a mind of her own.

'They're recognized here.'

'England is England and Cuba is Cuba. I can't talk to you about your legal position, but as a friend I must tell you that you should take no decision of any kind before you see Andrew. You must give this time. You've known Stilson a very short while. You might even change your mind.'

'I won't change my mind. There are reasons why we want to get this settled as soon as possible.'

'Well, you know my feeling on the subject. I'm sorry, Caryl, and also I'm a little alarmed. How does Dick view this situation?'

'He's taken it in his stride.'

'I'm agreeably surprised, from what I know of Dick.'

'Boys of his age can be very resilient. Would you like to see him?'

'I'd like to say goodbye if he happens to be about.'

She got up and went through to the second patio and heard Dick come scrambling down the steps. 'You were listening, weren't you?' she said.

He shook his head, feeling the blush in his cheeks. 'I went up to the roof to get some grapes.'

'I don't believe you,' she said. 'Come and see Mr Hollingdale. He wants to say goodbye. And run your comb through your hair.'

They went back together into the first patio, followed by the black shadow of the watchful Anna. Hollingdale was on his feet, waiting. 'Well, there you are, Dick. We don't seem to have had much opportunity for a chat, and now I must be on my way. Enjoying life in Cuba?'

'I'm getting used to it,' Dick said.

'Good. I'm glad of that. I hear you've been seen round town in the last few days.'

'I was staying with friends,' Dick said. He felt alarm flutter in the pit of his stomach, but his brain reacted to the emergency. 'We went down to the wharf to mess about with the boats. Had a pretty good time.'

'You can have a lot of fun in Havana,' Hollingdale said. 'Only one thing to remember: it's a lot easier to get into trouble than it is in Wimbledon. I should add it's also a lot harder to get out of it once you're in it.'

He kissed Caryl on the cheek. 'Take care of yourself,' he said.

Anna moved out of the background eagerly, carrying the key of the gate.

*

A noisy fly had found its way into the car and Sanger, a little concerned that it might bite or sting, was flapping at it ineffectively with a folded newspaper when Hollingdale appeared suddenly and got in.

'How was it?' Sanger asked.

'Depressing,' Hollingdale said.

Sanger persisted, knowing otherwise that no more would be said. 'As bad as you expected?'

'Worse.'

Sanger knew that in the ordinary way expressions of opinion or comment of any kind had to be prised out of his superior, and he was surprised when, after lighting a cigarette, Hollingdale said, 'As I remember telling you the day we saw that pair together down at the harbour, this is something that has the makings of a major headache.'

He took the folded newspaper from Sanger's hands, killed the fly with a single decisive swipe, and Sanger started the engine and they moved off down the dusty street. A cow cropping weeds in the middle of the roadway spread its legs to release a stream of urine before moving aside to let them pass.

'Not much of a place to live in,' Sanger said. 'What do you think made Mrs Frazer choose this of all places?'

Hollingdale stubbed the cigarette out in the ashtray with a vigour bordering on violence. 'It was chosen for her,' he said. 'She's a virtual prisoner in that house, in which she lives like a peasant.'

'Why? How could such a thing happen? Is she stupid?'

'She's not stupid. I think she's fallen into a trap.'

'Do you still feel narcotics may come into it?'

'All the more, now I've seen her. They use hallucinogens here. An overdose of datura can cause a massive loss of brain cells. That's the true fact behind the old zombie legend. It's something you can't help thinking about when you talk to her.'

'My God,' Sanger said. 'It's a terrible thought, isn't it?'

They had taken a wrong turning among the sombre buildings and found their way barred by a subsidence of the roadway into a broken drain.

'There's something gone,' Hollingdale said. 'Sometimes she talks like a schoolchild repeating a lesson. She goes in for little aggressive outbursts just as if she's been dosed with something to suppress the inhibitions. She used to be a good painter, but the picture I happened to see she's just been working on was nothing short of pitiable. For me it depicted merely a mental state. Now she's talking about a Mexican divorce.'

'Can she get one?'

'There's nothing to stop her. Something you can buy like a pound of butter over the counter.'

'Would this be likely to make life more difficult for us?'

'It would. In a number of ways.'

The grubby town had released them now from the hold of its tentacles, and they were in the cheerful countryside with mules turning the water-wheels and the brilliant blue of morning glory splashed over the hedges. Sanger broke the silence again. 'What's in this for Stilson?' he asked.

'Beautiful foreign women are status symbols. They're few and far between. There may be more to it than that, and it's the second possibility that rather worries me. Stilson's been heavily involved with the régime and all its misdeeds. I'm told that several of his kind have married foreigners as a kind of insurance policy.'

'Does this suggest that the possibility exists that the rebels could take over?'

'We don't think so for one moment, but it may well be that *they* do.'

'It's a disturbing thought.'

'I refuse to be disturbed by it,' Hollingdale said.

'Was the boy there?' Sanger asked.

'He was.'

'Did anything come up about the other matter?'

'No, on second thoughts I decided to leave it alone. I don't think there will be repercussions, so why bother?'

'And you expect the police to keep their word?'

'I think they will. They owe us a favour. What does it matter to them? A politician who's in the wrong party gets his head broken. They'll advise him not to press charges.'

74

'Easy, isn't it?' Sanger said.

Hollingdale put him in his place. 'That is what it is not. We've done a small thing for them, and now they do something for us. After that it's their turn again, and what's probably going to happen is that they'll back a visa application for some thoroughly unsavoury character, or something of the kind. At this point we shall have to say no, and that's when the war starts. No, I'm afraid it's far from easy.'

Sanger observed a moment of chastened silence before he came back to the topic of Dick.

'How did the boy seem?'

'Hard to say. People like that are like poker-players. They have a lot of practice at covering up what's going on in their minds. They're geysers. Everything's calm and quiet while the pressure builds up and then the explosion happens.'

'And you think there will be an explosion?'

'It's something I confidently await,' Hollingdale said. 'I think of that politician's fractured skull, and I wonder. Sometimes I'm not so sure I'd like to be in Stilson's shoes.'

Chapter Twelve

'I'd like to go hunting,' Dick said.

Stilson looked at him in total amazement. 'Well, you stagger me.'

Five quiet days had passed, with Stilson whenever present at his most genial, and his mother dreamily acquiescent in all Dick's proposals. In line with the new tactic of appeasement adopted since Dick had rejected the opportunity to return to England, Stilson insisted on making a great occasion of Dick's forthcoming birthday.

'I propose to take the day off,' Stilson had announced. 'You only have a sixteenth birthday once in your life. It's for you to say. Come on – what would you like to do?'

'I'd like to go hunting.'

Stilson, who had been talking about the air pageant in Matanzas, or bass-fishing in the Morón Lagoon, or alligator-shooting in the southern swamps, recovered from his surprise. 'Hunting what?' he asked.

'Deer,' Dick said. He looked at his hands and tried to make his voice offhand.

'And where would you hunt deer?' Stilson asked.

'Escambray. Is that very far away?'

'It's further than Morón, but not all that far. Whatever made you think they have deer down there?'

'A friend of Jerry Carmichael's told us. He goes down there hunting all the time. He said they have some kind of antelope someone brought over from the States thirty or forty years ago, and now the woods are full of them.'

'Well, it's always a possibility,' Stilson said. 'Escambray's a very wild place. It's also a very big place. I'd be happy indeed to take you over there hunting, Dick, but unless we could get something a bit more definite about the location it would be like looking for a needle in a haystack. You're quite convinced this buddy of Jerry Carmichael's wasn't some kind of big mouth out to make an impression?'

'I'm sure he wasn't. He showed us a picture of himself with a big buck he shot.'

'The thing to do would be to see him again, and nail him on the story. We need to be able to pinpoint the area where he does his hunting. Do you think there would be any way of doing that? If so, you're in business, Dick. Know what jack-lighting is?'

'No.'

'Well, jack-lighting is hunting at night with a light, and it's the most effective form of hunting as well as being the best sport. You carry a battery on your back, and you have a light strapped to your forehead and you just walk around, and any game that happens to be about is attracted to the light. When you see the light reflected in their eyes you shoot. That's all there is to it. How does that appeal to you?'

'Very much.'

'It does to me, too. There's nothing I like to do better. So what do we do now? Where do we go from here? Can you find this man again?'

'I'm sure I can. He's always down on the wharf with Jerry Carmichael.'

'Well, you should go and see him. Pin him down, though. Get all the details. I mean, the nearest village we have to go to, and preferably someone we could talk to there if he has any contacts. The last thing we want is to do this trip for nothing. Especially on your birthday.'

'Can I go in and see him tomorrow?'

'You can go in whenever you like. Do what you like. You know that, Dick.'

'Would it be all right, Mother, if I stayed the night with Jerry and came back next day? This man I was telling you about has a boat, and he's liable to be away on a fishing trip.' He asked as a matter of course, knowing that these days she would agree to anything.

Stilson answered for her. 'You do whatever you think fit, Dick. I'll run you in in the car in the morning.'

They settled down to an evening closely following the pattern of all the others. Anna cleared away after dinner, then Stilson turned down the lamps so that they should better appreciate the fireflies round the well, fetched his guitar, and sang for them. His voice was rich, but at the same time soft and persuasive, and Dick felt himself obliged to watch the little religious medal that he had been fiddling with a moment before striking up the first chords on the guitar, and which now dangled on his shirt front. He felt a little giddy. Once again his mother was wearing the long white first-communion dress he so much disliked. Her hair had been combed out to shoulder length in a way that seemed to Dick almost as indecent as if she had bared part of her body. Her thoughts seemed far away. A pretext was found on that evening, as on those preceding it, of summoning Simon into their presence and humiliating him. This time he was forced to go down on all fours and bark like a dog. Caryl covered her face with her hands while Dick looked away. After bullying Simon, Stilson was always in high spirits.

Simon was dismissed, and the guitar put away. 'Dick, your mother and I are planning to visit Mexico next week,' Stilson said. 'I'm not sure how long we'll be away, but I imagine you'll find ways of amusing yourself.'

'Am I to stay here?' Dick said.

'No, I don't expect you to do that. I have an aunt in town who'll be glad to put you up in her flat. She'll take good care of you.'

'Couldn't I move in with Jerry Carmichael while you're away?'

'Move in is hardly the right way of describing camping out on the wharf,' Stilson said. 'A night or two of it is all very well. I wouldn't recommend it for a longish period.'

'Is it all right with you if I stay with Jerry Carmichael, Mother?'

'I'd sooner you were guided by Juan about this,' Caryl said. 'If you were staying with Jerry's parents it would be a different thing, but I don't agree with boys of your age being left to fend for themselves. I'd far sooner you stayed with Juan's aunt.'

'Haven't you any idea how long you're going to be gone for, Mum?' Dick asked.

'I can't tell you exactly because we don't know ourselves, yet,' she said. 'Probably a few weeks.'

'And I couldn't come with you?'

'I'm afraid you couldn't, dear. We'd like to have taken you, but for all sorts of reasons I don't want to go into it's out of the question.'

'We've deferred leaving until the day after your birthday,' Stilson said. 'The way the flights are it would have been more convenient to make it two days earlier, but we decided against that because naturally enough we both wanted for us all to spend the happy day together.'

Stilson grinned genially, the light glinting in his eyes. An ample gesture, reminding Dick of a man rewarding a performing seal with a fish.

Dick said, 'It was very nice of you to think of that.'

'And we're going to have a great time on that shooting trip. A really great time.'

'I know we are,' Dick said. 'It's going to be very exciting. What am I going to do about getting a gun, Mr Stilson?'

'A gun, Dick? As a matter of fact that happens to be the least of our problems. I have a whole armoury full of them.'

'Well, that's all right, then,' Dick said. 'That was the only thing I was wondering about.'

He saw Stilson's glance shift, detected the slightest of nods, and in that moment he felt the shadow of Anna fall upon him, and he got up.

'Bright and early in the morning, Dick, huh?' Stilson said. 'I'll be knocking on your door at six.'

'I'll be awake,' Dick said. 'Good night, Mum. Good night, Mr Stilson. And thank you for thinking of my birthday. I'm looking forward to it very much.'

He went off quietly, following Anna to his room. When in bed he stuffed cotton wool into his ears to shut out the terrible sounds that sometimes reached him from the room in the first patio where Stilson and his mother slept.

Chapter Thirteen

Dick found Jerry on the wharf scrubbing a grimed shirt at the tap behind the poolroom. Absorbed in his task, he ignored a fly sucking at a sun-blister on his leg. 'I expected you to show a few days ago,' Jerry said. He straightened up, the fly still in position.

'I'm only staying the night,' Dick said. 'Going back tomorrow.'

'Decided to make the best of it, huh?'

'No.'

'Stilson still laying your old lady?'

'It's just the same.'

'You do what I told you? Give him the big smile, and let him think you think he's a great guy?'

'I smile at him when I have to. When he sings I clap and he gives us an encore.'

'He sings? For Chrissake.'

'We have dinner and then he gets out his guitar and sings.'

'I'd give a lot to see it,' Jerry said. 'You're buddies, huh? Or so he thinks.'

'He gave me a ride out here in his car today. Said he'd pick me up any time I liked if I wanted to go back. He's taking my mother to Mexico next week, making her get a divorce from my father. And I think they're going to get married.'

'They tell you this?'

'No, I'm not supposed to know. A man who works in our embassy came to see her, and I heard her tell him. They told me they're going away, but I'm not supposed to know why.'

'Looks like you have a crisis,' Jerry said.

'Do you think my father's got the letter by now?'

'I doubt it.'

'And there's no chance he could be here by next Tuesday?'

'Not a hope.'

'I was afraid of that.'

'Trouble is, Stilson's in a hurry,' Jerry said, 'and it all adds up. Remember that trial I told you about? It was in the paper again yesterday. Fixed for the 15th. Stilson must be aiming to get out of here before it starts. Figures he can get away to some place like Mexico and stick there till the heat's off. Your mother can get her divorce while they're hanging around.'

'He's taking me hunting the day before they leave.'

'He's *what*?'

'Taking me hunting. It's my birthday, and he says we ought to do something to celebrate it together.'

'Well, well. Going hunting with Stilson, huh? Hogs or deer?'

'Deer.'

'Over at Escambray?'

'That's right. You're sure they have deer there?'

'Positive. A guy on the wharf shot a big buck last month. Fella he was with got a 130-grain slug in the leg.'

80

'Stilson wanted to be quite sure about the location. Escambray's a big place, isn't it?'

'This guy said you find 'em around San Juan near Esperanza. Man called Rafael runs the local store and acts as a guide. Ask for him at the store.' A blister on Jerry's forearm attracted another fly. He cuffed it away. 'You sure you want to do this?'

'Unless my father gets here by Tuesday.'

'Let's go get a cup of something hot,' Jerry said. They walked back to the poolroom for coffee and sweet buns. It was full of fishermen with the fish-scales still on their clothing and the backs of their hands, filling their eyes emptied by the nothingness of the sea with the comforting sights of the land.

'I need to get some practice in a hurry,' Dick said.

'Practice at what?'

'Shooting. I'm not much of a shot.'

'For God's sake, Frazer, you're really going through with this?'

'I have to practise. The only thing I ever shot was an airgun.'

'Few weeks ago you couldn't hardly kill a rat, and now you're going hunting in Escambray. You've certainly come on fast. If you want to practise your aim they have shooting booths over at Luna Park.'

'That wouldn't be any good. Shooting at something only a few feet away isn't the same thing. Isn't there a real range anywhere? Where they give you proper instruction?'

'Only one I know of is at the American Club. A full-scale range. You can get a test there if you want to apply for a gun licence.'

'That's the sort of thing I mean.'

'But you only get ten shots. You can't just go there and practise. They have this arrangement with the City Hall. They test you and issue a certificate and then the City Hall gives you the licence. Ten shots going to be any good to you?'

'It's better than nothing,' Dick said. 'Can anyone use the club?'

'Not anyone, but my old man happens to be Vice-President so they won't turn us away. We could go over there now.'

'Great.'

They took a bus over to the American Club, where they were seen by an old Negro servant, reminding Dick of an aged lizard, with his green cut-away and darting eyes.

Jerry modified his accent and vocabulary under the influence of the surroundings.

'Good morning, Jim. This is my friend Mr Frazer who'd be very happy to be able to use the facilities of the range. Does Mr Charles Silver happen to be around?'

'He sure does, Mr Carmichael. Step this way, gentlemen.' He led them through the labyrinth of the ancient Colonial building to an office where Mr Silver awaited them. His face was strong, square and solemn, and he handled the weapons maintenance manual he was thumbing through with a preacher's reverence.

'Charles, this is Dick Frazer, an old friend of the family. He wishes to buy a gun, and they tell me the law says he has to undergo a test. Could you fix that for him?'

Silver brightened visibly at the prospect of deploying the small pomposities that went with his position. 'Well, I imagine that could be arranged, Mr Carmichael. I don't see any great problem about that. Mr Frazer, may I ask what is the purpose in mind for you wishing to acquire a firearm?'

'I want to go deer-hunting,' Dick said.

'What, here in Cuba?' Silver looked surprised.

'To be exact, in Escambray,' Jerry said. 'I don't know if by any chance you happen to know the locality? A friend who I can rely on tells me you can shoot all the deer you want in those woods.'

'Well, that comes as a surprise to me, Mr Carmichael. However, I'm sure you're right.'

'Proghorns,' Jerry said. 'Do you happen to be familiar with them?'

'I can't say I am. I guess I took my fair share of whitetails in the old days, including one or two trophy animals. We didn't have proghorns where I did my shooting. Mr Frazer, how's your eyesight? I imagine you don't suffer from an ophthalmic problem of any kind, or any such disability, huh?'

'My eyesight's good,' Dick said. 'As far as I know.'

'Well, seeing all this has to go into the book, and the book's always liable to be inspected, why don't we take a quick check on it?' Silver lumbered comfortably to the end of the room and pulled open an optician's chart.

'Happen to know Buck Mountain, Idaho, Mr Carmichael? Pity, not many people do. You're talking about deer . . . Mr Frazer, let's start with the fourth row down. Can you read that?'

'UFDZNR.'

'And the one below?'

'ZNPHEDRY.'

'Good. I guess there's no problem there. I'm now going to expose you to a little invention of my own.' Silver gave a dry routine chuckle. 'It's liable to cause a little trouble if you happen to be suffering from a hangover, that's all.'

He put an object like a wand, about a yard long, in Dick's hand, pressed a button on his desk, and a point of red light appeared on a darkened screen above the chart.

'What you have there is a torch throwing a very narrow beam,' Silver said. 'I want you to switch on, hold it with your arm fully extended and endeavour to hold the light so that it exactly covers and cuts out the red light. OK?'

Dick did as instructed. Silver timed him for a minute on his stopwatch, during which time only the briefest and thinnest arc of red peeped from under the total eclipse of torchlight.

'Looks like your nerves are in good shape,' Silver said, 'so why don't we go through to the range now and take a few shots at a target? Any previous experience of target-shooting, Mr Frazer?'

'Only with an air rifle.'

'Well, anyway, you know how to handle a gun. The principle's the same.'

They went into the gallery. 'Let's advance to the barrier

and take up a stance,' Silver said. He picked a gun out of the rack, caressed its stock, lips pursed in admiration, slapped in a charge, and put it in Dick's hands. 'That,' he said, 'is the latest Marlin. You're going to like it. Treat it as a friend, and it'll treat you as one. Target is fixed at thirty yards. You have five shots, taking your own time, and after that another five, rapid fire. Maximum score is fifty and you need twenty-five to qualify. This gun is semi-automatic. You require to shoot the bolt once only. I'll demonstrate how that's done.'

Silver took the gun from Dick's hands, worked the bolt and handed it back. 'Be prepared for the double pressure on the trigger. All right, Mr Frazer, whenever you're ready, then.'

Dick laid his eye along the sights, nestling his cheek on the stock. He felt the give of the easy first pressure on the trigger. 'Breathe normally,' Silver said. 'Hold the breath before firing.'

Jerry had moved up close behind him, giving Silver an opportunity to air his philosophy. 'You're going to laugh at me when I tell you this, but every gun has its personality, just like you and me . . . Mr Frazer, better take another breath, you're getting all tensed up.'

The easy movement of the trigger had stopped. Dick breathed out, drew in his breath, and jerked with his finger. Silver whistled. 'Well, I don't know what happened there. You're right off the target. Seems like you yanked at that trigger instead of squeezing it. You have to co-operate with a gun, Mr Frazer. You have to fall into its mood. OK then, let's try again.'

Dick fired again, and there was a moment of silence while Silver scrutinized the target through his binoculars. 'We have a mystery here. Something seems to be seriously wrong. This time you're just on the target, with no score. The impression I got was you jerked the gun. For me, you weren't even pointing at the centre of the target. I'm sorry to have to tell you this – in any case I guess you know already – but I'm obliged by law to enter your score up in the record book. You have three shots left and to qualify they have to be three nearly perfect ones. I hope you're going to surprise me.'

The foresight of Dick's rifle wavered about over the general area of the bull. Silver and Jerry, behind him, had moved closer. He could feel the impact of their mixture of derision and anxiety. When he drew in his breath they drew in theirs. Now he had begun to tremble in earnest.

'You're not even holding the gun still,' Silver said. 'You gotta be able to hold it still. Do you want to rest and relax for a coupla minutes? Maybe you'd like to visit the washroom, huh?'

'No, I'm all right, thanks. I'll rest for a moment and then try again.' He lowered the gun.

'Mr Frazer, you seemed to be chasing that bull round like it was on the move. Can you furnish any explanation maybe why that should be?'

'I think I had what they call double vision,' Dick said. 'When I was concentrating I saw two targets and I didn't know which to fire at. Is this the kind of thing that can happen sometimes?'

'I've heard of it,' Silver said, 'but I have to say it's nothing I've ever encountered before. From what you tell me it's something that could seriously hamper your shooting. If this is going to happen all the time you ought to get a medical opinion as to what's going wrong.'

'That's what I'll have to do,' Dick said. 'I feel better now. Shall I go on?'

'Go ahead by all means. But take your time, huh? This time has to surprise us. This has to be a great shot. Ten if you can. Nine, minimum.'

Dick fired. He heard Silver's sigh. 'Well, Mr Frazer, I'm afraid that's it. You scored a two, which I regret to say rules you out. No point in going on, I guess.'

'I suppose there isn't,' Dick said. 'I'm sorry. I'm sorry for wasting your time.'

'No cause for you to be sorry. That's what I'm here for. What I feel badly about is that you're not going to be able to get that certificate. I'd like to be able to help out, but I can't. You realize that, don't you?'

'I know you can't. I understand that. And thank you for giving me the test. Do you think perhaps I could get a little practice somewhere and come back and have another try?'

'Nothing whatever to stop you. But on your present showing you'd have to work hard at it.'

'I suppose I'm about the worst shot you've ever come across.'

'You sure are the worst I've ever come across,' Jerry said.

'Well, I don't know about that,' Silver said. 'I've known guys, you put a gun in their hands and they couldn't hit the side of a house at thirty yards. Let's say this, there's scope for improvement.'

'You're a diplomat, Silver,' Jerry said. 'That's what you ought to be, a counsellor or something over in the Embassy.'

'As you tell me,' Silver said, 'you're aiming to shoot deer, which is an intelligent and elusive animal. Take a whitetail, or an antelope, for instance; you're lying out there waiting for them and they can see you move your hand to scratch your ass when they're a mile away. You gotta have a great gun and a good relationship with it, a good score on the book, a lotta practice, and you gotta be able to think with that animal's mind. You have to ask yourself, are you ready to meet this challenge?'

'No, I'm not,' Dick said. 'The whole idea was a bit of a mistake.'

'To be brutally frank,' Silver said, 'you got about as much chance of shooting a deer right now as you have of creeping up on it and scaring it to death.'

They all laughed.

'That's not meant to be rude, Mr Frazer. I know you can take a joke.' He laid a consoling hand on Dick's arm.

They walked back to the wharf, taking cuts across several parks to shorten the distance.

'I was bad, wasn't I?' Dick asked.

'You were bad, all right. I never saw anybody so bad.'

'Mr Silver said he'd seen worse, but he was being polite.'

'They have to be in that business. Don't worry, Frazer, you took him by surprise.'

'He'll remember me, won't he?'

'OK, he'll remember you. You've established the fact you're a truly terrible shot, but right now are you being rational? Are you using your head?'

'In what way do you mean using my head?'

'What about all that fantasy stuff you went in for? That have anything to do with this?'

'I don't think so. It's going to be my birthday and I want to go deer-hunting. Let's leave it at that.'

'OK by me. I'm only trying to help, but I guess this is your baby, huh? You gotta do what you think, Frazer, but stop thinking like a kid, and start thinking like a man.'

They walked on. 'So you're taking off tomorrow?' Jerry said.

'Yes, I want to get back.'

'Done all you came for, huh?'

'That's about it.'

'You ought to stick around a day or two and think about things. Give it another day, so we could chew the fat a bit. I was kind of looking forward to your visit. What's all the hurry?'

'I said I'd go back. I've only got a few days left to be with my mother.'

'You make it sound like the wait in the death-house. Listen, Frazer, you're starting to depress the hell out of me. And I got enough bad news lately. Remember that buddy of mine from Paris, Missouri, I told you about, went off to the Sierra? I just heard he's missing. Went out with a patrol, and never came back.'

'I'm sorry,' Dick said. 'Let's hope he turns up. The fact he's missing doesn't mean he's dead. Perhaps he's been captured.'

'That could be worse. Anyhow, the way things are I have this feeling I might run out of friends. When am I going to see you again, Frazer?'

'I don't know,' Dick said. 'I wish I could think of anything further ahead than next Tuesday, but I can't.'

Chapter Fourteen

They headed eastward, backs to the setting sun, through the passive yellows and greens of the evening spectrum towards the blue and the violet of night. The Central Highway was straight and empty; a white-faced straying cow, high-wheeled carts spilling their corn into village streets, a Greyhound bus carrying in its silver facets all that was left of the light of the sun.

Dick invented and resolved unlikely situations.

'Your mother didn't want to tell you before but I better now,' Stilson said. 'You'll be attending the American School while we're away. As a day boy. And staying as was suggested in my aunt's flat. Any comment?'

'No.'

'She's a nut-case. But don't let that bother you. Anna will be there to look after you and cook your meals.'

'I don't want to be left with Anna. I don't like her and I know she hates me. If she could hurt me in any way, she would.'

'What gives you that idea?'

'The way she looks at me. It's easy to see when anybody hates you. She must be jealous.'

'You're quite wrong there. She may be a little possessive where I'm concerned, but she takes quite an interest in you. You'll get along fine together. Anna is a remarkable person. There's a good deal more to her than meets the eye.'

They could hear the sound of the dog scuffling and whining in the back, and Simon's scolding gibberish above the noise of the tyres. 'Stinks, doesn't it?' Stilson said. 'It's hungry. They won't hunt if they're well fed. You're not much of a one for dogs, are you?'

'I'm a bit afraid of that one. I don't like Simon much, either. He gives me the creeps.'

'I had the impression that you were both surprised and disappointed to hear that I was bringing them along,' Stilson said.

'I didn't know we needed them.'

'The dog is indispensable,' Stilson said. 'It goes off into the woods, sniffs out the deer, and drives them in front of the guns.'

'I see.'

'And only Simon can talk to the dog.'

Stilson turned his head towards Dick. His smile had widened, thinning his lips. 'It would have been nicer to be on our own,' he said. 'However, there it is.'

They charged into the small town of Esperanza, with every star alight in the sky, and the houses strung out like white cubes all along the road. Stilson pulled into a filling station and Simon got out with the dog and led it in the direction of a tree, while the attendant topped up the tank.

'Something wrong with him tonight,' Stilson said. 'He's in one of his funny moods. Hated having to come on this trip. He's afraid of the dark.'

Simon came back, dragging the dog, and Stilson started up. 'Never believe that guy back there used to be a student revolutionary. Like all the kids still are in this country. Used to be one myself. You don't have politics in your country, do you?'

'Not like they have here. You vote when there's an election, that's all.'

'Good thing too,' Stilson said. 'Far better off as you are.'

They turned off into a third category road winding into the hills, and soon San Juan showed in a few doubtful lights and a police station with hammocks hung in its porch.

The store they had been directed to was closed, so Stilson went into the police station to enquire, then came back and climbed into the driver's seat again.

'I have news for you,' Stilson said. 'The store's changed hands. Rafael hasn't been around for months. And that goes for the deer too. They seemed surprised at anyone going deer-hunting round here. How long ago was it when your friend is supposed to have shot that buck?'

'A few weeks, I was told.'

'Well, I've got a terrible feeling it may be a piece of ancient history. Our only hope, they say, is Los Altos. There's a dirt track going up to it a couple of miles up the road.'

They took the track which stopped in deep jungle five miles further up where a village was marked on their out-of-date map. Of this a single hut had survived.

'From now on we walk,' Stilson said. 'Something tells me we're going to be lucky if we shoot a deer on this expedition. How are you feeling now? You look kind of funny. You've been looking kind of strange to me all this evening.'

'I'm all right.'

'Sure?'

'Quite sure.'

'This is your birthday trip. You're supposed to be enjoying yourself.'

'I am.'

'Good. Because I'd hate to think something had happened to disappoint you. What's your leg shivering and shaking like that for?'

'It's the way I'm sitting.'

They climbed down. 'Right,' Stilson said. 'What we do now is eat. We sleep in the back of the car after Simon has washed it out. I'll fix the alarm to wake us at two, and we'll go and see if there are any deer to be shot. The best hunting's just before dawn. According to the map there's a path down to a river. If there are any deer at all, that's where we're going to find them.'

Simon had come from the back of the car, dragging the dog on its chain. Stilson summoned him with a snap of the fingers, and gave a curt order.

'I told him he'd have to wash the animal and also wash out the car before he got any food,' Stilson said. 'He took it badly.'

Stilson went to the car for a pressure lamp and lit it, after which Dick helped him set up a folding table and two chairs, and to unpack the hamper. In the background Simon was trying to wash the dog, which resisted his advances with fearsome growlings.

'See the way he's going about it?' Stilson said. 'Notice how half-hearted he is? It's his way of telling me to go to hell. Let's take a little walk to try the lights while he cleans up. Then we'll have supper and go to bed.'

Stilson went to the back of the van, hoisted himself in, and came back carrying the rifles, two battery haversacks, and the jack-lights on their headbands. He lifted one of the haversacks and buckled it to Dick's shoulders. Then he slipped the padded lampbands over his forehead, tested its tension and adjusted the straps. 'Comfortable?' he asked. 'OK then. You can give me a hand with mine.'

Dick helped Stilson put on the equipment, and Stilson put a gun in his hands. 'That's a Ruger mini-14. Not much bigger than a kid's toy, is it?' he said. 'But it's all you need. I go for a small calibre gun because I hate meat destruction. Two-four-three cartridge which is enough. It puts a neat little hole through the target without smashing it up.'

He showed Dick how to load, and reminded him to keep the safety-catch on. 'Let's go and take a look at the forest from the inside.'

They found a jungle track. 'Switch on,' Stilson ordered. Dick pressed his switch, and light beam, hard, clean-edged and full of brilliant motes, punched into the foliage a hundred yards ahead. Stilson overtook, then passed, trudging softly through the light-frosted undergrowth and fallen leaves. He waved for Dick to come up, the dazzling halo from his lamp mounted on utter blackness, and when he spoke his face remained invisible. 'We're on our own at this moment,' Stilson said. 'As much I guess, as we'll ever be. Simon's out there somewhere but he's behind about a million trees. Listen, hold my gun a minute. I need to take a leak.'

Dick groped into the light, found the gun and took it, and Stilson turned away, suddenly appearing as a dark cut-out against the trees as his light swung with him. He walked a few paces to stand with his back to Dick, and unbutton, then was back. He took the gun from Dick's hand. 'Let's go back and eat,' he said. His voice which had been quiet and low-pitched, was now suddenly cheerful.

They walked in silence for a few moments. 'Well, that was quite an experiment you just took part in back there,' Stilson said.

Dick could find no reason for the new, breezy confidence. 'You mean trying out the lamps?'

'No, I do not mean that. I just won a fifty to one bet with myself, namely that you wouldn't try to shoot me even if I gave you the chance. I guess I like to find I'm right in my judgements.'

Suddenly the mechanism holding Dick's thoughts together lost control, and they fell apart. In a moment of fractured concentration and the dispersal of ideas he felt the sudden clench of the jack-light headband tightened by the swelling veins in his temples. He took a deep breath as he had learned to do in psychological crises, then swallowed, and the muddle in his head began to unravel itself.

'It's too much to expect you to own up,' Stilson said. 'I'm not even going to ask you. Anyway, nobody can be put on trial for having bad intentions. Dick, let me ask you something. Did you ever hear what I did for a living way back nearly twenty years ago?'

Dick found the words and assembled them into a sentence. 'Someone said you were on the stage.'

'Well, not quite that. I used to appear at the Victoria Theatre in the guise of a mind-reader. It was a good act, Dick. So much so that the scientists came down from Boston to check if I wasn't actually reading minds. Which I wasn't. Let me say that here and now. Mind-reading is crap. Nobody reads minds. What I did was to study people. I studied them until I could tell when there was a change in their pulse-rate, or their breathing rate, or the sugar in their blood, or the electrical fields in their bodies, or even their bodily odour, Dick. Imagine that. I watched the way they shifted their eyes, and how the muscles in their faces moved when I asked them questions. And how they twiddled their fingers, and crossed and uncrossed their feet and how they moistened their lips, cleared their throats, or coughed. That's the way I watched you, Dick. I knew when the pressure started in your bladder and when you were going to have to get up to go to piss. You haven't said or done anything that went unnoticed, and in the end I just about knew what you were going to say before you said it . . . And guess what all these things told me when I added them up? That you wanted to kill me. You made it as clear to me as if you'd taken me aside and told me so. And naturally, once you got this idea into your head, and you being you, there was some pretty wild planning.'

Listening to his jaunty tone, Dick knew that Stilson was enjoying himself, and he understood that this was one of his ways of displaying power. Stilson was turning his mind inside out, moved to laughter rather than anger at what he found there.

They traipsed on through the crackling branches and dead leaves. 'But that, as I knew, would be about as far as it would ever go,' Stilson said. 'Most hundred per cent planners tend to fight shy of action when it comes to the crunch. The thing to remember is that half of you didn't want to kill me anyway. When I told you Simon was going to be included on this trip your subconscious relief was as strong as a smell. You'd been given a way out. It was an excuse to drop all your ridiculous plans. I brought Simon into this just to be on the safe side, just the way I made sure that the top cartridge in the clip in your gun was a blank. It was a kind of a routine thing, like a safety-line in a trapeze act, but I knew it wasn't necessary.'

They were at the end of the track now, about to enter the clearing. 'Do you still want to go ahead with this, Dick? I mean, this hunt?' Stilson asked. 'We can call it off and go back if you want. Say what you want to do.'

'I want to go ahead with it.'

'Good, I'm glad to hear that. I admire that attitude. We've defused the situation and I have a strong feeling that things are going to be better between us from now on. The only time you pushed yourself to a violent solution of your problems it didn't work out for you. I'm sorry I didn't know you in those days, Dick. My hunch is you would never have gone to Stoneyfields.'

'My mother promised me she would never tell you about that,' Dick said.

'And she didn't, not at first. The way things were shaping I felt I had to make a few enquiries, and I was bound to find out. All she did was to confirm what I already knew.'

They crossed the clearing together. Stilson turned up the lamp to inspect the cutlery he unwrapped from the linen napkins, the glasses and the plates. 'Never believe in leaving anything to chance,' he said. 'Just to make sure Simon hasn't touched anything with his filthy paws.'

He gestured to Dick to sit down. 'Half the pleasure of hunting trips,' he said, 'is the food that goes with them. I can put away double the amount of food I normally do. We have roast chicken, sucking pig, two kinds of ham, and one or two local specialities you may or may not like.' Simon, who had carried out the hamper, awaited further orders, attached to the long shadow projected from his body by the lamp. He was bloated and blue-lipped in this light. Stilson dismissed him. 'You still stink, go away,' he said. He began to arrange the food with almost finicky concern for order. 'Pull up your chair and pitch in,' he said.

They had begun to eat when Simon made a stealthy and cautious return edging towards them, foot by foot. Now he squatted on his heels to watch them on the perimeter of the lamplight. A great white owl, lit from below, flopped over their heads on wings of cotton wool.

'Curious, isn't it, this fear of the dark he has?' Stilson said. 'We fell out yesterday when I caught him stealing the dog's food, and as I believe in making the punishment fit the crime I'm just about to give the dog a chance to get his own back.'

He signalled to Simon, who limped towards them, head askew, drooling from the lips, one arm dangling six inches lower than the other from the dropped shoulder, one toe turned in so far that he seemed to have difficulty in not tripping over his feet.

'He's all out of shape, but he's a strong man for all that,'

94

Stilson said. 'You'd never believe how fast he can move when he has to.' To Simon he said quietly, 'Get the dog.'

Simon shuffled away to untie the rope fastening the dog to the tree-trunk. He looked back at them, wincing and grinning with anxiety.

'Bring it here,' Stilson said.

Simon brought the dog, which was one of the ugliest Dick had ever seen. Its legs were too long and its head too small for its body. Its shoulders were covered with thick matted hair, like a lion's mane, but its flanks and belly were obscenely bare. It growled continuously. Stilson took the rope and holding it in his left hand he tore a leg off a chicken and threw it into the air. It fell to the ground seven or eight yards away. 'Get it, it's yours,' he said to Simon.

Simon went skipping and hobbling away.

'You see,' Stilson said. 'He runs nearly as fast as I can.' He waited until the old man was within a few feet of the chicken bone, the dog whining and tugging, and then let go of the rope and the dog went bounding after him.

Simon, hearing it coming, let out a blubber of dismay. He straddled the chicken leg to snatch it from the ground and hold it as high as he could out of the dog's reach, and the dog sprang, landed on his shoulder and knocked him off his feet. The man and the dog wrestled and scuffled together on the ground, the dog kicking out and thrusting with its muzzle after the bone into Simon's folded body, and the man jabbing with fingers of his free hand into the dog's eyes. Sickened and horrified, Dick realized how agile and powerful this near cripple was when relieved of his dependency upon his legs.

A screaming and yelping began and Stilson jumped up and ran to pull the dog away. He dragged it to the car and tied it to the rear bumper. 'Had to move fast,' he said. 'The old man would have blinded it.'

He tore the other leg off the chicken and threw it and Simon, continuing to blubber, caught it with the perfect judgement of a trained dolphin catching a fish.

'He never misses,' Stilson said to Dick. 'Go and wash that

95

blood off yourself,' he told Simon, 'and then clear away this mess.'

He sat down again. 'Another chop?' he asked Dick.

Dick shook his head. 'I couldn't eat any more.'

Stilson stared at him with curiosity. 'Not worried, were you?'

'Not really,' Dick said. 'I was afraid the dog was going to kill him.'

Stilson laughed. 'You ought to have more faith in me. I know what I'm doing and the dog knows what he's doing. If he'd wanted to, he could have bitten the old man's throat out. That's a tear in an arm muscle anyway. I'll stitch it up when we get back. The man was getting out of hand and I've put him in his place.' He looked at his watch. 'Ten thirty-five. Let's grab a little sleep.'

Dick helped him lay out the bedding rolls in the back of the Range-Rover, and tie up the mosquito nets. Stilson set the alarm for two.

'Where's Simon sleeping?' Dick asked.

'Under the car. He likes to keep as close as he can.'

Stilson had brought up one of the folding chairs, and they both took their shirts off and hung them on the back of the chair, and then crawled under the nets.

'Quiet, isn't it?' Stilson said. 'I don't hear the old man around anywhere.' He groped through his net to put out the lamp. 'He's going to be shaking in his shoes out there in the dark,' he said.

Dick listened. All he could hear was the soft creaking of the trees' branches moved by the breeze that had arisen. A feeling of guilt, of frustration, of failure and of hopelessness was added to the normal physical fatigue of the long day. He fell asleep.

He was awakened by torchlight in his eyes. A moon of aching light swelled up, then shrank in the darkness, and a voice he was unable for a moment to recognize spoke close to his ear. 'Two o'clock. Time to get up.'

Footsteps clanked on the metal floor and the torchlight bobbed away. Dick pulled the mosquito net open, got up and stood swaying, brain fuddled, bent double under the low roof. He groped his way to the back of the truck and dropped to the ground. A few yards away Stilson was busy with the Primus. He straightened himself and half-turned, his face chiselled by the lamplight with a kind of Indian stoicism.

'Sleep well?' Stilson asked.

'Yes, I did.'

'You must have done. I suppose you didn't hear anything?'

'No.'

'Well, I did. I heard the dog, but I didn't wake up enough to do anything about it. It's dead.'

'It's *what*?'

'It's as dead as a doornail.'

'What happened?'

Stilson turned to finish pouring a cup of coffee. He motioned Dick to take it. 'Simon cut its throat. He probably put nigger poison in its food to paralyse its legs. I heard a couple of yelps, and that was that. It's lying over there.'

Dick turned his head cautiously, holding his breath, afraid of what he might see. The dog lay, a shapeless heap a dozen yards away. The rope still trailed from its neck. 'Poor dog,' he said, more in comfort to himself rather than to Stilson. He was sickened by the thought of this powerful animal being dragged helplessly to a bloody end. And on the heels of sorrow and disgust came fear. He wanted to jump to his feet and run away.

'Coffee all right?' Stilson said. 'Not too sweet, huh?'

Dick had been sipping mechanically. 'It's just right,' he said. 'Where's Simon?'

'He's gone,' Stilson said. 'He dragged the dog away and killed it, and then he came into the truck and stole everything he could lay his hands on, and we didn't wake up. We were sleeping as peacefully as babes. He could have cut our throats too, if he'd felt like it.'

'What about the guns?'

'They're OK. He couldn't get at them because I pushed them down between my bedding and the side of the truck. But he did get my watch and a gold pen and the cash I left in my shirt pocket. Better check whether he took anything from you.'

'I didn't have anything to take. What are we going to do now?'

'The best we can,' Stilson said. 'We came here to hunt and unless you've had enough of it that's what we're going to do.'

'Are we going to get anything at all without the dog?'

'It would be one hell of a chance if we did. We'd practically have to bump into some animal that happened to be walking around in the same sector of wood. The chances are kind of remote.'

'Did the dog suffer much, do you think?'

'If you're paralysed you suffer. You're going to suffer when somebody cuts your throat, too. Go and take a look for yourself.'

He handed Dick a torch, and Dick walked across the clearing to the place where the dog lay on its side at the end of the rope, eyes bulging and tongue hanging out, in a dank, black patch of grass.

Stilson had followed him. 'He could never have got to it to cut its throat if he hadn't poisoned it first,' Stilson said. 'I guess it wobbled away from him all it could when it saw him coming with the knife, but didn't have the strength to fight him off.'

'Where do you think Simon went?' Dick said.

'Not far, that's for certain. I know his mentality. He has this phobia about the dark. Right now my bet is he's not more than fifty yards away. Somewhere in the trees over there, just watching us. And he's going to stay around until it's light. I have a feeling it's a good thing for us he didn't get his hands on one of those guns.'

He could be watching us. Dick stared into the encircling trees. There were many rents in the whitened texture of their foliage, at the mouths of dark places, in any of which Simon might be laying in wait.

'This for me,' Stilson said, 'is a failure. A mistake. Something that should never have happened. It's brought me to the sad and sudden conclusion that I know just a little less about the human race than I believed I knew . . . Why are you trembling, Dick? What's the trouble?'

'I'm a bit cold, that's all.'

'Know something? I worked on the assumption that that old guy hadn't a will of his own left, and I was wrong. That was an experiment that didn't quite come off.'

He threw the dregs of his coffee away and got up. 'Well, no use sitting around here beefing on about one thing and another. Let's get the gear on and make a move.'

'What about Simon? What's he going to do?'

'My hunch is as soon as we move off, he will. He'll tag along and try to keep us in sight if only because it would drive him crazy to have to stay here by himself in the dark. I've got the car keys. He's stolen everything worth having anyway.'

'Are we going to do something about the dog?' Dick asked.

'I was forgetting. Maybe I should bury it,' Stilson said.

He went for the shovel in the car, and a moment later Dick heard the sound of digging. Stilson came back. 'Well, that's done,' he said. 'Let's get going.'

They switched on. Saplings appearing in the light of their lamps to be made of shining plaster had planted themselves at exact distances, and the lianas hanging from the high branches above were like brilliant stalactites, sometimes even like icicles.

'In the end it makes you sleepy to look at it,' Stilson said. 'Walk far enough through this kind of thing, and you're practically asleep on your feet.' He glanced at Dick, plodding silently over the carpet of fallen leaves. 'You take anything that shows on the right. I'll handle this side. And by the way, I've taken that blank cartridge out of your clip.'

Ahead of them to the left, points of light pricked from the relative shade under a swathe of incandescent foliage. 'Let that one go,' Stilson said. 'Whatever it is, it's too small. Some kind of forest rat.' The little reflections were switched off as the animal, whatever it was, made its unseen escape.

'Never believe you could pick out an animal by the colour of its eye reflection, would you?' Stilson said. 'Red eye

99

reflections are cats, and orange reflections are owls. A fox is white, like a deer, but you can't make a mistake because a fox keeps down in the underbrush, and a deer lifts its head to look at you . . . Tell you something, I've never been on a hunt that looked less promising than this. Listen, did you hear that?'

They stopped and Dick felt his breathing speed up. He realized how incomplete was the silence he had accepted as total. From all directions came the faint, mysterious sub-sounds of the night. A breeze that was suddenly cool stirred the down on the nape of his neck.

'The question is, are we being followed?' Stilson said. 'When I give the word, swing round with me, and let's see if there's anything to be seen . . . now.'

They turned together sweeping a great saturation of light through the trees to shine on the path. Dick stared into the glowing, frosted monotony of trees, branches, saplings, vines, bordered with a frothing collage of leaves. Nothing moved.

'See anything?' Stilson asked.

'No.'

'Nor do I. I heard something though. I have exceptionally acute hearing. Sounded like someone treading on a dried branch.'

They turned back again. Two points of light were dancing in a pocket of shadow. 'Only a pig,' Stilson said. 'That's the way they jerk their heads about. You want to take a shot at it for kicks, go right ahead. But what's the point?'

The jungle closed in on them and then opened out, with its endless glittering vistas and its endless repetitions.

'I hear you went to the Poste Restante to collect a letter,' Stilson said. 'From your father, huh?'

'Yes.'

'Havana is a small town,' Stilson said. 'Everybody knows everybody knows everybody else's business. Was there any news to report?'

'He was upset because he hadn't had any of our letters.'

'Strange.'

'It isn't strange,' Dick said. 'The letters weren't sent.' He

100

was amazed at his boldness, while half understanding that in some way Stilson had been damaged and weakened by Simon's revolt.

'Did you reply?'

'Yes, I did. I told him he ought to come back here as soon as he could.'

'We may just miss him, which will be a pity,' Stilson said. 'I haven't any doubt that your father and I could reach an agreement.'

'You mean he'd agree to you marrying Mother?'

'I think he would. I believe I could convince him it would be a good thing for all concerned. I expect you don't think so.'

Dick wanted to say, 'No, I don't,' but his little accumulated store of resistance had been used up. He said nothing.

'I'm still convinced we're being followed,' Stilson said. 'If Simon's back there, he's closer than he was. Let's try again. Ready?'

They swung round together again, the lights with them. 'There you are,' Stilson said. 'Over to the left of the track, between those two trunks. Something moved. Did you see it?'

'I thought I saw something move.'

'It's gone now. It could have been an animal, but I don't think it was. It looked like a man pushing his face from behind the trunk and pulling it back again. Is that what you saw?'

'It was just a movement. I'm sure I saw something move.'

'That's our friend, be sure of that,' Stilson said. 'It's easy enough to follow us, but he may find he has a problem on the way back to keep far enough ahead to be out of sight. Let's push on a bit further. This track is going to take us down to a stream, if we keep going. If there are any game at all they'll be down there, and if not we'll throw it in.'

They reached the stream and the ruin of a bridge. There was nothing but frogs and a few rodent eyes flashing back their lights from the waterside thickets.

'Well, that's it,' Stilson said. 'Want to rest for a bit?'

'No, I'm all right.'

They started back up the slight uphill slope, and had covered about a mile when Stilson gave a warning hiss. A figure was scampering in and out the trees a hundred yards ahead. Stilson raised his rifle, then lowered it. The running man was lost in the dim patterns of the forest. 'That's the last we'll see of Simon,' Stilson said. 'Get light soon, and he'll take off.'

They reached a clearing where saplings grew to ten feet in height, miniatures of the great trees that surrounded them, and there were dense clumps of bushes having no part of the real jungle but which had grown here because falling airborne seeds had discovered space and light. Dick did not know why they had come to a stop. He was drugged by fatigue, and the brilliant monotony of the long walk. His mind had begun to wander and his tensions to dissolve. Stilson was no longer an object of hatred, but an anonymous human presence.

Dawn had come, shafting thinly through the trees, and the lights were out. Stilson had taken his gun from him and stood it against a tree-trunk, before starting a conversation not a single detail of which Dick could remember. Sometimes Stilson's lips moved as if in speech, although not a word was to be heard. Now he lit a cigar blowing out the smoke in such a way that it hung coiled in soft, sluggish currents before his face, and only his eyes showed through. When Stilson's silent mouthings turned to words, Dick understood that what was being said was in continuation of a theme that had been under discussion. 'The fact that you are highly suggestible,' Stilson said, 'is nothing to be ashamed of. Most imaginative people are. Don't attempt to resist it. It is for your good.'

Stilson reached in the opening of his shirt for the religious medal and held it close to Dick's eyes. A shaft of light stabbed out from the trees to shine on a woman's head shown in profile on the medal. 'I am a Christian,' Stilson said, 'but I am also a member of the cult of Santeros, and this is our saint. She came to us from Africa, and she is *vodun*, or as you would say, voodoo. When I spin the medal you will see the head come out. If you were an *iluminado* you would hear it speak to you. But to be *iluminado* one must be chosen.'

He spun the medal on its chain, and Dick watched the woman's head. The thick lips appeared to move but he heard no sound. 'All is in the mind,' Stilson said. 'The past, the present and the future.' Dick closed his eyes. He felt himself swaying like a pendulum between two walls of darkness.

Stilson threw away his cigar. He bent down to pull up his trouser-leg, and drew the heavy knife carried in a sheath strapped to his leg. Then he went over to the nearest sapling, slashed through it at its base, and cut from it a wand about four feet in length and as thick as his thumb. He walked back to Dick.

'Open your eyes, Dick, and tell me about this plan you had to kill me. I'm most interested. Just what were you going to do?'

Dick was suddenly flooded by the urge to lay bare the secrets of his innermost being. 'Shoot you,' he said, almost with eagerness.

'We know that,' Stilson said in his friendliest voice. 'But how? In what circumstances?'

'Hunting,' Dick said. 'Like this. It was a place just like this, with some bushes. We would be out in the open talking like we are now. You would put down your gun to light a cigar, and I would shoot you through the heart.'

'Well, I'm going to light a cigar right now. And my gun's over there. I'm at your mercy. Why do you favour this particular scene? And why the bushes?'

'I was going to drag your body into the bushes. That's where a deer would have been. It wouldn't have been out here in the open.'

'Of course it wouldn't. So a deer came into this, huh? I get it, you saw something in the half-light, moving in the bushes, which you took to be a deer. You fired at it, and to your horror, you found you'd hit me. That was to be your story?'

'That's what I was going to tell them.'

'Wouldn't there have been some evidence to show I'd been

103

killed elsewhere? Where I'm standing now. Blood on the ground, for instance?'

'It would be very easy to clear it away.' Dick scuffed with his boot among the decaying leaves and smiled vacantly. 'When I got you into the bushes,' he said, 'I was going to tear up my shirt to make a bandage before going for help.'

'To give the impression you'd done what you could for me, I gather. You think of everything, Dick.'

'Before going for help I'd have looked round for another bush about twenty or thirty yards away.'

'You mean like the one with yellow flowers over there.'

'Or the one behind it. I was going to tread down the undergrowth a bit, break off a twig or two and leave the gun there.'

'Why?'

'Because if I was going to mistake you for a deer I would have to be quite a long way away. And the deer wouldn't be there anyway if I was out in the open. Another thing was, everybody knew I was a bad shot. They wouldn't believe I'd be able to shoot you through the heart at a distance like that unless it was a fluke.'

'How come everybody knows you're a bad shot?'

'I made sure they would because I went along with Jerry Carmichael to take a test at a range. I made one of the worst scores there the man had ever seen. He put it in a book.'

'And you were faking all the time? This was all part of the cover-up? You fill me with admiration. Pity in a way it was all so much wasted effort, huh, Dick? That's the trouble. Waste of energy. Waste of everything. Do you know what my feeling is? My feeling is we shouldn't allow this kind of thing to run on, and if you and I are going to co-operate in future in every way – which we are – we have to do something to get it out of your system. And the quickest, the most painless and effective way of doing so is to act the thing out the way you planned it while in your present receptive state. You have to do exactly what I tell you without hesitation or question of any kind. That way we can wipe the slate clean, we can straighten this thing out once and for all.'

104

'I'll do anything you want me to do,' Dick said, in his new piping voice.

'Of course you will, Dick, and the first thing I'm going to do is give you a gun, which is indispensable to your plan. Am I right?'

Stilson put the length of sapling in Dick's hand. 'Well, here it is. The nicest little weapon of its kind in current production. Reliable and accurate in the extreme.' He stepped back a couple of paces. 'Decide where my heart lies and point it at me. Up fairly high and a shade to the left of the centre of my chest.'

Dick held the length of sapling as if it had been a rifle, and aimed it as directed.

'Finger on the trigger. Safety-catch off, right?'

Dick's fingers moved in response to Stilson's command over the smooth surfaces of the wood.

'When I give the order to fire, you will pull the trigger,' Stilson said, 'and I shall drop dead. It's as simple as that.' His tone was pleasantly conversational. 'After that you will do what you planned to do with my body. In due course I shall resurrect myself. You will have no recollection of what has taken place, and our relationship will be renewed on a fresh and more rewarding basis.'

Stilson raised a hand, 'Are you ready, then?'

'Ready, Mr Stilson,' Dick piped.

'Here we are then, Dick. Your greatest moment of release has come. Right through the heart, huh? Fire.'

Dick tugged with a crooked finger along the under surface of the wood. Stilson let out a theatrical gasp, grabbed for his heart and fell to one knee.

Dick watched him cautiously, keeping the length of sapling pointed at his chest. He made an urgent, frustrated sound, and went through the mime of firing again.

'Well, if you insist,' Stilson said. He lowered himself comfortably to lie on the ground. 'All right, I'm dead now. You've killed me. Let's get on with the next part.'

Dick moved forward. 'You're not dead, Mr Stilson,' he said. With the sapling pointed down and the imaginary sights within a foot of Stilson's ribcage, he pressed the imaginary trigger again.

Stilson sat up, laughing. 'Something sure went wrong here. No way of stopping you now, is there? Ninety per cent of my little experiments work out right, but once in a while one has to fail.'

He was on the point of hoisting himself to his feet when Dick threw the stick down and made a dash for the guns Stilson had left standing against the tree-trunk.

Stilson went after him. 'No, Dick, no,' he screamed. 'No, no, no.' Dick reached the nearer gun, picked it up and turned. He snapped off the safety-catch and took aim. A flame not a half-inch in length leaped from the barrel, and the echoes barked in falsetto, like a jackal among the trees.

Stilson stopped dead, skewered in space. His jaw snapped open and an unhinged tongue dropped on his lower lip. Dick waited and watched while Stilson's fingers began to strip petals from the air – she loves me, she loves me not.

Dick held the gun pointed at the centre of his chest, his finger tightening again on the trigger, while Stilson, speechless and rolling his eyes, began a kind of slow, jerking dance, torso held stiff, but squirming and bouncing like a rumba dancer from the waist down.

Dick took a small step backwards, still aiming the gun.

Stilson's mouth had twisted into a smirk of agony. He threw out an arm in a drowning gesture. 'Help me, Dick, for Christ's sake. You just put a bullet through me.' He stopped his prancing to guffaw blood, catching as much as he could of it, as if precious to him, in a cupped hand.

'Please help me, Dick,' he wheezed and wheedled through the bubbles of mucus rising in his throat.

Dick watched him warily. In the minutes that had passed since he had looked into the childish face of the African goddess locked in the medallion's silver core, the million facts and episodes of a whole lifetime had emptied into oblivion, to be replaced with sixteen years of a shadow existence of absolute credibility. The natural evolution, the causality, the interlocking experiences of this second life into which the smiling African had led him had reached their culmination in this moment. Only the simplest of questions remained to be answered.

'Are you going to die now, Mr Stilson?' Dick asked.

A rush of weakness had knocked Stilson's legs from under him. He had crumpled into an awkward sitting position, blowing a little pinkish spray before being able to reply.

'I don't know. Yes I am. I'm going to die. Don't shoot any more. Oh my God, why can't I get through to you? Why can't I make you understand?'

'I understand you, Mr Stilson.'

'Listen to me, Dick. You *must* listen to what I say, because it's getting hard for me to speak. The medal I showed you. Take it out again. I want you to look at it while I talk to you.'

Stilson fell back to lie full length, his eyelids were half-closed and his moustache and chin were flecked with a murky frothing from the lips. Dick put down the gun and squatted to watch him with curiosity. 'Please get the medal out, Dick,' Stilson whispered. 'I have to talk to you.'

Dick carefully undid the buttons of Stilson's shirt. The silver medallion on its chain hung down to the right side of the chest. He picked it up, then let it drop again, his attention wholly absorbed by the revelation of a tiny black, dribbling indentation left by the entry of the bullet. Excitement broke into the piping monotone of his voice. 'I've found the place where the bullet went in, Mr Stilson,' he said.

'Oh God, Dick, never mind. Just get out the medal and look at it, so that I can talk to you.'

'The hole is so small you can hardly see it,' Dick said. He smiled and nodded. 'You were right, Mr Stilson, there's no meat destruction, is there?'

'Dick, listen. This is what you have to do. You have to go to San Juan as fast as you can. Remember the police station there? You have to go to the police station and ask for the *encargado*. Tell him there's been an accident and to bring a doctor. This cuts out all the other things I've told you to do. You're to forget about them. They never existed. Got that? There's been an accident, and you're going to San Juan to bring a doctor. That's all you have to think about now.'

Stilson's voice was getting fainter and Dick had to hold his face very close to Stilson's to be able to hear. He began to take off his shirt.

'Why are you doing that?' Stilson whispered.

'I want to bandage you up.'

'Please leave me alone, Dick,' Stilson said. 'It's useless and it's a waste of time. Bandaging won't do any good. Please don't touch me.'

'You must be bandaged, Mr Stilson,' Dick said.

Stilson let out a groan as Dick lifted him by the shoulders and held him in a sitting position. He passed the sleeves of his shirt behind Stilson's back and tied them as tightly as he could with a granny knot, so that the back of the shirt covered the black morass on Stilson's chest. The operation was a clumsy one.

'You're hurting me, Dick. I'm in pain.'

'I'm sorry, Mr Stilson. I'm being as gentle as I can. I thought you were dead.'

Agony had resculpted Stilson's face. It was white and as stiff as cardboard, and the bones of the skull, the forehead, the cheekbones and the chin jutted from the taut chalky skin. Suddenly, funnelling his lips between groans, he sprayed Dick's mouth and chin with a little geyser of frothing blood.

Dick lowered Stilson's torso to the ground, and took him by the feet and began to tug.

Stilson opened his eyes. 'Please don't, Dick. Please let me alone. I want to die here where I am.'

'I have to take you to the bushes,' Dick said.

'For God's sake don't! Don't touch me any more. I can't bear it.' Stilson continued to moan for a while as Dick dragged him foot by foot towards the cover. In the end Stilson fainted. The rough and ready bandage had come adrift before the bushes were reached, and Dick had to tie it more firmly in position. 'Can you hear me, Mr Stilson?' he asked, but there was no reply.

He went back, removing very carefully any signs of disturbance he had caused to the forest's carpeting of leaf-litter and rotting branches. There was no trace of blood where Stilson had first lain after being shot. Dick took the gun standing against the tree and dropped it into the bush where Stilson lay, close to his right hand. The gun with which he had shot Stilson he threw into the bush some twenty yards away, behind the one bearing the yellow flowers, after he had trodden down the undergrowth in the vicinity and snapped off a few small twigs.

Chapter Fifteen

Dick set out on the walk which took him through the clearing where they had left the car, which showed no signs of having been disturbed, and thereafter down the dirt road to the small town of San Juan some six miles away, and a little over two hours later, at seven in the morning, he walked into the ugly little concrete fortress which was the headquarters of the Rural Police.

His reception was sympathetic. The Rural Police of Escambray were engaged in a losing battle with guerrillas. When cornered and captured, they killed them after inflicting the most fiendish tortures. Perhaps as a reaction to these professional cruelties they were mild, forbearing and even generous in their relationships with the general public. Enough English was spoken by the men at the station between them to piece together Dick's story, to which they listened unsurprised. The *encargado*, a genial old paterfamilias with a tobacco-stained moustache and a pearl-handled antique pistol stuck in his belt, clicked his tongue in a show of concern, but whatever had happened in the woods up at Los Altos was to him a matter of unimportance. Life in the backwoods of Escambray was for most of its inhabitants brutish and short, with sudden death as familiar as the hurricanes of autumn or the drought that ravaged the crops almost every spring. Only the most atrocious of crimes awakened police interest. If hunters shot each other, what could be less important? It happened all the time.

A doctor was called, young and enthusiastic, and happy not to have been summoned for once to carry out a routine examination of a murdered rebel, prior to certifying death from natural causes. He took Dick's temperature, noting that this, as well as his pulse rate, was subnormal, examined the whites of his eyes and tested his reflexes, finding them sluggish almost to the point of non-existence. He formed the opinion that Dick was suffering from severe shock and, puzzled by the gaps and inconsistencies in his account of what had happened, deduced the existence of a partial amnesia. There was little in the way of medicaments in the backward village of San Juan, so he gave Dick a couple of aspirins and a drink of bitter-flavoured restorative containing a dash of strychnine, a drug favoured locally for the small violence it administered to a jaded nervous system.

Ten minutes after Dick had staggered into the police station he set out in the police van for Los Altos. With him went two policemen, the doctor and a thin Negro with enormous hands and feet, in charge of a stretcher. Dick led the party straight to the place where Stilson lay among the bushes. The doctor, at his side, noticed with some curiosity the way he walked, a little like a blind man, oblivious of his feet, searching with eyes half-closed for traces of vanished light. Stilson was dead, the tip of his nose already gnawed off by some rodent animal, and his lips coated with flies. The police treated the body with indifference, poking at it with their boots and then drifting away to resume conversations about other matters such as women and gambling, and a suspected rebel they had captured on the previous night, whose throat they had cut. Dick went with them to show them the place where he had thrown down the gun, and a policeman picked it up, ejected the spent cartridge, sniffed at it and dropped it into his pocket without comment.

No one paid the slightest attention to beaten-down vegetation or snapped-off twigs. This was in theory off-duty time. The time to play dominoes and cards and boast of sexual adventures, and they hated to waste it in this way.

Minutes later the younger policeman and the thin Negro lifted Stilson's body, dumped it face downwards on the stretcher, the arms hanging down, and began to walk back to their van. The others followed.

Complications now arose. Had Stilson been a local man the *encargado* would have simply telephoned the magistrate at San Juan to tell him what had happened, and inform him of the negative result of his investigations, to enable the magistrate to issue a certificate of death by misadventure. After that the body would have been released to any relative who could be found to claim it within the next twenty-four hours, otherwise, in accordance with law, the police would have arranged for its burial.

But where the Rurals were all-powerful in these country parts, and could dispose of unwanted bodies almost as they pleased and with absolute immunity, they were powerless in towns where a state of almost open warfare existed between them and the Investigational Police, solidly entrenched in all urban areas. The *encargado* rang his chief in Cienfuegos, who showed agitation when he learned the dead man's name, and some dissatisfaction at the nonchalance with which the affair had so far been handled.

'There's no problem about a certificate,' the *encargado* said. 'Why don't we just bury him after the twenty-four hours?'

'You're off your head,' the captain said. 'Any form of refrigeration up there?'

'None.'

'What's the weather like?'

'Warm.'

'Get hold of some ice and keep the body as cool as you can. Put all the material evidence under lock and key, and get ready to answer a few questions.'

'What do I do about the lad?'

'Hold him until we decide what to do.'

Dick spent what remained of his birthday being entertained by members of the Rural Guard. They fed him with bread, sausage and coffee, displayed the souvenirs taken in action with the rebels, their weird and wonderful

111

homemade guns and bombs, the thumb of a dead rebel chieftain pickled in spirit. He was entertained by card tricks, taught to play the local version of dominoes, and visited several times by the doctor, whose interest in psychiatry had been rekindled by this experience. He found Dick increasingly alert but remained perplexed at his continued inability to supply any solid details of what had happened in the period between Dick's shooting at what he believed to be a deer in a thicket and his arrival at the police station.

In the mid-afternoon a detective in a dark city suit and bow tie arrived with an ambulance to take Stilson's body back to Havana. The coolness of his reception bordered on hostility. He arrived at a time when the *encargado* was away on a wild-goose chase after rebels, and the junior NCO left in charge refused to look at the Ministry's order the detective held under his nose, and told him he would have to wait until the *encargado* returned. He waited fuming in the anteroom for two hours, having had to ask for a chair, and even being denied the ritual coffee. When the *encargado* finally appeared, hot and depressed, after his wasted foot-slogging in the mountains, he refused to answer questions of any kind. The case had been investigated and a report would be submitted to his superior and that was that. The detective was welcome to the body but he would not be allowed to see the young Englishman, nor would he be taken to the spot where the accident had taken place, because all this was no concern of his.

When Stilson's body was carried out to the ambulance the detective was horrified to discover that it had already been prepared for burial in local style, having been stripped and wrapped in sacking, the anus plugged with wood and sticking-plaster over the eyes. What was far worse, Stilson's shirt – which might have provided certain vital clues for an expert on the nature and effect of gunshot wounds – was missing and not to be found. The encounter between the detective and the *encargado* ended in a brisk exchange of insults, with the *encargado* finally reaching menacingly for his pearl-handled pistol before recovering his control, and turning his back to walk away.

112

Dick slept comfortably on a bunk bed, heavily sedated by the doctor who was never far from his side. Next morning a chauffeur-driven car arrived with Sanger from the Embassy, to take him back to Havana. Bearing in mind Hollingdale's prediction of trouble to come, Sanger found it hard to believe that what had happened had really been an accident, although the *encargado* assured him that this was the case, and had had no objection to giving him a copy of his report. Sanger and Dick talked about sport, particularly football, and although Dick told Sanger that he did not play himself, he followed the fortunes of a number of league teams and showed remarkable memory for games won, and lost, and even the number of goals scored in these matches.

Sanger took Dick straight to the Presidente Hotel, introduced him at the reception desk, gave him a hard handshake, then left.

A bell-boy took him up to the seventh floor to a room of the better sort that he and his mother and father had occupied when they had first stayed in the hotel. Here his mother was awaiting him.

PART TWO

Chapter One

Dick's reunion with his mother was almost a wordless one for both of them instantly understood the defensive value of silence. They sat together, first clutching at each other, then holding hands. Dick was puzzled by a lack of any sensation of a clean and clear-cut break with the past, and by the feeling that the shadows were still over him. Stilson was dead, but a voice deep down in his subconscious murmured, 'Dick, I'm still here. I'll always be with you.' It was a voice that not even the sight of Stilson's coffin being lowered into his grave would have silenced. In life Dick had always associated him with the house at Villa Maria and once outside the house he had sometimes been able to put him out of his thoughts. But death had released Stilson like a genie from its bottle. Now he was everywhere, and Dick waited for his footsteps in the passage outside, and his hand on the knob of the door, and the confident, challenging voice, 'Dick, I told you I'd resurrect myself, and here I am.'

It was inevitable in the end that the uses of silence should wear out, compelling them to experiment with cautious small talk, in which the art consisted in avoidance of association of words or ideas likely to drag them in the direction of the unmentionable topic. Chance conspired against them in small ways. The radio might have provided a diversion, but the first station Caryl tried offered a guitarist not only playing one of Stilson's favourite songs, but in a florid style that was indistinguishable from Stilson's. She tried again and found a talk in English on the unspoiled beauties of the countryside within reach of the capital. For both of them rural Cuba had become out of bounds, and they moved together to switch off.

Caryl ordered a light meal to be sent up to the room. After they had finished with it she suggested rest, and Dick eagerly agreed. Sleep was a temporary solution.

By this time it was early afternoon. He went to bed, slept for the rest of that day and right through the night, awakening next morning with warm sunshine striping his face through the slats of the Venetian blinds. He heard his mother moving in the sitting-room between the two bedrooms. 'Mum,' he called. She came through, smiling. There was something brisk and determinedly cheerful about her now that reminded him of a trained nurse.

'I thought you were never going to wake up.'

'I was dreaming I was riding a horse. What time is it?'

'Nearly nine. Ready for breakfast?'

'Please. It's Thursday, isn't it?'

'Friday.'

'Oh yes, Friday,' he said. 'Mum.'

She came over and kissed him. 'What is it?'

'Nothing.' He had just remembered that every word must be watched. She would have gone away to Mexico the day before, and she was here, and she was staying. But he could only half believe in her presence.

He found many changes in her. Her quick, vivacious way of talking – jumping as she sometimes did from subject to subject – had returned, and her almost un-English use of gestures to emphasize a point of view.

'You've done something to your hair,' he said.

'I had it cut off. Yesterday. Most of it. Do you like it this way?'

They were on a dangerous subject. Stilson had sat for what seemed to Dick hours on end, just staring obsessively at his mother's hair. 'I like it much better,' he said.

A cheerful girl brought the tray. 'They're nice here,' she said. 'They can't do enough.'

'Are we going to stay here for a bit?' he asked warily. He sensed that all references to the past were taboo, and even the future lay in dangerous, uncharted country.

'I think so. For the time being, anyway.' For a moment her expression was under a cloud.

'That's good,' he said. 'It's a nice hotel.'

'Mr Hollingdale made all the arrangements. He's been very kind.'

She picked up the copy of the English-language *Havana Post* sent up with the breakfast, instantly discovering a mine of trivia to be used as ammunition in the fight against ghosts. The front page headlines said, REBELS IN FULL FLIGHT. PRESIDENT SAYS END IS NEAR. This she ignored. The news on page two and the subsequent pages was more entertaining. 'They're planning seventy-five floats for carnival this year at a cost of two million dollars,' she said. 'It should be a wonderful sight.'

She turned over the pages, sifting the columns in search of diversionary material. COLOURED GIRL CHOSEN AS MISS CAMAGUEY SETS OFF RACE RIOT . . . PINEAPPLES AND COLOUR BLINDNESS, NEW MEDICAL DISCOVERY . . . NUDE BATHER PANICS VILLAGERS – FLIGHT FROM 'RIVER GOD' . . . ALARM CLOCK IN PIG'S STOMACH. Watching her as he listened, Dick made a tremendous discovery. She was untouched by sorrow. He sensed that, like him, what she most craved was to find some way of dismissing even the memory of Stilson from her life.

They strolled on the Prado in the afternoon, and Dick noticed that men no longer turned their heads as his mother passed. The canaries sang in the shade trees that held their great parasols over the street; perfect strangers exchanged smiles, congratulating each other, as they always did in this city, on being alive; and great cardboard cut-outs of Fred Astaire and Ginger Rogers, endlessly gay and free, pranced hand in hand over the heads of the crowd to announce the revival of *Top Hat*. For a moment they were received into the heart of the warm, secure world of pleasure. Then Dick's heart thumped as a black Cadillac slipped past, as silently as a shark through the traffic. He felt his mother's grip tighten on his arm. 'Let's go back now,' she said.

They turned and began to walk back to the Hotel

Presidente, where a very worried Hollingdale, accompanied by Pelham Craker, legal adviser to the Embassy, awaited their coming in the lobby.

Hollingdale had just arrived by taxi from police headquarters in Mercedes Street, where he had had a disquieting interview with the Assistant Chief of Police, after which he had immediately telephoned Craker to arrange this meeting. Within minutes Craker had come skipping through the door, dressed absurdly as usual in brown denims and a flowered shirt. 'Thank you for coming to the rescue, Pelham,' Hollingdale said. 'Do forgive me for bothering you in this way. The news, as you gather, is none of the brightest.'

'How did you find my old friend Gomez?'

'Desperately polite as usual over the undercurrents of menace. The fact is, we've the bad luck to be caught in the crossfire between the P.I. and their sworn enemies, the Rurals. The Rurals' report put poor old Dick absolutely in the clear, and I'm informed the P.I.'s are ignoring it. They're doing their own investigation. As Gomez put it, "we propose to look a little behind the scenes."'

Craker laughed easily. He was an old man who did all he could to deck and disguise himself with the trappings of youth, and who pursued all the things pursued by youth, among these a facile optimism. 'What if they do?' he asked. 'What is there to find?'

'More than we suspected, I'm afraid,' Hollingdale said. 'I have an uncomfortable feeling they've already stumbled on something we don't know about, because the deal I was proposed doesn't make sense if they haven't.'

'What sort of deal?'

'A very special friend of Gomez's urgently needs a UK visa. They're prepared to do a swap. They get the visa and we get Dick.'

'A bluff, would you say?'

'I wouldn't think so. We know each other too well. There was even talk about whether or not the Embassy would put up bail. They were asking us for an important favour in exchange for what they considered an important favour, and remember Gomez has already helped us out with Dick in a small way by agreeing not to press a GBH charge.'

'Can't we let them have their visa?' Craker said.

'Gomez's very special friend happens to be the top gangster on this island. He's said to control the world trade in narcotics. Cardiello. You probably know him.'

'I know him only too well,' Craker said. 'So the famous deer-hunting accident may not have been an accident after all. What do you think?'

'I haven't any views on the subject. One of our nationals is in the soup, and that's what concerns me. Between you and me and the gatepost I believe young Frazer is quite capable of murdering anyone. I also think it was high time Stilson was murdered.'

Craker looked at him with a flash of admiration. 'Our views exactly coincide,' he said.

'Supposing there is a trial?' Hollingdale said. 'What are the chances? What can one expect from the processes of law in this country?'

'Very little,' Craker told him. 'There is no presumption of innocence. The system's a century behind the rest of the civilized world. It's in a mess. The prosecution normally opens the case by a job of character assassination in which hearsay is treated as evidence.'

'Anything we can do at all?'

'You can sometimes get to the examining magistrate. You write something out for him saying what a nice chap your client really is and why you think he should be let off the hook. Naturally it's accompanied by a small present.'

'How much?'

'Oh, I don't know. Say a hundred pounds.'

'Could you arrange for that to be done?'

'I imagine so. We have to remember that the magistrate will be under pressure by the prosecution. It's a pity we can't do anything about the visa.'

'Forget it. We can't.'

'Let's hope that if there's a charge it will be culpable homicide, not murder.'

'Why do you say that?'

119

'Because if he's sent for trial at the preliminary hearing on a murder rap, he wouldn't get bail.'

'That's pretty grim.'

'You can spend up to two and a half years on remand waiting to go to trial. About ten per cent of the people held on remand are never tried in the end. They die of one or another of the unpleasant things that happen to people in prisons.'

'Hardly bears thinking about, does it?'

'It doesn't. And I gather we're here to break the news to Mrs Frazer that something like this can conceivably happen.'

'Well, I thought we should prepare her. And him, of course. I felt I needed your support.'

'What a pity it all is,' Craker said. 'Charming woman, Mrs Frazer. A tragedy she should have run into that awful Stilson fellow.'

Chapter Two

Dick felt the presence of the two men in the instant before he saw them as he and his mother passed through the hotel door, and he knew that his future was involved with their visit and that they were messengers from a world in which carnival floats and Ginger Rogers in her sequins and feathers had no part.

Hollingdale, wearing his ill-fitting outmoded tropical suit like a uniform, advanced to meet them. Craker at his heels might have been a barfly from the Beach Club. 'Caryl, Dick,' Hollingdale said. 'I don't think you know Pelham Craker. Mr Craker handles our legal affairs.' They shook hands. Craker achieved the wraith of a boyish smile, then his features surrendered to the ingrained shrewdness and calculation imposed upon them by the long years at his trade.

'Dreadfully sorry to butt in on you like this,' Hollingdale said, 'but we are faced with a problem. Do you think we could find somewhere quiet?'

A fair proportion of the English colony came here regularly for tea, and the area set aside for this leisurely ritual excluded all disturbance. They moved to a corner and settled at a table.

'We've been completely taken by surprise,' Hollingdale said. 'Hence the absence of any warning. I felt we had to meet as soon as possible. Pelham, would you perhaps explain?'

Craker's insistently amicable gaze, lifted to Dick's face over the rim of his teacup, was switched to his mother. As ever in his encounters with young and beautiful women he was prepared to indulge in an instant of fantasy in which chance was midwife to an involvement. 'I'm afraid I have to prepare you for a rather unpleasant possibility,' he said. 'As you know, we all counted on a straightforward coroner's verdict . . .'

Dick glanced at his mother. Make-believe was at an end, and they had been hunted down and cornered by truth. There would be no more evasions. The debarred topic was about to be exposed to the frigid climate of reality. He would have expected from her some dramatic recognition of this, but she showed only marble calm.

'. . . all the more so,' Craker said, 'as the original police report treated the case as death by misadventure.'

Hollingdale had twisted his head sideways as if on guard in this sedate environment against the presence of an enemy, but a fragile old couple occupied the only table in their vicinity, nibbling in a misty, desultory fashion at their egg and cress sandwiches.

'There are now indications that a charge may be brought,' Craker said.

'Do you mean Dick's going to be charged with a crime?' Caryl said. 'I don't see how he can be.' There was a trace of anger in her voice.

'We don't either,' Craker said. 'The trouble is, this is a country where justice is different from justice as we

121

understand it. The way things are moving, it seems likely that Dick will at least appear before a magistrate's court for a preliminary hearing. This being so, we ought to decide what our strategy's to be.'

'What would the charge be?' Caryl asked.

'Manslaughter, perhaps,' Craker said. 'We should hope for that, but at the same time we should be prepared for the worst.'

'And what does that mean?'

'Culpable homicide,' Craker told her.

'Would that mean a prison sentence?'

'If you're found guilty, yes.'

'Dick's only a young boy.'

'In this country a male becomes a fully responsible adult at the age of sixteen.'

'He was sixteen last week. The accident happened on his birthday.'

'I know,' Craker said. 'It's very sad indeed. A few hours would have made all the difference.'

'Isn't the Embassy doing anything about it?' she asked.

'Be sure the Embassy will do everything it possibly can, Caryl,' Hollingdale said. 'I've just had a long interview at Police Headquarters to try to get them to see reason. You can be quite certain we have no intention of letting the thing rest there.'

'Can I see the Ambassador?'

'I'm sure H.E. will ask to see you,' Hollingdale said. 'Be sure he's as worried about this business as we all are.'

'I don't want to depress you too much,' Craker said. 'We're only talking now of what could conceivably happen, not by any means what is certain to happen. The legal system here is so very different from ours. In England the police don't press a charge unless they feel pretty sure of a conviction. Here people are arrested and charged on the flimsiest of evidence. Happily, three cases out of four are thrown out at the preliminary hearing.'

'What *are* we to do?' she asked.

'We can prepare ourselves for any eventualities,' Craker

said. 'That, until we know which way the cat is going to jump, is all we can do.'

'Would you be able to act for us, Mr Craker?'

'I should be very happy to do so,' he said.

'Thank you.'

'And now,' Craker said, 'if you've no objection, I think I'd like to borrow Dick for an hour or so for a little private chat.'

Craker's new car stood encircled by respectful onlookers in the drive of the hotel. 'Does your Thunderbird Really Thunder?' read the advertisement for an exhaust system conversion Craker had recently bought in the belief that a noisy sports car would contribute to his image. They drove in local style, tyres squealing, Craker's finger on the button of the three-tone horn, to the calm and shaded gardens of the Cap de Vila where Craker parked and they settled themselves on a stone bench.

'Questions will be asked,' Craker said. 'I'm obliged to know all there is to know about you, Dick. I want to understand what makes you tick. Tell me, for example, about that trouble you were in in England. I've been given a garbled version. What I want is the facts.'

'I fired a rocket at a man's house,' Dick said.

'I heard that. And you made the rocket, didn't you? What was the idea?'

'He was cruel to my dog.'

'Did you damage the house in any way?'

'No, it fell in the garden. It started a fire.'

'A big one?'

'Pretty big. The rocket fell in some rubbish and set it alight, and the fire spread to a car and its petrol tank exploded and two other cars went up.'

'Quite a blaze, in fact,' Craker said. His attention was suddenly distracted by the passing of a splendidly arrogant mulatta girl. Dick was astonished as he followed her with his eyes by the hunger of his gaze.

Craker's dream faded and a touch of severity expunged the wistfulness in his expression. 'Do you think you might be a psychopath?' he asked.

123

'I don't think so. They say if you're a psycnopath you stay that way. I've been getting better all the time. One of the doctors explained to me that the main difference was that I wasn't born with any mental defect.'

'What was the illness that gave rise to all this trouble? Encephalitis, wasn't it?'

'I had measles when I was five, and then encephalitis. That left me deaf, and I think I had a breakdown in what they call idea-association. The trouble was that nobody knew there was anything wrong for a year or two, so I didn't get any treatment. My father used to say I was unlucky.'

'How right he was. What happened when you went to school?'

'Well, I was partially dyslexic, but I got over that. I didn't play games, or do anything like that for a few years. It was just that I didn't want to.'

'When they sent you to Stoneyfields did anyone take into account your history of bad health?'

'They don't go into that. If you'd been ill that was just too bad.'

'And at school you'd always been rather the odd man out?'

'The boys said I was skiving. Some of the masters did too. I used to keep out of the way as much as I could.'

Craker opened a monogrammed notebook and wrote in the big, showy handwriting that went with the flowered shirt and the noisy car: 'Bad mixer, shy and retiring.' 'You seem to have had a raw deal, right from the word go,' he said.

'I used to be kicked around,' Dick said, 'but I have forgotten about most of it. You do forget.'

'*Tout passe*,' Craker said. He made the passing of sorrow sound more sorrowful than its reality. 'Tell me, did you really want to blow up that man's house?'

'I knew I couldn't. It was impossible. The most I could have done was break a window. It was just a warning to him not to hurt dogs again.'

'You seem to feel rather strongly on the subject of animals. I believe your mother told Mr Hollingdale there'd been some upset over Stilson and a shark.'

'Mr Stilson took me fishing and he had his man cut the fins and the tail off a shark and throw it back in the water alive. It made me feel sick.'

'It would have made me feel sick, too,' Craker said. He opened his book again and wrote in it: 'Obsessed with cruelty to animals.'

'Otherwise how did you get on with Stilson?' Craker said.

'We got used to each other after a bit.'

'I've been told of the relationship between Stilson and your mother. Did you object to it?'

'I didn't like it but I knew there was nothing I could do about it.'

'You took a philosophical attitude,' Craker suggested.

'I tried to,' Dick said. 'He was nice enough to me in his way.'

'Anyway there was nothing like open warfare between you at any time?'

Dick hesitated. 'No,' he said. 'We had a sort of man-to-man talk, and after that we kept off the subject of him and my mother. I wouldn't say either of us was wild about the other, but there wasn't any fuss.'

Craker wrote: 'Mutual tolerance soon established.' A thought occurred to him. 'What was the idea of going deer-hunting with this man?' he asked. 'Especially taking into consideration your views on the subject of animals and, I would have imagined, blood sports in general?'

'When Mr Stilson wanted something he always got his own way,' Dick said. 'He got this idea into his head of doing something for my birthday, and it was either going fishing, which I hated, or alligator shooting which would have been worse, or this deer hunt. There was no way of talking him out of it, so I settled for the trip we went on because I was sure we wouldn't see any deer. Even if we did, I knew I couldn't hit one because I was a bad shot.'

'And yet what happened, did.'

'It was a fluke,' Dick said. 'It must have been a one in a thousand chance. When I went to have a test at the range at the American Club I only hit the target once out of five shots.'

125

Craker wrote again. 'One other question,' he said. 'Were you ever surprised at the extraordinary hold Stilson seemed to have over your mother? Did it ever occur to you that there might have been something there apart from the normal attraction between a man and a woman?'

'I didn't think much about it. What I mean is, I tried not to. As soon as we went to live in Mr Stilson's house my mother changed. You wouldn't have recognized her. She stopped doing all the things she used to do. She hardly ever went out of the house.'

'Do you think she wanted to live in this way? Was she happy?'

'I don't think she was happy,' Dick said. 'If anything, I think she was miserable.'

'I never met Stilson,' Craker said, 'nor did I want to, but there were a lot of stories around about him. He was a great one for conjuring tricks. Did he ever show you any?'

'No, he didn't.'

'That surprises me for a man who liked to show off.'

'He used to play the guitar and sing every night. The same old song. We had to listen whether we liked it or not.'

'Do you remember what it was called?'

'It may have been *Sueños*,' Dick said. 'The word *sueños* came up all the time.'

'*Sueños*, eh? That sounds like the old hit *Sueños y Ilusiones* – Dreams and Illusions. Suitable in its way, when you come to think about it. And you had to put up with regular doses of *Sueños* whether you felt like it or you didn't? I've just thought of something. Have you ever heard of hypnotic suggestion?'

'I saw a programme about it on the television,' Dick said.

'It's had quite a vogue in this town,' Craker said. 'One of the dentists still uses it to pull teeth out. Does it occur to you that Stilson may have used these compulsory guitar recitals of his as a way of attempting to hypnotize your mother? And you, too, Dick, by the way. It may sound far-fetched, but I'm beginning to be convinced that something like that happened to her.'

An association of memories formed in Dick's brain, then

dissolved. 'There was the guitar,' he said, 'and there was something about a medal, too. A medal came into it, but I can't remember how.'

'Let's have a nice quiet drive back,' Craker said, 'while you try to remember just what went on in that sinister house.'

They got up and began to walk towards the car. 'The more I hear about Stilson,' Craker said, 'the more I'm inclined to believe he was mad.'

'What do you think's going to happen to me now?' Dick asked.

'Well, I hate to say this, but I have a feeling that that terrible luck of yours hasn't quite burned itself out, Dick. I'm sure it eventually will.'

'That's what I was thinking, too. Are they going to arrest me?'

'They may do, Dick.'

'Soon?'

'It could be quite soon. You're not afraid, are you?'

'I am a bit, but I oughtn't to be. I know you'll be doing what you can for me.'

Craker squeezed his arm. 'Be sure of that, Dick. We'll all be in there pitching. It'll come out all right in the end.'

Chapter Three

Next morning at eight a studious-looking and bespectacled young agent of the Investigatory Police came to the hotel to arrest Dick and take him to Police Headquarters on Mercedes Street. Although it was not expected to rain for another three months he wore a blue nylon raincoat over his plain clothes. He was courteous and considerate, inviting Dick and his mother, after impounding Caryl's passport, to breakfast at their leisure. He then suggested, to avoid embarrassment to them, that he should leave the hotel ahead of them, and wait in the police car which had been parked discreetly round the corner.

The journey to headquarters was a leisurely one, the siren mute, and traffic lights treated with respect. Despite the building's frightening reputation, the office Dick and his mother were shown into could have belonged to an investment company. It was presided over by a motherly-looking woman seated under a picture of the President taken in the good old days when he had charmed the nation into submission and been affectionately known as *El chico lindo* – the handsome kid.

'I must ask you questions,' the agent said. 'Please to follow me.'

Dick disengaged himself from his mother's anxious clutch and followed the agent into a room full of burly genial men in shirt-sleeves at typewriters, of tobacco smoke, of the clatter of laughter, of ringing telephones and the regular shrieks of a grey parrot in its cage. The agent took him in search of a quiet corner, but one could not be found, nor were there any chairs free, so they stood uncomfortably for the interrogation between a coffee machine and a hatstand. 'I am sorry, there is not much convenience,' he said.

A man wearing an enormous pistol in a shoulder-holster screwed a sheet of paper into a ball and threw it at another man and laughter came and went in eddies and gusts. The agent shook his head at the thrower reprovingly. 'Shirt off, please, sir,' he said to Dick.

Dick took off his shirt.

'Now, sir, please turn round.'

Dick turned, and the agent took off his glasses, polished the lenses with his handkerchief, and studied the skin of Dick's back. He then turned to Dick's hands with a careful inspection of the fingernails. He nodded as if pleased at the confirmation of a theory. 'All right, sir, shirt on again, please.'

Dick got into his shirt.

'So when you shoot Señor Stilson, he grab you, huh? He make marks on your back.'

'I scratched myself on the bushes,' Dick said.

'Then you get on top of him. You grab his neck.'

'I didn't touch him except to bandage him.'

The agent shook his head sorrowfully. 'Why you shoot this man?'

'It was an accident.'

'You shoot him close. You point gun in his chest.'

'I wasn't close at all. I was thirty or forty yards away.'

'You burn his skin. You must be very close. For why you don't say me the truth?' The agent's tone held nothing but mild reproach. 'You know Isle of Pines?' he said. 'For murder a man like this you can go there for twenty years.'

'I'm telling you the truth,' Dick said. 'I didn't murder anybody. Please believe me.'

'After you kill Señor Stilson you walk to the police barracks of the Rural Guard. How long you take?'

'I think I took about two hours.'

'This is not true, also. You take about four hours. When they go for body it is stiff.'

'It wasn't. When they put it on to the stretcher the arms hung down.'

'You don't say the truth again. You left Señor Stilson for four hours to be sure that he must die. You kill him because you hate him, no?'

'No, I didn't hate him. It was an accident.'

'I think that is not true,' the agent said. 'But now we must go to the Matricula office to make the *denuncia*. Please come.'

They went first for routine photographs to be taken, Dick full-faced and in profile against a screen marked off in centimetres. After that the agent led him back to the first office, where the lady seated under the picture of the President as the brave, kind and witty man he had once been, typed out those details of place, date of birth, parentage and religion called for in any involvement with bureaucratic routine anywhere. Having finished with the form she took it out of the typewriter and handed it to the agent, who made a couple of alterations with his pen, and gave it to Dick to sign. He then blinked nervously, coughed behind his hand and, speaking first in Spanish, and then in English translation, he charged Dick with the murder of Juan Stilson. While this was going on the woman at the desk stood up as if they were taking part in a church ceremony. She then sat down again.

'Do you understand what I say you?' the agent asked Dick.

'I understand, but there's a mistake,' Dick said. 'You don't understand what I say to *you*, because you don't speak English properly. If you ask the other policemen they'll tell you it was an accident. They were there, and they know. There was a doctor who spoke English. Why don't you speak to him?'

The woman at the typewriter, no longer motherly-looking, was watching him sternly. She picked up a pencil and struck her desk-top sharply with it, as if in reproof. His mother put her arm round him in defence.

'There's nothing to worry about, dear. It's only a form. Something they have to go through with. Our Embassy will look after us. We're in good hands.'

The agent, appearing nervous and embarrassed, signalled to them. 'We shall now go,' he said, 'to speak with the people who have come to pay bail.'

Hollingdale and Craker were waiting outside. 'Well, there we are, Mrs Frazer,' Craker said. 'I'm afraid things have turned out to be rather as we feared. The preliminary hearing has been fixed for Thursday. Bearing in mind what I told you yesterday, I wouldn't be too despondent.'

He managed an aside in her ear that went with a squeeze of the wrist. 'Just managed to track down a chap who knows the magistrate and I'm seeing him this afternoon. May or may not come to anything, but I'm keeping my fingers crossed.'

Chapter Four

Hollingdale held on to his seat as Craker accelerated away with a squeak of rubber from the Embassy gates, braked for the bend, then eased the Thunderbird, finger on the horn, into the fast lane of the Avenida. The speedometer showed sixty-seven miles an hour, and buildings seen through the windscreen began to rock and shudder as though a major earthquake were in progress.

'Why the hurry?' Hollingdale asked.

'I don't know. It's the way I feel,' Craker said. He made a racing change-down and the car lurched wildly into the arc of a roundabout.

'Temperament apart, we'll be there too soon,' Hollingdale said. 'The hotel's just down the road. They're sure to be out there waiting for us and it's only five minutes to the court.'

'We'll drive round the block a couple of times,' Craker said. 'It's my way of letting off steam.'

'Anything wrong?'

Craker slowed and made a dangerous left turn in the path of oncoming traffic. 'The magistrate's been changed. I tried to get you to tell you. I only found out this morning.'

'Is that bad?'

'It's a catastrophe,' Craker said. 'The regular man was a friend. A decent, honourable chap. He would have helped in any way he could. I wrote out something as best I could for him to go on and sent it with a couple of hundred cigars and that small contribution you agreed should be made out of special funds. Not a matter of bribing anyone. These are common courtesies. The way things are done.'

'You just ran over a pigeon,' Hollingdale said.

'Where I went wrong was not putting his name on the package. This is a normal precaution. If there's a mistake

131

and the wrong person opens it he can always say, "This isn't for me." I addressed it to the Magistrate of the Third District Court. When I rang this morning to see how he felt about things, and what the prospects were, I was told he was in a car crash at the weekend and a new man had taken over *pro tem.*'

'So the new man now has the package?'

'Right.'

'Does that necessarily mean all is lost?'

'Let me explain. We now have a fellow called De Pina, who is a political showpiece. He was put in when that big scandal over the judiciary blew up a few years back.' Craker produced a dry cackle of laughter. 'To see that justice is done. Before that he was a professor of English at the University. Within a couple of minutes of meeting you for the first time he says, "Look at me, my hands are clean." They only use him for odd jobs like this. Can you imagine what he's going to do to us if he gets the chance. This is his day. For once in his life he's someone.'

'Nobody's going to be charged with bribery and corruption over three hundred dollars and a box of Corona Coronas.'

'No,' Craker said, 'they're not. But I happen to become involved in the fortunes of any client of mine, and this means we've taken a bad knock. It would have been nice to have the magistrate on our side. Now he'll be batting for the prosecution, and if they've got something up their sleeve that may be all that's wanted to tip the scale.'

'Can we appeal if necessary?'

'Against the findings of a magistrate's court? How can we? There's nothing to appeal against. There's no verdict. All they do is throw the case out or send you for trial.'

'In which case you're held without bail for two years or more.'

'In deplorable conditions. A young boy with Dick's background would never survive.'

'And nothing whatever can be done about it?'

'Not unless you happen to drink at the same water-hole as the President.'

132

The hotel came into sight and Craker slowed.

'There they are, at the top of the steps,' Hollingdale said. 'Pathetic, isn't it?'

'Five minutes to go,' Craker said. 'That Cardiello visa remains our only hope.'

'You can forget about it,' Hollingdale told him.

The magistrate's court reminded Dick of a church. The seats were in rows like pews with a hint about them of a possible confinement to come. Thin, distant light squeezed through pointed inaccessible windows high up in the wall, and there was a smell of imprisoned air, vestments and dust.

The brief conference at the hotel before setting out had been a dispiriting one, Craker having fallen under the shadow of a sudden dejection. 'From an English point of view the law here is hopeless,' he said. 'Hearsay and miscellaneous denunciations of all kinds are treated as evidence, and one has no opportunity to cross-examine witnesses. The whole object of the prosecution is to catch you off guard. I have a feeling that we could be in for unpleasant surprises.'

Dick sat between Craker and his mother in the front row, with Hollingdale, wearing the haunted look with which he awaited any emergency, on his mother's far side. The young police agent who had arrested Dick had placed himself immediately behind. For this occasion he had exchanged his plain clothes for a blue uniform, stiffly buttoned at the neck. They faced a low platform in the centre of which had been placed a small table bearing a green tasselled cloth, and behind this stood a wicker chair.

Time passed in fidgeting minutes. A dog barked, a baby cried somewhere in the hallway, and an old man with a dustpan and broom arrived to sweep listlessly in a corner. Officials in faded green livery began to drift in from one of the other courtrooms and presently the magistrate, De Pina, who was round-bodied, pink and dishevelled-looking, made his sudden entrance through a door in the back of the court, glanced round anxiously as if doubtful whether he had come to the right place, then stumbled up the platform steps and

133

slumped in the wicker chair. Everybody stood up. De Pina stared down at them, blinking. Then he held up his hand and they sat down again.

De Pina took some papers from his briefcase, laid them on the table and began to rustle through them, pausing occasionally to rub his scalp through thinning hair as if in perplexity. Presently he looked up. 'Richard Frazer?' he said. Dick found himself nudged to his feet.

The magistrate seemed agreeably surprised to find Dick present. 'Come and take the stand, Frazer,' he said. A separate pew had been placed, somewhat to the right, in the space between the front row of the court and De Pina's dais, and an usher bustled forward to show Dick to this. He found that from this position, while facing the magistrate, he could still find reassurance in the presence of his mother, Hollingdale and Craker, seen out of the corner of his eye.

De Pina picked up a paper to glance at it before going on. He appeared to shake himself as if to rid himself of boredom, muddle, and even the ill-effects of insufficient sleep, then smiled in a slow, reflective manner. 'Richard Frazer,' he said, 'you have been charged with the murder of Juan Stilson.' He spoke with a soft American accent having its origins in the cool and equable climate of New Hampshire, and his tone was pleasantly matter-of-fact. Dick might well have been charged with stealing a bicycle. 'This is a preliminary examination conducted in accordance with Cuban law,' he said, 'to decide whether there is a case for you to be sent for trial. Do you understand this?'

'Yes, sir,' Dick said. Nothing had been said to him or his mother about De Pina's reputation. He associated all round-bodied, pink and dishevelled men with a tendency to benignity.

'The charge arises,' De Pina said, 'from an incident that occurred during a hunting expedition undertaken by you in the company of the late Juan Stilson. In the course of this Stilson received a serious gunshot wound. When questioned by the Rural Police you admitted to the shooting, but claimed that it had been an accident. This explanation was not challenged by the Rural Police who carried out an investigation on the spot. However the autopsy revealed that although Stilson would almost certainly have died from the gunshot wound the actual cause of death was asphyxiation by manual strangulation.'

Dick felt rather than heard his mother gasp. Craker was on his feet, loud-voiced in his protest. De Pina, gesturing weariness and indifference, was thrusting his objection aside.

'But, sir, this is the first we have heard of manual strangulation as the cause of death.'

'Is it, Mr Craker?'

'Surely I should have been notified of the result of the autopsy?'

De Pina's expression reflected a looseknit amiability. He took the objection like a performing animal accepting a titbit. 'I don't see why,' he said.

'Can application be made for an adjournment?'

'On what grounds?'

'I should like to interview the doctor who carried out the autopsy and see a copy of the medical report.'

'Application refused,' De Pina said. 'This is a preliminary hearing, not a trial.'

Craker sat down, grunting his dissatisfaction, and De Pina turned to Dick again. 'In view of the findings of the autopsy, Frazer, do you wish to withdraw or in any way modify the statement you made to the Rural Police?'

Dick's lips were numb. He shook his head.

'Say yes or no,' De Pina said. There was no loss of kindliness in his tone.

'No, sir,' Dick said. Could this be some trick they played on anyone in these foreign countries to confuse people and trap them into self-incrimination? He risked a glance to his left, eager for comfort and succour. 'Face the court,' De Pina said.

'I told the police the truth,' Dick said. 'They wrote it all down. That was what happened.'

'You didn't strangle Mr Stilson?'

'No, sir.'

'The more I think about this story the funnier it sounds,'

De Pina said. 'You're supposed to have mistaken a man for a deer. Have you ever seen a deer?'

'Yes, I have.'

'Where?'

'In a zoo.'

'Well, tell me what a deer's like? Is it a big animal? What colour is it? What sort of noise does it make? Does it bark? Does it moo? Does it have udders and teats like a cow? Any horns? You must know if you've seen one. I'm waiting for an answer.'

Craker broke in with his protest. 'I think my client is rather confused by the questioning, sir.'

'Mr Craker, please be quiet. I will deal with you in a moment. I can't understand how anybody with two eyes in his head can possibly mistake a man for a deer.'

'It was half-light, sir,' Craker said. 'Just about dawn. The visibility was very poor. Very little of Mr Stilson's body would have shown through the undergrowth.'

'I'm putting my questions to Frazer, not to you, Craker. Stop interrupting.'

'Very well, sir. I'm sorry.' Craker sat down.

'Frazer, you saw Mr Stilson, whom you took to be a deer, moving among the bushes some distance away. You pointed your gun at him and shot him. What happened then?'

'I went to the bush where he was lying, and I bandaged him up with my shirt.'

'Was he conscious?'

'Yes.'

'He spoke to you?'

'Yes. He told me to get help.'

'And off you went. How long did it take you to get to the police post in San Juan?'

'I don't remember very well, sir.'

'The Rural Police say you took about two hours. The Investigatory Police claim it was four hours. They employed a tracker who said you went off, then you circled round and came back from another direction to the spot where Mr Stilson was lying. Finding him still alive, you then strangled him. In a moment my friend Mr Craker is going to tell us you are physically incapable of strangling anyone. Before he does that I want to refer to a remarkable document I have received from him, although I cannot imagine why he should have sent it to me.'

De Pina found Craker's letter, held it up, nodded in Craker's direction, then let it drop. He returned to Dick.

'For some reason Mr Craker seems anxious that I should believe you to be a physical weakling with a shy and retiring disposition. Tell me, have you at any time since residing in this country worked as a bootblack?'

Dick raised his hand to cover his mouth as he swallowed. De Pina, in a sudden fluttering of the perspectives, had become half gargoyle, half elf. He was watching in the same way that Stilson had watched, and not the slightest indication would be lost on him.

'Yes, sir,' Dick said. Now he knew that he'd been followed and spied upon since the moment of his arrival in Havana.

'My congratulations, Frazer,' De Pina said. 'Shy and sensitive as you are, you could break into the toughest juvenile fraternity in this city. However much they may have resented your presence as an interloper, you could hold your own against them. As for your poor physical strength, I have here a statement from Senator Aragon, who, when staying at the National Hotel, was violently assaulted by a bootblack he accused of attempting to pick his pocket. He's been shown your photograph and believes you to have been his assailant . . . Yes, Mr Craker?'

Craker was on his feet. 'Surely, sir, no one can be positively identified in this way from a photograph?'

'Of course they can't, Mr Craker. Which is why I used the word believes . . . Frazer, do you deny you assaulted a guest at the National Hotel?'

'I didn't assault him, sir. I was with a friend and this man was trying to pull his ear off. He was beating us up. I hit him in self-defence.'

'Well, I suppose you can't be blamed for defending yourself and your friend, but surely there's a limit to the amount of violence you're entitled to use. You hit Senator Aragon with such force that he spent a week in hospital. Mr

137

Craker has described you as a weakling, but all I hear of you from other sources suggests to me you're a very dangerous young man to come up against.'

De Pina picked up a sheaf of papers and waved them at Craker. 'Mr Craker, I can't imagine what was your purpose in sending me this communication.'

'It was intended to assist you,' Craker said.

'Well, it did that, although not in the manner you probably hoped. I'm not at all sure after reading this piece of uninspired fiction how much you yourself really know of the character of this shy and sensitive lad you've taken under your wing. You say he has an obsession about cruelty. Did you know he obtained employment in the municipal slaughterhouse in this city?'

'No, I did not, sir.'

'I had a feeling you didn't. Frazer, did you assist in the killing of animals in the municipal slaughterhouse?'

'A friend took me to the slaughterhouse.'

'Answer the question,' De Pina said, not unkindly. 'Did you or did you not help to kill animals?'

'I pulled on a rope, that's all. We were only there for a short time.'

'Did you do this for payment?'

'They gave us some meat.'

'I see. Well, working for a wage of any kind at the slaughterhouse isn't a crime, but unless you're pushed for the money or its equivalent it's the kind of employment most people I know would want to avoid . . . Mr Craker, would you willingly pull on a rope at the municipal slaughterhouse?'

'Is pulling on a rope actually to be classed as killing, sir?' Craker asked. He had picked up Hollingdale's hunted expression as if through physical contagion.

'Oh, I think so,' De Pina said. 'It's all part of the process. Somebody does one part of the job, and somebody else another. But I repeat that it's no crime to help to kill the animals we all eat. If you feel able to do it, all well and good. It's a matter of temperament. What I'm saying is that working in the slaughterhouse doesn't fit in with the picture you painted of your client's character. Another thing you ask us to believe is that Frazer is bad at all forms of sporting activity, particularly shooting. I ask myself continually why you should wish to stress this point.'

'Because only a first-rate marksman could have shot Mr Stilson with intent through the chest at nearly forty yards.'

'It had to be a fluke, in fact. An accident, and you mention the incident of Frazer's failing a simple test at the range of the American Club. Well, Mr Craker, this was a piece of information I was glad to have and I took the trouble to telephone the man who runs the range there. He remembered the occasion very well. He confirmed that Frazer's score was about the worst ever, but he couldn't understand how it could have been so bad because he tested his vision and his nervous co-ordination, and these were normal. His opinion was that for some reason best known to himself he may not have been trying.'

De Pina turned to Dick, whose power to think had suddenly shrivelled away. He was mesmerized by certain details of the magistrate's slipshod appearance; the red stripe left across his forehead by his hat, a food stain on his jacket, a gaping sole that had opened like a small mouth under his shoe.

'Anything to say, Frazer?' De Pina asked. 'Were you trying?'

Dick's jaws oscillated to produce a faint yammering.

'Is that meant to be yes or no?'

'Yes, sir. Yes, I was.'

'I wish some of your replies carried more conviction. However, we'll pass on to what Mr Craker describes as the bonds of affectionate comradeship existing between you and Mr Stilson. Tell me in your own words how you felt about this man.'

'I . . .' began Dick. 'I . . .' A slow thudding pulsation of pistons had begun remotely in his head. He found it impossible to form a sentence.

'When I ask you a question you must reply directly and without hesitation,' De Pina said. 'Otherwise you are bound to produce an unfavourable impression on the court. Did you like him? Did you admire him as Mr Craker seems to think?'

The distant thump of pistons passed its crescendo. The thoughts were flowing again. 'I think I admired him,' he said. 'In a way.'

'You only think you admired him. You sound a lot less enthusiastic about the relationship than Mr Craker does. I want you to be very careful how you answer the next question. Did you and Mr Stilson ever quarrel violently?'

'Only once,' Dick said. What was the point of further evasion or denial? Stilson had said that no man could read another's thoughts, but if anyone could it was this little dandruff-shedding magistrate.

'Well, you managed to clear that hurdle,' De Pina said. 'And it's just as well you did, as I've an account here of what happened on an occasion when you and Mr Stilson came to blows. Before considering this I must ask Mrs Frazer to leave the court. I will send for her when she can return.'

De Pina signalled to the usher, who crossed over to his mother, and she got up and followed him. Dick heard a door close behind her. The usher came back. The magistrate held up a paper. 'This is a statement made by Mr Felipe Mendoza who was a close associate of Mr Stilson's. In it he says that Mr Stilson confided in him about certain disturbing matters arising from his liaison with your mother. Do you know what a liaison is?'

'No, sir.'

'It means that they were sleeping together. Or so Mr Stilson told Mr Mendoza. Mr Mendoza states that on one occasion when Mr Stilson and your mother were having intercourse, you attempted to break into the bedroom and you struck Mr Stilson in the face with a stone. Is this true?'

'I was trying to break the door open with a stone and I hit Mr Stilson by accident. Mr Stilson came out while I was smashing at the door, and he was hit in the face.'

'Another accident, Frazer? You seem accident-prone. Were you an admirer of Mr Stilson at the time when this was happening?'

140

'No, sir.'

'The true fact of the matter is you detested him. Isn't that so?'

'Yes, sir, I did.'

Dick heard Craker give out a sound like a groan, then he was on his feet waving his arms and trying to attract De Pina's attention. De Pina finally noticed him. 'Yes, Mr Craker?'

'I wish to ask leave for Mr Mendoza to be called to be questioned on his statement, sir.'

'No, certainly not, Mr Craker. You know as well as I do what the procedures are.'

'With respect, I understand that procedural changes were to be made.'

'They are, Mr Craker, but they're still in the pipeline. You'll have to put up with things the way they are for a little longer.'

'I apologize for the interruption,' Craker said.

'It further alleges in this statement, Frazer,' De Pina said, 'that your mother discussed with him certain psychopathic tendencies she believed you to possess, among these being incestuous feelings displayed towards her. You were always pestering her to allow you to sleep in her bed.'

Dick felt the blood burning in his cheeks and the sensation that every eye was turned on him in loathing and horror. He risked a guilty, shame-stricken, surreptitious glance first at De Pina, who had returned to his papers, and then at the others, each in turn. Hollingdale and Craker, heads together, whispering moodily on the topic of defeat, might have forgotten his presence entirely. The police agent, arms folded, inspected his knees. The usher, supremely indifferent to all that was going on, was picking his teeth with a finger. Dick gathered a little strength. 'I wasn't always pestering her,' he said.

'Did you sometimes come into her bed while she was asleep?'

'Once or twice, that's all.'

'Why did you?'

'I used to have bad dreams. She didn't mind.'

141

'Mendoza says Mr Stilson told him she did. *He* certainly minded. He told Mendoza his solution was to pack you off back to England, but you refused to go, so he was arranging for you to go to a boarding-school in this country. He said he could see a battle ahead . . . Mr Craker, I do wish you'd allow me to continue.'

'With respect, once again, sir, I find it hard to see what relevance these random allegations can have.'

'They have no less relevance, Mr Craker, than your glowing evaluation of the defendant's character.' Displeasure had underscored the latent intelligence in De Pina's features.

'You have offered us one side of the character picture, and Mr Mendoza has shown us another. Your version fails to match the facts. Mr Mendoza's statement is relevant and valuable because it points to a motive, namely the extreme jealousy – possibly sexual in character – felt and demonstrated by the defendant. When Mr Stilson told Mr Mendoza, as I am prepared to accept that he did, that he could see a battle ahead, my feeling is that this was an unconscious understatement.'

De Pina reached down for the briefcase he had propped against a leg of the table, grabbed up a handful of papers and began to stuff them back into it. There was a suggestion of finality in the action. He puffed out a sigh. 'I see no reason why Mrs Frazer should not return to the court,' he said. He signed to the usher, who stopped exploring his mouth with his finger and went off, returning in a moment with Dick's mother. She walked with caution, as if on ice, and a sudden inflammation underlined her eyes. Dick's smile as he turned his head towards her was as stiff as if he had just been given an injection for a tooth extraction. She replied with a quick, half-hearted wave.

'However we look at this case it is unsatisfactory,' De Pina said. 'You've done your best, Mr Craker, to make the court believe Frazer is quite incapable of committing any crime, which clearly he is not. This, in its way, may be understandable. What is neither understandable nor pardonable is that the police, too, can't be cleared of the

142

suspicion of attempting to deceive the court. We have the Rural Police telling us Frazer shot Stilson at a distance of thirty-three metres, and either overlooking or preferring not to see that he'd been strangled as well as shot. The Investigatory Police say the gun-barrel was practically touching Stilson's chest when Frazer pulled the trigger. They had a ballistic expert's report in support of this claim.'

'Sir,' Craker began, 'is it possible . . .'

'If you're about to ask me whether you can see the report, Mr Craker, the answer is no. I may as well tell you I've rejected it because I regard it as dubious. To be on the safe side the court called in another ballistics expert, and the second, as is sometimes the case, disagreed with the first. The court is of the opinion that more positive evidence of whether or not the fatal shot had been fired at close range would have been provided by an examination of the clothing worn by Mr Stilson at the time. It is highly unsatisfactory that this could not be produced.'

'Is it suggested that the clothing was intentionally destroyed, sir?' Craker asked.

'It could have been, Mr Craker, although don't ask me why, or it might even have been quite simply stolen. The only result is the court's work is made harder. I would recommend both the prosecution and the defence to abandon tactics designed to confuse the issue, and manœuvrings behind the scenes. I would not advise the prosecution to produce their ballistics expert's report in evidence, after my comments, nor would I suggest to you, Mr Craker, that you dress your client up in Sunday School uniform to go into court.'

Craker stood up. 'May I request fifteen minutes' recess at this point, sir, to confer with Mr Hollingdale who represents the British Embassy?'

'Certainly you may have fifteen minutes if you wish, Mr Craker,' De Pina said.

The usher took them into a room cluttered with brooms and pails, tins of paint and a step-ladder.

Hollingdale was irritated and suspicious. 'What's all this in aid of?' he asked.

'We're in a spot,' Craker said. 'You know what's going to happen now?'

'I have a fair idea. Your strategy collapsed, Pelham.'

'If things had gone as planned we'd have been on our way to the Tropicana to celebrate by now.'

'They didn't. End of story.'

'It has to be the visa. Now or never.'

'You don't give up easily. I've already told you, it can't be done. *Pas possible*.'

'H.E. ought to be given a chance to decide.'

'If you were a member of the Embassy staff you'd realize how totally out of the question your suggestion is.'

'What's to be lost?'

'Well, in a sense my own reputation, among other things. H.E. is a very straight up and down man. An approval of that kind would impair our relationship.'

'Look at it from the purely practical point of view. Couldn't the visa be eventually withdrawn, and the man deported?'

'I wouldn't even dare to hint at it.'

'This is a crisis, make no mistake about it. De Pina's about to send Frazer for trial. That means he'll spend two years on remand in conditions you can't begin to imagine. Mrs Frazer is bound to move heaven and earth. At the very least, questions are going to be asked in Parliament.'

'It's all very unpleasant,' Hollingdale said. 'Even if this could be done – and I know it couldn't – there'd be no guarantee Gomez would fulfil his side of the bargain.'

'I'd guarantee that. All I'd have to do would be to get him on the phone and the case would be dropped. Tell you what, Paul, supposing I go to H.E. and tell him just what's involved. Would you have any objection?'

'No,' Hollingdale said. 'No objection at all. Be quite sure, though, you leave me out.'

They went back into the courtroom and sat down. Craker reached for Caryl's hand again, as much to reassure and comfort himself as her. Hollingdale thought of Dick's predicament and his future. What exactly were Craker's unimaginable conditions? He had never been inside a prison but had read lurid stories of the degradations and the indignities committed within them by the strong upon the persons of the weak. Perhaps H.E. could be moved in some way to surrender an iota of his rectitude in such a cause. The silence in court was heavy and dutiful, like that of a church service in an interval of silent prayer.

The magistrate reappeared briskly, climbed the platform and fell into his chair. Two men in grey cotton uniforms with braided collars and cuffs, of the kind worn by ticket-collectors on the State railway, had followed him through the door and, advancing stealthily in rubber soles, had placed themselves in the third row of seats, immediately behind the young agent of the Investigatory Police.

De Pina raised a hand as if about to conduct a concert. 'Mr Craker, following your conference with Mr Hollingdale, is there anything you wish to say before the court announces its decision?'

Craker got up. 'Yes, sir. On behalf of the British Embassy, I should like to apply for twenty-four hours' adjournment of this hearing.'

'On what grounds?'

'The Embassy asks for time in which to present new evidence in support of the defence's case.'

De Pina shook his head. 'It's out of the question. Even if the normal procedures of the court allowed for such an adjournment, which they don't, I cannot conceive of any new evidence that the Embassy or anybody else might present that would in the slightest way influence my decision . . . Mr Craker, please pay attention.'

Craker, who had given up, and was using the handle of a silver teaspoon he carried for the purpose to press back his cuticles, looked up. 'I'm listening most carefully, sir.'

'Good, because what I have to say is concerned with principles, and I want to make quite sure you appreciate them. This examination is concerned with the probability of guilt and it is only when such a probability can be excluded that it is entitled to dismiss a case and discharge the defendant. No amount of fresh information at this stage can override the body of circumstantial evidence reinforcing the

145

probability of guilt. I'm therefore obliged to make an order for Richard Frazer to be sent for trial for the murder of Juan Stilson, and I direct that such a trial be held as speedily as it can be arranged, and that the prisoner, Richard Frazer, be held on remand in custody, to await the verdict of the assize court when this is pronounced.'

The two men in grey uniforms had moved forward in absolute silence to stand behind Dick's chair, and one of them now placed his hand lightly on Dick's arm at the moment when a babel broke out. De Pina had disappeared, snatched from their sight like a puppet that had played its part in a show that was at an end, and now Dick's mother, Craker, Hollingdale, and the police agent were talking at once, while the two men in grey uniforms tried to impose calm with patient and placatory gestures.

His mother tried to push the man who was holding Dick's arm away, and the man smiled back at her, embarrassed and a little hurt. 'But surely I can go with him?' she appealed to Craker.

'I don't think they'd agree to that,' Craker told her. 'I'm sure you'll be allowed to see him tomorrow. They'll probably let you see him whenever you like.'

'How long are they going to keep him there?' she asked.

'Well, at this stage we don't know,' Hollingdale said. 'It takes a little while to organize whatever has to be done. The thing to remember is this is not a prison, it is a remand centre. Something entirely different. I have an idea it's a big house, standing in its own gardens. Probably not all that different from a boarding-school.'

'Sir, you must go with these men now,' the police agent said to Dick.

'But can't our Embassy do anything at all for us?' she wailed.

'I'm quite sure it can,' Hollingdale said. 'A matter of setting the wheels in motion.'

'How do I know he'll be given proper food?'

'Nothing whatever to stop you bringing in food parcels yourself. Take him anything he fancies. We'll tip whoever it

146

is looks after him. They'll make him comfortable,' Craker assured her.

'He won't be in a cell, will he?'

'No, he'll be in an ordinary room. A small ordinary room with a proper bed and a wash-basin and a picture on the wall. Dick hasn't been found guilty of anything. He won't be treated as a prisoner. This is a remand centre, not a gaol. Cubans are very advanced in this way. We probably have a lot to learn from them.'

The police agent had taken Dick by the other arm. 'Sir,' he said, 'these men are waiting. You must please go with them now.'

Craker, whispering consolation and hope, was manœuvring Caryl to the door when the usher came scuffling up to him, and he found himself holding a loosely-packed and badly-tied parcel. There was a note pushed under the string, and, excusing himself, he took it out and unfolded it. A much crumpled 500-dollar bill – the one which, in better condition, he had enclosed in his letter to the magistrate – was pinned to the top of the sheet of paper. He read,

> Dear Mr Craker, I hope you will not be offended if I return the cigars. As I do not normally afford Corona-Coronas I prefer not to develop expensive tastes. It was kind of you to suggest a contribution to my favourite charity, but I am an uncharitable man.

Chapter Five

The silent, creeping war fought in the mountains and forests pushed forward its frontiers towards the cities. Few battles in the field produced prisoners, for the rebel taken under arms had little to hope for, but those who supported the rebel cause in the cities were rounded up by the thousand.

The problem arising from these efficient nocturnal operations was what to do with all those who had fallen into the police net.

Havana's gaols overflowed, and every few days convoys slipped quietly out of the city heading for Batabanó on the south coast from which the detainees were shipped in dismal conditions to the Model Prison and its sinister satellite camps of Nueva Gerona, on the Isle of Pines. A majority of the prisoners arrived at their grim destination, but a few did not, and many of those who did had reason later to decide that fortune had not necessarily favoured them in their surviving the informal process of selection conducted en route.

Accommodation in the city for prisoners awaiting trial had been pared away until finally only a wing borrowed from the Lunatic Asylum remained to be shared with political detainees waiting to be packed off to Cuba's Devil's Island. The Asylum had once been a rich man's palace, a place of lavish interiors, gay laughter and sweet music, but now all parts of it were disturbed by the bayings, the blubberings and shrieks of inmates under restraint, some of them in the cages in what had been the rich man's zoo. Into this building Dick was hustled after being hauled from the van in which he had been transported from the magistrate's court.

The two men in grey, furiously transformed in this climate of mania, half-pushed, half-carried him up a marble and gilt staircase to the reception centre, where, to avoid complication, detainees, whether sane or insane, were accorded identical treatment. Here, watched by attendants armed with knuckle-dusters and clubs, he was inscribed in the register, then told to turn out his pockets, the contents of which were listed and placed in an envelope, to be sealed and then locked in a safe.

A short passage led to a room full of sweating pipes where he was ordered to strip and get into a rusted bath half-full of grey water rimmed with scum, to be scrubbed with a floor brush by a tattooed Chinese in boxer shorts. When this was over the Chinese gestured to him to touch his toes, put on a

148

rubber glove and prodded deep into nis rectum for concealed objects. Frog-marched naked into an adjoining room, his clothing was next snatched from him in exchange for a suit of threadbare pyjamas. Putting on the trousers he found that they were a number of sizes too large, and had to be held up by hand. He was given a wooden platter, ladle and mug.

Up to this point Dick had been at the mercy of the Asylum staff, but now the moment had come for the Remand Centre personnel to take over. A warder in a blue uniform arrived with a huge bunch of keys dangling at his side. He was full of the shallow laughter often employed as a defence by people compelled to pass their lives in the twilight of human misery. The warder, the bath attendant and the man in charge of stores chatted and giggled for a moment, and then the warder gestured to Dick to go with him and they set off. The rich man's zoo came first, and the warder, pushing him ahead broke into a canter as they went through the doors. The madmen in the cages were ready for them and, naked and screeching behind their bars, they bombarded them with their fæces. Dick and the warder passed through a steel gate into the Remand Wing, which after the resounding hubbub of the Asylum was chillingly silent. The light turned grey, and the air smelt of fungus.

They reached a row of doors in the wall, and the warder stopped before one of these, unlocked it and nodded to Dick to go in. Doing so, Dick crossed over a threshold of ammonia-saturated gloom into a room that was about twelve feet square, with brick showing in patches where the plaster had fallen from the wall, a tiny window-opening draped with a cobweb, a bed covered with a stained blanket, and a bucket in the corner. The warder, twittering, slapped him on the back and went off, and Dick stood there holding up the pyjama trousers, drawing into his lungs the rancid, poisoned air, staring in horror at the brown streaks covering the wall like a form of surrealist decoration, left by prisoners who had cleaned the excrement from their fingers in this way. A notice said, in two languages, '*Es prohibido hablar*. It is forbidden to speak.'

149

Dick sat on the bed and closed his eyes, and what was left of the day fell into its slow, wasting decline of seconds, minutes and hours. This nothingness, this unfocusing of time, bred its single event – the arrival of a meal, produced by the warder with a theatrical flourish. It was a sour, steaming mess of rice and beans, among which floated a cooked cockroach. Dick shook his head in disgust, and the warder laughed full of raillery and good-humoured contempt. His meaning was clear from his gesticulations. 'You'll come to it sooner or later. Why not now?' He then went over to the bucket in the corner, unbuttoned and urinated into it, seeming in this act, and with the proprietorial smirk in Dick's direction that accompanied it, to be marking out his territory in the way of a dog or a skunk.

The man buttoned up, executed a few jaunty dance steps, picked up the food pail and went off, the clump of his boots and his laughter echoing in the passage, leaving Dick to the day's slow ebb in silence, stench and gloom. He could only be sure that night had come when the tiny electric bulb in the ceiling began to glow, and the hunting spiders ceased to dart over the walls and withdrew into their cracks.

He slept tormented by fresh and familiar nightmares, and awoke full of hunger, thirst and fear, and blistered by insect bites on all parts of the body.

The day began with the solemn prison ritual of slopping-out, and the warder came skipping to take him to the latrine and watch, ogling, with his secret, possessive smile, while Dick emptied the contents of the bucket into the fæces-encrusted hole in the floor. Dick left untouched a breakfast of greyish bread and fermenting maize gruel, and then the warder was back to lead him off to the visiting room, where Craker, dressed as if for a regatta, awaited him.

Craker jumped to his feet. 'For heaven's sake, Dick, why on earth have they made you wear those things? I'm going to lodge an immediate protest. Never mind, first things first. I've got tremendous news for you. Your father's been located in Tokyo. He should be on his way by now, and if everything goes well he could be here by Friday.'

'When's Friday?' Dick asked.

'It's the day after tomorrow. This must be a great moment for you.'

Dick nodded. 'When Dad gets here everything will be all right.'

'I'm sure it will.'

'He knows a lot of people,' Dick explained, 'and he knows how to get things done. People listen to him.' He got up to hitch the prison pyjama trousers higher into his crutch and sat down again. 'He'll come here straight away, won't he?'

'Straight away,' Craker said. 'Straight from the plane.'

'I hope I won't still be wearing these dirty pyjamas. Is my mother here?'

'I didn't bring her because I didn't think it advisable,' Craker said. 'And I knew you'd understand. She wanted to come but I managed to put her off. I wanted to see how you were and talk to you first.'

'When is she coming?'

'Tomorrow.'

'I don't want to stay here.'

'I know you don't, Dick.'

'This is a madhouse. They keep mad people in cages, and they throw their shit at you whenever you go past.'

'How truly shocking. Are you receiving proper food?'

'They gave me some horrible stuff with a beetle in it. I haven't eaten anything since I came here.'

'Well, anyway there'll be no problem about food. I've brought something to tempt your appetite.' Craker put a parcel down on the splintered table top that separated them. 'That,' said Craker, 'contains among other things a whole roast chicken. Have to eat to keep your strength up.' He forced a broken laugh. The atmosphere of the place was beginning to sop up his reserves of optimism.

'Getting all the exercise you need?' he asked.

'I've only been let out of the cell to empty the lavatory bucket,' Dick said. 'You can't even see the daylight. I think the warder's a pansy; the way he looks at me all the time. He comes into my cell and uses the bucket when he wants to go to the lavatory. There are spiders and fleas everywhere.'

151

'That's terrible. That's really terrible, Dick. They've no right to keep anyone on remand in conditions like this and I'm going to see that something's done about it. If necessary, I'll ask to see the Minister himself.'

'It's a pity Dad isn't here,' Dick said. 'Friday's a long way away. I don't see how I can wait until Friday. If I could prove I didn't strangle Mr Stilson do you think they'd let me out before then?'

'Well, Dick, I suppose they'd really have to, but it might be very, very difficult to produce the proof.'

'You can't be kept in prison for something you haven't done.'

'I'm afraid you can, Dick, and many people are. Justice is very fallible. It makes mistakes all the time. If you didn't strangle Mr Stilson – and I know you didn't – the question is who did?'

'A man called Simon.'

'And I imagine you're quite sure of that.'

'Quite sure, Mr Craker.'

'Perhaps you should have mentioned this before.'

There was a moment of distraction for them both as an outcry started at the far end of the room when a man who had refused to be parted from his visitors was pounced upon by two warders and dragged away by the hair, screaming.

'Surely this is something you should have brought up in court?' Craker said.

'I wasn't given the chance, and I didn't even have time to think about it while we were there. When they said Mr Stilson had been strangled, I didn't know what to think. The first thing I thought was they were making it up, but now when I think about it I know just what happened.'

'You'd better tell me, then.'

'You see, Simon was following us all the time. He saw the accident, and when I went away to get help he strangled Mr Stilson.'

'I'd like to know all about this Simon. Who was he?'

'He was Mr Stilson's servant in the house at Villa Maria. He went with us on the trip.'

152

'Well, now, Dick, this is something quite new,' Craker's voice was as indulgent as if he were talking to a young child. 'You told the Rural Police that you and Mr Stilson were by yourselves. It's in your statement.'

'I didn't want to bring Simon into it unless I had to because I was sure they would pick him up somewhere and start asking a lot of questions and that business about my mother and Mr Stilson would come out. He saw me hit Mr Stilson with the stone. I didn't think that would come out in court, either.'

'What reason would Simon have had for killing Stilson?'

'Mr Stilson treated him like an animal. He did all the dirty work round the house and when Mr Stilson was angry with him he used to make him do silly tricks like going round on his hands and knees, and pretending to bark. He used to be a captain in the Army once. Mr Stilson had a picture of him on a white horse. Another way he used to punish him was to make him sleep in a dog kennel.'

'A strange story, isn't it?' Craker said. Sympathy and scepticism fought for control of his expression. 'Many people might find it incredible.'

'Do you find it incredible?' Dick asked.

'I wouldn't say that,' Craker said. 'The world's a strange place. But it is a trifle fantastic. The thing is, you believe this Simon killed Stilson?'

'I'm sure he did. He's the only one who could have.'

'How could it have happened? In your statement you said that you and Stilson had a kind of picnic supper, and then you went to sleep in the van. What's the new version?'

'Simon was there. That's the only difference. Mr Stilson was angry with him because he said he'd been stealing the dog's food. We had Mr Stilson's hunting dog with us, and Mr Stilson punished Simon by making him fight with the dog for his own food and the dog bit him.'

'Go on,' Craker said.

'Well, then we went to bed, and in the night Simon gave the dog some poison to paralyse it and then he cut its throat. After that he got into the van while we were asleep and took Mr Stilson's watch and his gold pen and went off.'

'What happened to the dog?'

'Mr Stilson buried it and then we went hunting.'

'And how does Simon come into the story from this point on?'

'He followed us. We heard him crashing about in the undergrowth behind us, and when we turned round we saw him hiding in the trees.'

'Why should he have followed you?'

'Mr Stilson said he was afraid of the dark, and he thought he was going to keep near us until it was light. He might have hoped we were going to get separated in some way so that he could kill Mr Stilson.'

'And then the accident happened and you did what you could for Stilson and went for help, and this was Simon's chance to get his revenge.'

'That's what must have happened.'

'Describe this man,' Craker said. 'I'd like to know what he looks like.'

Dick tried to recapture the details of Simon's brutalized, malevolent face and of his ungainly body. 'He was pretty ugly. He wasn't exactly a cripple but he used to walk badly. It was more like a hobble, like that hunchback in the film about Notre-Dame.'

'Old or young?'

'Old. Anyway he looked old, but he was quite strong. There was something wrong with his leg, and he was all pulled down on one side as if he was carrying something heavy. I think he must have been out of his mind.'

'Dick, the moment's come to say that we might have difficulty in proving your Simon ever existed, let alone that he killed Stilson.'

'Don't *you* believe he existed, Mr Craker?'

'I believe that Simon's very real for you, and I know you can make him real for me. But he sounds just a little too much like an ogre out of some old folk legend. You see, Dick, we can't afford not to be absolutely frank with each other at a time like this. I'm told there have been instances in the past when you seemed unable to separate fact from fancy. I doubt whether we'd ever induce any

154

judge to accept him as a real flesh-and-blood human being. If this Simon sounded a little less horrific he'd be more convincing.'

'You think I made all this up?'

'Not consciously, but I'm not sure that Simon isn't part of a mental process. I must tell you that I investigated all the circumstances of that farmhouse at Villa Maria. I was told that it was looked after by an old caretaker called Anna, who lived alone before you arrived and who's now disappeared. Nobody spoke of any Simon. I'd be prepared to wager any sum that there was no Simon at that address on the electoral roll for the village.'

'Mr Stilson kept him out of sight. He didn't want people to know about him.'

'That's the trouble, and he appears to have done it so thoroughly you might as well say he had no existence.'

'My mother will tell you all about him.'

'I've already questioned her very closely about life at Villa Maria. There was no mention of any Simon.'

'Mum may not have wanted to say anything about him for the same reason as I didn't. Anyway, he killed the dog, didn't he?'

'According to your version number two, yes.'

'Mr Stilson was mad about it. He was really wild about that dog. He wouldn't poison his own dog and then cut its throat; would he?'

'I wouldn't expect him to, no.'

'The dog would be there where he buried it. That proves that we weren't alone, doesn't it? That proves someone was with us.'

'Alas, it proves nothing. After all, *you* could have poisoned the dog, and cut its throat.'

'Jerry Carmichael can tell you all about Simon. He can prove to you he exists. Jerry's father owns a property near Villa Maria.'

'Well, I think perhaps in the circumstances I'd better get over there right away.' Craker got up. 'I'll do my best to see Jerry and have a chat with him. I'll let you know how I get on.'

155

'Do you think you could come back again today, Mr Craker?'

'I don't know about that, but I'll see. I'll do my very best.'

'You see, I'd like to know what happens. I'd like to see my mother, too, if she could come.'

'Well, we'll see what can be done about it. I'll go straight round to the hotel as soon as I've been over to the wharf.'

The warder, simpering, one hand in his pocket covering his testicles and jingling his keys with the other hand, shuffled closer.

'I think your time's up, you'd better go, Dick,' Craker said. 'Is that the man you were telling me about?'

'That's the one. I hate him.'

'He's not a very attractive person, is he? Perhaps I'll give someone I know in the prison service a ring about him, and see if something can't be done . . . Ah yes, one other thing. This was sent to you to an address in the city. A house owned by Stilson's aunt. Would you know what it's all about?' He handed Dick a picture-postcard of a crudely coloured landscape. It showed misty fields, a blurred river and a rainbow. 'Read it,' Craker said.

Dick turned the postcard over and read. 'Well, here it is as advertised, but I can't recommend it with enthusiasm. As you can see, the views are pretty and it's easy on the nerves, but not entirely my scene, I'd say. Be nice to see you again, Dick. And pronto, eh? *Hasta luego*.' The signature was an undecipherable flourish.

'It's from Stilson,' Craker said.

'I know.' Dick let the card drop.

'Someone's taken the stamp off, and there's no postmark, but I believe it's from Mexico.'

'It can't be. They were going there, then this happened.'

'We're dealing with a very tricky individual. I don't suggest he personally sent this. He could have arranged for a number of these things to be posted from Mexico, purely with the idea of putting people off the scent. It could have been something to do with being involved in this unsavoury court case. He may have been planning to go somewhere like Reno, and this was intended to cover his tracks.'

156

He got up. 'Well, I must leave you. I can see your man's getting impatient.'

'Come back as soon as you can, Mr Craker.'

'Be sure I will, Dick.'

'And thank you for the parcel.'

'I hope you enjoy it.'

Dick got up and went after the warder and Craker stood watching until they went through the door. At this point the warder snatched Dick's parcel from his hands. '*Para mí*,' he said. 'For me.'

Craker had the luck to find Jerry Carmichael in his usual poolroom. He bought two small mugs of cane spirit at the bar and took them to a corner table where they settled under the amazed glances of the regulars who only expected to see a man dressed like Craker on the deck of a passing cruise ship. Craker was delighted with the place: the ruined pin-tables, the broken-throated jukebox, the rumbustious drunks, this young man with his burned-up skin and his mystic's eyes.

'Your friend Dick Frazer's been sent for trial for the murder of Stilson,' Craker said.

'That's too bad,' Jerry said. 'I heard something about it.'

'He's supposed to have strangled him. Do you think he did it?'

'It's kinda hard to believe.'

'Why?'

'Frazer was soft. He tried to be tough. He wanted to be tough, but he couldn't make it.'

'Well, I personally don't think he strangled Stilson either. Have you ever heard of a man called Simon?'

'Simon who? I heard of plenty of Simons.'

'An old man who is said to have worked for Stilson.'

'That one? Sure I heard of him. Yes.'

'Have you ever seen him?'

'No, but I can tell you all about him. Frazer used to talk about the way Stilson gave him a rough ride.'

'Frazer was a bit of a romancer, wasn't he?'

'Yeah. He was imaginative.'

'So there's always a chance that he only existed in Frazer's imagination?'

'In his imagination?'

'In fact, he made it all up.'

Craker waited, feeling himself on the threshold of defeat. The great blood-red sail of a schooner passing the wharf drew a triangle of colour across the window behind Jerry's head. 'Simon was real enough,' he said.

'Ah.' Craker emptied his lungs with relief. 'How do you know?'

'Everybody used to know this old guy. Simon Veragua. He ran a private army for Machado and when Batista took over he put a price on his head. My old man found him in a cave on his land. He lived on tree-frogs for fifteen years and nobody knew he was there. Stilson asked my old man if he could have him.'

'Why should he do that?'

'Stilson said Simon killed his brother when he was a kid. I guess it was nice to have him about so he could knock him around when he felt that way. Stilson used to use him in his hypnotism cabaret act until the police closed it down.'

'Why did they do that?'

'He couldn't keep it under control. He had politicians' wives standing on their heads and guys who'd paid twenty bucks cover charge lapping their soup up out of saucers. It was irrational.'

'I see,' Craker said. 'Frazer says Stilson took Simon with him on that hunting trip.'

'He would, wouldn't he, if it was another chance to make his life miserable.'

'What chance do you think we have of finding this man?' Craker asked.

'This is a big country,' Jerry said. 'They tell me about a third of it is swampland or forest. Where are you going to look for him?'

'The place where your father found him. The cave. Do you think there's any chance of his returning to his old haunts?'

'He's crazy, but not that crazy.'

'No, I suppose he's not. Well, it doesn't matter.'

158

'What did you have in mind? Do you suppose that if they ever picked up Simon Veragua it might help Frazer in any way?'

'No, frankly I don't. Not the way the law operates in this country. Anyway, it's not important. Why don't we have another drink?'

'OK, Craker, why don't we do that?'

Craker filled the mugs at the bar and came back.

'Got on well with Frazer, didn't you?'

'I wouldn't have had him around the place if I didn't.'

'And you don't think he could have strangled Stilson?'

'Not in my opinion. Physically he was only a kid.'

'What about that time you were working together in the National, and he hit the senator and put him in hospital for a week?'

'This guy had his hand in my crotch and when I kicked him he started to tear me to pieces. All Frazer did was to drop his shoe-cleaning box on his head. He didn't have to be Charles Atlas to do that. He probably saved my life.'

'And naturally you felt grateful towards him.'

'Frazer was a spoilt kid and he couldn't help that, but he was basically OK. We had a guy down on the wharf with a bullet through his neck and we had to get out past the police and Frazer changed clothes with him, and we got him out that way. A lotta guys woulda been kind of nervous about doing a thing like that.'

'That would have been a rebel, would it?'

'We never ask questions like that, Craker.'

'No, I suppose we don't. Apart from that, the impression I get is that Frazer was ready to help anyone whenever he could, even at risk to himself.'

'Yeah. That's about the way it was. You could say that. He was no chicken.'

Chapter Six

On his way back a generous impulse stoked by the raw esters in the cane spirit made Craker stop at a shop in the jewellers' arcade at the top of the Prado. As he did so a man came out and got into the Lincoln Continental drawn up at the kerb ahead of him. Craker noted the CD plate and also a badge issued by the Secret Police, the Servicio Investigación Militar, to top government officials enabling them to pass without undue hindrance through the frequent road-blocks that were a feature of the times. When the car made a U-turn to pass him he recognized the powerful man seated at the chauffeur's side.

The encounter intrigued him and, as a superstitious man he wondered as a matter of course if Fate could have taken a flattering hand in the episode. He went in and the jeweller materialized like a spirit at the entrance to his curtained alcove; a soft-eyed ruminative Syrian who wore his many-pleated Cuban shirt like a kaftan and who might have been disturbed while at prayer.

'Good morning, Antonio,' Craker said.

'Good morning, Mr Craker.'

The jeweller stood looking past Craker into the street. 'I was admiring your car,' he said. 'The first of this model I've seen.'

'I've just taken delivery,' Craker said. 'A modified exhaust system had to be fitted, and it's taken a little time.'

'Mr Craker, you always have the best of everything. I admire you. That's the way it should be. I'm still running a '39 Mercury.'

'Display doesn't go with your religion, Antonio. I admire that, too.'

'Will you take a coffee with me?'

'If you have any on the premises, yes please, but otherwise don't bother. I'm in rather a hurry. As usual, I'm looking for a gift for a lady.'

'A dark lady, Mr Craker? Don't be offended. It helps me to help you if I know.'

'You mean a Negress, I imagine. Yes, and she's a dancer at the Copacabana with certain pretensions to style. This has to be something I can ill afford.'

'Then for once I can't help you,' Antonio said.

'What do you mean, you can't help me?'

'I have nothing suitable. Nothing worthy of your taste.'

'I still don't understand. I've always believed this to be the best-stocked jeweller's in the country.'

'Thank you. I think that in normal times it is. These aren't normal times. Everything of real value's been bought up. The items I have left are in nine carat gold. Not at all suitable for an occasion like this.'

'Well, it's all very strange, but if you've nothing, you've nothing. Where am I going to look?'

'I don't know where to send you, Mr Craker, the plain fact being that all my friends are having the same problem. I can tell you that this is so. Jokingly we refer to ourselves as Akhuyat-al Dhahab. That means the Brotherhood of Gold. We know each other's business. There is no gold to be had. Neither necklaces, nor bracelets, nor even coins.'

'Nor presumably jewels of any kind?'

'No jewels either. Nothing.'

'Antonio, you know me for a discreet man, and I know you for one, too, and I'm not asking for names. A customer came out of your shop just before I came in. Was he buying or selling?'

'Like everybody else, he was attempting to buy.'

'Only attempting?'

'Only attempting.'

'Gold is an international commodity commanding a fairly stable world price.'

'That is just the point, Mr Craker.'

'Dollars are just as good.'

161

'If you can get them. If I had been able to serve you on this occasion I should have asked you for dollars.'

'I can take my pesos to any bank and exchange them for dollars at par.'

'In theory, yes. In practice you will find that the banks have run out of dollars, or are running out. They may change a hundred or two hundred as a favour to a customer. If you want to change a large number of pesos you must go to the black market, and the price is very low.'

'What's happening, Antonio? Please tell me. You people of the – what do you call it?'

'The Akhuyat-al Dhahab. The Brotherhood of Gold.'

'You people have your ears to the ground. What is this? The writing on the wall?'

'I'm afraid so, Mr Craker. That's what I would call it. Do you think that instead of buying a piece of jewellery for this lady she might like to receive a this year's model Cadillac car, or, say, a beach cottage at Varadero?'

'It hadn't occurred to me. Why?'

'Because things like that are for sale very cheap indeed. They are wonderful bargains. Five hundred dollars for a beach cottage is not dear. You will find that anything within reason will be accepted.'

'And I can guess why,' Craker said, 'in view of what you've told me. You can't take them away.'

'Exactly that. You can't take them away.'

Craker bought the late edition of the *Diario de la Marina* on a bookstall outside the jeweller's shop. He glanced at the headlines, then picked up the pay-phone provided and phoned Hollingdale at the Embassy. 'I've just come from seeing young Frazer at the Asylum,' he said. 'Have you any idea what this place is like?'

'I'm told it's bad, even as asylums go,' Hollingdale said.

'Have you ever read of the way it used to be possible to smell a slave ship two or three miles away at sea? Well, it stinks like that, or so I imagine. Of excrement and misery. I can't get the sound of the screaming out of my ears.'

'In a way the Isle of Pines might have been better.'

'I doubt it,' Craker said. 'I had the occasion to talk to a man who'd done three years at Nueva Gerona yesterday. The old lags cast lots for any young boys who get sent there. They make them dress up as girls.'

'The trouble is they probably do much the same in any of these prisons,' Hollingdale said.

'Let's only hope it doesn't apply at the Remand Centre. Have you tackled H.E. yet?'

'Not yet. This is a busy moment. I will as soon as ever I can get to him. I thought *you* intended to.'

'I will when I've anything positive to suggest, but I'd like you to prepare the ground. Have you seen the midday *Diario*?'

'I haven't.'

'You'd better get one. You're in for a shock.'

'I doubt that, but what's happened?'

'It says the rebels' advance has been broken at Limonar.'

'Is that supposed to be bad news?'

'Limonar's about sixty miles from here. Escambray's the best part of double the distance. The rebels were routed at Escambray last week.'

'Why worry? They'll be back in Escambray after this kick in the teeth. They've let themselves be drawn out of the mountains into open country where the air force could take them on, that's all. Everything's gone according to plan.'

'Paul, I've just tried to buy a present for a girl in a jeweller's I know, and they've got nothing. They've sold out the whole of their stock, and so has every other jeweller. People are buying up transportable wealth in any form.'

'You're over-reacting, old man. These things happen all the time. It's the way these people rig the market. They sell out their stock and then buy it back again at half price. Don't believe half the things you read in the papers, either.'

'My information is that a run on the banks has started, and the shops aren't accepting pesos any more. Do you realize you can pick up a Varadero beach cottage for five hundred dollars? Dollars, by the way. Not local currency.'

'Buy one if you can,' Hollingdale said. 'Buy one for me, too, while you're about it.'

'People are getting out. They have the feeling that the world is falling about their ears.'

'They're the victims of rumours put about by the enemy, which is about the most effective weapon they've got. It's the military situation that counts. I may as well tell you, I've just had a word with my opposite number in the US Embassy, and he's entirely confident. They have a huge stake in this country, and the last thing they're going to do is see it go down the drain. I can't say any more on the telephone, but I'll tell you the true story when I see you.'

'I want to discuss our next move over Frazer,' Craker said, 'and I can't talk to you about that over the phone either. Can I come over now?'

'Well, the thing is I have to pop out for a while, and I'm not sure when I'll be back. Do you think we could make it this afternoon? Shall we say five o'clock, at the usual place?'

'I'll be there,' Craker told him.

Chapter Seven

Hollingdale's mood was one he had never experienced before, the alerting of an instinct to trouble ahead affecting him like the first warning twinges of an unsuspected disease. Like a famous prime minister, he had always thought of himself as unflappable. Slowly over the years, wearing the Old Etonian tie that abetted a conviction that the world would not let him down, he cultivated this unflappability to a point where it freed itself from the guide-lines of judgement to become pure habit. If unpleasant things were ignored they might, and often did, go away. But sometimes they didn't.

The patrician calm, the unconsidered optimism with which he confronted crises of all kinds without examining their nature made him popular with his chiefs, who naturally hoped for assurance that all was well at the conference with which working days began. Like his predecessors, this particular ambassador had gratefully exposed himself to the anodyne of Hollingdale's reports and then, on this particular morning, a request from London for urgent information combined with the alarming newspaper headlines had recalled him to a harsh reality.

He had sent for Hollingdale's sit-rep file and re-read it, then rang for Hollingdale. 'Paul,' he said, 'these reports of yours date from December 1956. I want you to go over them again and tell me what you think of them.'

Hollingdale took the file and began to read.

5 December 1956

It is reported that on the 2 December a small force of revolutionaries landed from a boat on a beach near Santiago. These were immediately attacked by Government troops, and it is believed there were no survivors.

20 March 1957

The number of rebels in the Sierra Maestra is put at 20 at most. It is stated that these are survivors of the ill-fated Santiago expedition. A peasant who strayed into their camp said that among their weapons he saw a 16-bore air rifle.

15 September 1957

American intelligence contacts inform that the rebel force does not exceed 200. They are short of ammunition and supplies of all kinds, and there are many cases of sickness. A Government spokesman has stated that a rebel appeal to be allowed to surrender 'with dignity' has been turned down by the President's order.

26 May 1958

The big push in the Sierra goes ahead as planned. About 2000 rebels are surrounded by 17 armoured battalions with aerial and naval support. Total war will be followed by total victory, says the Government communiqué.

Colonel Schultz of the US Embassy confirms that US involvement in the Government's war-effort is now wholly accepted by the White House. Combat divisions have been stiffened by men trained in the US, and have been equipped with the latest weaponry. The despatch of a guerrilla force to Escambray is described as a propaganda exercise.

While he read the Ambassador studied the map of the great sprawling island that covered half the wall, and pondered the matters that were troubling his heart. The emergency had leaped on him suddenly like a wolf from the darkness. He had read only of skirmishes and ambuscades until the May offensive and its collapse, and of all he had read and heard only one fact had emerged to encourage him. The rebels were daring and resourceful and intrepid, but in the two long years of their harassments and their attacks, they had never built up the strength to capture a single town.

Hollingdale closed the file and looked up. 'Makes extraordinary reading, now, doesn't it?' the Ambassador said.

'I'm afraid it does, sir. It doesn't seem possible that things can have gone the way they have.' Hollingdale handed the Ambassador a folded sheet. 'Today's sit-rep,' he said. 'I had a word with Colonel Schultz before doing it.'

The Ambassador unfolded the sheet and read.

3 January 1959

It is absolutely incorrect to say that Sancti Spiritis (Pop. 115,000) surrendered to the rebels without a shot being fired, when in fact the city was by-passed and only occupied after being found untenable by its defenders. Colonel Schultz describes the rebels' unconsolidated advance as a primary strategic error, and the whole of this phase of their campaign as 'a gambler's last throw'.

He put it down. 'As Colonel Schultz would say, Paul, "who is trying to kid whom?"'

166

'Is there anything you want me to do, sir?' Hollingdale asked.

'Yes, there is, Paul. I want you to go out personally today and find out what is really happening in this war. I want you to go down to the front, if there is a front left and you can find it, and talk to the people who are fighting it and then come back and tell me what we can expect.'

Hollingdale picked Caryl up at the Presidente. 'I thought you wouldn't mind,' he said. 'Things here are moving very fast, so I was obliged to kill two birds with one stone. H.E. gave me a job to do in a hurry, and I wanted to talk to you as soon as possible.'

'Where are we going?' she asked.

'To the front if we can find it. It's somewhere down the Central Highway. There's no risk involved. The MPs see to it that you don't get yourself shot up. I have to be back for a meeting with Pelham Craker by five.'

'Did he see Dick this morning?'

'Yes, he did, and that's one of the things I want to talk to you about.'

'When can I see him?'

'Whenever you want. He's naturally very upset and he wants to see you. You'll have to be prepared for a shock.'

'I am prepared. Is it very bad?'

'Dick's standing up to things very well, but according to Pelham the place he's in is very depressing. You're bound to find it a painful experience.'

'When can I go?'

'Tomorrow if you like. I'll get Pelham to apply for permission.'

'He's a good friend, isn't he?'

'None better. He's made a kind of personal crusade out of this.'

'He's been very kind.'

She looked straight ahead, her fine eyes fixed in contemplation of the empty, polished rectangles of the Vedado suburb. Her long ordeal had left no trace whatever in her face, which was as serene and composed as a Botticelli

Madonna's. Hollingdale believed that she had summoned up a woman's biological defences, to repair and recreate a life that would shortly reveal no outward sign of blemish. Women, who largely remained mysterious to him, were more efficient in these matters than men. 'I refuse to panic,' she had said firmly. 'Andrew will be here in two days.' His coming was to provide the grand solution.

The Central Highway, freed from its burden of traffic, had fallen into the hush, the strange moment of peace that descends in those last moments before the onrush of war. The sun at close quarters was yellow on the peasants' cabins and the ripe maize, loping then across the plain to a frontier of distant green hills, and to the remote glitter on the left of Matanzas along the edge of its bay.

'He might even make it by Thursday night,' she said, 'depending upon connections. Andrew knows so many people through his business contacts. He has a wonderful way of getting things done.'

She spoke of her husband with unmistakable pride. He wanted to ask her, 'Did you really mean to go through with that divorce?' He suspected that she was busily readjusting to perspectives of memory. Soon so many things would be forgotten.

They passed the first military vehicle they had seen, a command car with a flat tyre facing away from the battle with an unshaven soldier at the wheel drinking from a bottle. Nothing could have painted a clearer picture of what had happened to the war, not even the conclusion of the secret despatch passed on through Schultz from the Cuban High Command. 'The Army is losing its will to fight.'

'Don't feed them that stuff, feller,' Schultz had said. 'It's kind of bad for morale.'

'To return to our problem, we're faced with a dilemma,' Hollingdale said. 'Andrew's a resourceful man with valuable contacts, but I suspect he could find this a hard nut to crack. I offer this with some hesitation, but do you know what is meant by plea-bargaining?'

'I've never heard of it.'

'It's a widely practised system. It means we'd go cap in

168

hand to these people and offer to change our plea to guilty in exchange for concessions on their part. We'd plead guilty to a lesser offence. In this case culpable homicide.'

'But how can we do that if Dick isn't guilty?'

'Our great predicament is that Dick could stay in prison while on remand for up to three years. Coming to an arrangement might be the lesser evil. The thing's decided then and there. There's about a one in fifty chance he'd even get a suspended sentence.'

'And what's the worst we'd have to expect?'

'A year. Eighteen months. If they were ready to do business.'

'Who would do whatever has to be done?'

'Pelham Craker.'

'And this is something you advise?'

'At this moment I don't see any alternative. There's not a lot to be lost.'

He was wondering about that one in fifty chance of a suspended sentence. 'Could you put your hands on a large sum of money?' he asked.

'I have a few hundred dollars.'

'It wouldn't be enough. Anything of value? A piece of jewellery perhaps? Something to tempt the eye of one of the local magpies if need be.'

'My engagement ring, that's all,' she said. She held out her hand, and he slowed to inspect it.

'The stone's a nice one,' she said. 'Andrew bought it when he went to South Africa.' She slipped the ring off, held it to' the light, rotating it so that the facets of the diamond released their small, sudden gushes of fire.

'It looks most expensive,' he said.

'They let him buy it for a lot less than the market price. Some special pumps had to be fitted in the mine and he was the only one who could show them how to do it. It was a way of showing their appreciation.'

Again the pride in her voice. 'It could make just that bit of difference,' he said.

'Take it. Do what you like with it,' she told him.

169

He took the ring from her and dropped it into his pocket. 'Let's hope we can find a magpie,' he said.

A movement in the corner of his vision made him slow again and pull in to the verge. Six planes were flying over, very low, heading in a south-easterly direction. 'Hold on,' he said. 'I just want to see what's happening. Won't be a moment.' He took his binoculars from the glove box, got out and climbed a bank to scan the distance. According to that morning's news the fighting should have been among the lemon groves and peach orchards of Limonar, but Limonar was over the far horizon, and what he saw now was a chain of little pyramidical hills not five miles away, with a sparkling on their flanks as the planes that had passed overhead only seconds before unloaded their bombs. This, he realized, was a distant view of a battle that was being fought many miles from where it should have been. Probably the last battle, he thought, because after this there were no more hills to slow down the advance on the capital.

He got back into the car. 'The war's just down there,' he told her. 'Do you mind if we push on a bit further? See how the fighting's going if we can get close enough.'

They drove on and turned a bend and there was President Batista's army in full flight. This was a village with an empty market-place, closed shops and the chairs on the tables outside the only café, and the soldiers were coming up the street singly or in ragged groups, no longer marching, but making for Havana in a stolid, patient trudge. Their faces carried growths of beard, and were strangely alike, simplified as if sketched by a cartoonist, emptied by the battle of individuality, and saddened by the memory of tragic sights. Hollingdale stopped the car and they watched the defeated soldiers pass in an immense silence, broken only by the shuffle of their boots. A jeep coming from the direction of the capital stopped just ahead of them and three MPs dressed like Americans with white bucket helmets and gaiters, jumped out waving their pistols. The soldiers simply pushed them aside and walked on.

Hollingdale started up and they drove on to the end of the village where looters had smashed into a liquor shop and were carrying away the bottles, and boys tore down a recruiting poster under the pacific eye of the village policeman. He turned the car round. 'I've seen all I need to see,' he said. 'We may as well go back.'

Chapter Eight

The five o'clock meeting with Craker was to be at the Spanish bar just round the corner from the Embassy. Craker was there when Hollingdale arrived, and he was just in time to see his friend hang up a Sevillian hat. They sat in chairs made from sherry barrels and ordered the thick Pyrenean wine that contributed to the atmosphere sketched in by the old bullfight posters and the tattered goldfinches in their tiny cages.

'I hear you were sent to see the war,' Craker said. 'So what's the verdict after all?'

'It's over,' Hollingdale said.

'Do you really mean that?'

'I'm afraid so. I wanted to talk to Caryl and I took her with me. We weren't able to reach Matanzas.'

'How far did you get?'

'About thirty, thirty-five miles. A place called Matruga.'

'The Government can use its tanks in the plains.'

Hollingdale laughed.

'Aren't you being a shade defeatist?'

'I saw what was left of the army at Matruga.'

'So you of all people have given up hope?'

'Yes.'

'How long will they take to get here?'

'It depends on how much of a hurry they're in. You remember the much-advertised armoured train that was sent to Santa Clara?'

'I do.'

171

'Well, it got there all right. The assault troops it was carrying threw their guns away and handed it over to the rebels.'

'Anything we're planning to do will have to be done rather rapidly, won't it?' Craker said.

'Very rapidly,' Hollingdale said. 'Did you see H.E. after all?'

'With difficulty. It's the only time I've ever found him somewhat overwhelmed.'

'And did you talk to him as planned, about the visa for the gangster?'

'That, in the circumstances, I feel would have been most unwise.'

'Yes, it would,' Hollingdale said. 'In any circumstances.'

'In any case there wouldn't have been any point. Gomez has gone.'

'What do you mean, gone?'

'Gone. Departed. He's in Miami now. And not only Gomez, alas. Remember that girl I was interested in – that dancer at the Copacabana? She's gone too. She left a message in lipstick on her bathroom mirror and a trunk containing thirty-six ostrich feathers and fourteen pairs of shoes with broken heels, and that was it. I've been deserted.'

'The world really *is* falling about our ears,' Hollingdale said.

'I have some more bad news,' Craker said. 'The *Post* reported another escape attempt yesterday by political prisoners being taken in convoy to the Isle of Pines. A number were shot dead.'

'It's one way of reducing the prison population,' Hollingdale said. 'Let's at least be thankful young Frazer is not a political.'

'For all that, it's most alarming. I think my next move has to be to get over to the Ministry right away and see if I can talk to the man I saw come out of the jeweller's shop this morning. It could be our last hope. How much could we raise in cash in an emergency? If, for example, we had to go to people like the Community Chest and the White Heather

172

Club? Assuming, too, that we could hope for a sub from the special fund?'

'I don't know,' Hollingdale said. 'There are two or three thousand Scots in this city who could be counted upon to do what they could, but it's largely a question of time. Say ten thousand dollars. Twenty at most.' He took Caryl's ring out of his pocket. 'And this, too, might help. Caryl's engagement ring. Andrew bought the stone in South Africa.'

Craker took the ring and turned it over in his hand. He whistled. 'I think it might, too,' he said.

He took out a handkerchief, wrapped the ring in it and pushed it into the breast pocket of the blazer he wore, then he got up and reached for the Sevillian hat. 'Society here is corrupt,' he said, 'but it is divided into a majority who are dishonestly so, and a small minority who are relatively honest in their corruption. My friend is one of the latter. Let us hope that he, at least, has not already gone.'

Craker drove in his Thunderbird straight to the Ministry of the Interior, where packing cases almost blocking access to the lifts reflected the stirrings of alarm, and the normally crowded anteroom was empty. He was shown without delay into the presence of the under-secretary, Carlos Prieto, an American-educated sugar aristocrat with a clipped Bostonian authority of manner, and a decisive profile of the kind shown in the graffiti decorating the walls of the art school.

Prieto took Craker's hand in a prolonged grip. 'It's been a long time, Pelham,' he said. 'A very long time.'

'I knew you'd been kept busy,' Craker said, 'and now when I do come to see you I'm sorry I have a favour to ask.'

'I'm delighted to hear it,' Prieto said. 'I'm glad you came when you did. There's some talk of shifting the Ministry to Pinar del Rio. As you see, we're anticipating a move.'

Craker glanced round. Prieto's office was hardly recognizable in the shadow of impending change. He remembered the clutter of polished mahogany and the oil paintings designed to overawe the visitor already numbed by the long ritual wait in the anteroom. All this was gone, leaving an almost monastic interior, presided over by an object Craker had never seen before. This was a plaster statuette of the voodoo Santa Barbara, of the kind Cubans hurried to Woolworth's to buy when they felt themselves threatened by disaster.

'Pinar del Rio's a most picturesque town,' Craker said. 'I once spent a holiday there. I presume the move, if you go, will be a temporary one.'

Prieto's eyes creased in a defeated smile. 'Even death is temporary if one is a believer,' he said.

'Carlos, I've come running to you,' Craker said, 'over the sad business of a young man by the name of Richard Frazer, who's been charged with murdering a compatriot of yours, Juan Stilson.'

'I followed the case,' Prieto said. 'I was particularly interested because I happen to have been at college with Stilson. He showed promise in those days. Wasn't there something going on between him and Frazer's mother?'

'She fell under his influence. I've always suspected he employed narcotics, or even hypnotized her.'

'It's on the cards,' Prieto said. 'Something similar was alleged in an earlier case.'

'Is it true he was involved in a secret society?'

Prieto gave a slight start, as if in touching a piece of furniture he had received a small electrical discharge. 'Yes, he was,' he said. An infusion of respect had entered his tone. 'He was high up in one of the cults. This alone made him a powerful man. These are things we don't usually speak about.'

Craker had suddenly discovered the similarity in the two men. A thirty-second or sixty-fourth part of African blood in their veins would account for it. There was a slave ancestress somewhere in the leafy recesses of both ancestral trees.

'I'm certain that Frazer didn't kill Stilson. A man called Veragua did.'

Prieto nodded.

'They were on a hunting trip. Frazer wounded Stilson

174

accidentally and went for help, and Veragua strangled him and decamped.'

The Under-Secretary nodded again. 'Yes,' he said.

He's going to say yes to everything, he's going to agree to everything, but nothing's going to happen about it, Craker thought. The men who had emptied this room of its desks, its bureaux, its pictures and its telephones had carried away the power with it. The power now was with Santa Barbara with her pink cheeks and her doll's painted mouth, simpering down at them from her shelf.

'Carlos, this is a terrible injustice,' Craker said. 'Something must be done.'

'Of course,' Prieto said. He had taken his half-smoked cigarette from his mouth, and now he reached up to drop it in the ashtray at the statuette's feet. A tiny feather of smoke drifted up to the saint's retroussé nose. 'Something must be done,' he said.

'Have you heard of Veragua?'

'I've heard of Veragua,' Prieto said. 'He went to prison for freedom and justice forty years ago, and then he became what he was.' A grimace of self-pity suddenly weakened the authoritarian mask. 'I went to prison for freedom and justice when I was a student, and many of my friends did, but will anyone remember it?'

Craker ignored the diversion. 'Veragua stole a number of articles belonging to Stilson before taking off. If we could find him that would be the answer.'

'You're crying for the moon, Pelham. Nobody who decamps in these times will ever be found again. They've gone for good.'

'Young Frazer's going to spend two to three years in prison waiting to come to trial.'

'Catching Veragua wouldn't make any difference even if he confessed. It would only complicate things. We live in a legal morass. An innocent man should never get himself into prison. Especially if he's argumentative. Far better to be guilty and keep clear of complications. You should know that by now, Pelham. You've lived in this country long enough.'

'Time is short, and there's no room for manœuvre,' Craker said. 'What would you do?'

'Avoid any attempt to fight the system.'

'I've tried always to do that.'

'This is a beehive of a place in which most things can be achieved by understanding and a sensitive approach.'

'It's a lesson I've done my best to learn.'

'Take the simple matter of applying for a driving licence,' Prieto said. 'How would you set about it? Would you fill in all those forms they give you, take a test and wait a month or two to be told you can drive?'

'No, I'd pay five dollars to the right person in the licensing department.'

'Good, that's exactly what I do. So does the Minister himself. The poor man in the department has to get together a dowry for his daughter.'

'You have three daughters, haven't you, Carlos?'

'I have three. The Minister has five.'

'They must involve you in a financial problem.'

'They do, although I'm devoted to girls. The compensations are considerable.'

'The problem so often,' Craker said, 'is to find the right person in the right department.'

'Especially as they can't advertise themselves,' Prieto said. 'Frequently there is more than one person involved, which makes for added complications.'

Encouraged and emboldened, Craker decided to move closer to his objective. 'Carlos, excuse me, but could this room possibly be bugged?'

'It isn't, rest assured of that. Bugging starts at one grade lower down in the Ministry. I bug the others. They don't bug me. You can always speak freely in this office. Go ahead and say what you like.'

'I don't want to offend you as an old friend.'

'It's practically impossible to offend me at a time like this. Emergencies cure one of over-sensitivity.'

'To get down to brass tacks, how many people would have to be squared to take care of young Frazer?'

'Quite a number. Five or six at least.'

176

'And could you help?'

'I could help to a certain extent. As an old friend, understand? I would not be directly involved myself.'

'I realize that.'

'We would have to come to an arrangement now, because with every minute that passes things get worse. Last week I could have picked up the telephone and made a couple of calls to get certain things done. This week I may have to phone five or six different people because half my contacts have gone.'

'I want to come to an arrangement now. To put it bluntly, how much?'

'Fifty thousand,' Prieto said. Looking at him, as he had done a moment before with a tinge of anxiety, Craker decided that he was one of the few men he had ever known who could speak of the rewards of corruption without seeming to demean himself in any way.

'That's an impossibly high sum, Carlos,' Craker said.

'If you say it's too high, it's too high, Pelham,' Prieto said. There was no guilt, no dissimulation, no calculation in his face. 'Why don't you suggest whatever you think fit? We can but try.'

'They tell me,' Craker said, 'that jewellery is in great demand at the moment.' He took the handkerchief from his breast pocket, unfolded it and put the ring on the table, and Prieto's hand moved towards it like some cautious animal tempted by bait. He prodded at it gently with the tip of a well-manicured finger. Nothing altered in the benign indifference of his expression, and Craker, who had lived in India, was reminded of a Brahmin priest taking an offering of fruit.

'What it's worth, I wouldn't like to guess,' Craker said, 'but I believe it's a good deal. Perhaps it could be sold, and the proceeds split up.'

'Yes,' Prieto said. 'That might be the answer.'

'Can you tell me at this stage what are the chances of success?'

'The chances are good, but not certain. At this moment no one can be certain of anything.'

He had taken the ring delicately between thumb and forefinger, smiling down at it almost shyly, in the way a man might have shown tenderness to a new-born babe. 'A nice little thing, isn't it?' he said. 'Be sure we'll do what we can.'

'I know I can rely on you.'

'Of course you can rely on me. What we can't rely on is the times we live in.' Their eyes met, Prieto's sincere and unwavering. 'I may find it impossible to help,' he said, 'but if something can be done, you must promise me one thing. You must see to it that young Frazer leaves this country immediately. The same day if possible.'

'Of course, but why?'

'Because Stilson has friends who will seek to avenge him. Not necessarily because they want to do so, but because they are bound to do so as members of his cult.'

'He'll be safe as long as he's in prison, won't he?'

'He wouldn't be safe anywhere, because no one knows who these men are. The prison governor could be a cult member. The magistrate who heard his case could have been, and probably was. Even I could be. If in some way this should turn out well, you must see to it that he leaves on the first plane bound for any destination.'

Chapter Nine

Dick picked up the piece of bread and broke it open, and as he did so some small black flies flew out. He found that the flies had made little cavities or cells in the bread, and in these they had laid clusters of minute eggs. Dick broke away small pieces of bread, crumbling them for evidence of the presence of flies before putting them into his mouth.

He next turned his attention to the dollop of meat that sat in a pinkish slobber on his platter. It was soft and spongy, with white tubes of empty veins twisted round a core of gristle. He jabbed into it with his wooden spoon, breathing through his mouth to avoid an odour which was not one of decay but of something strange, and even evil. The spike of a red pepper showed from beneath the meat, and he scraped it clear, picked it up and put it into his mouth. An instant later he spat it out, his tongue on fire.

He was besieged by a terrible hunger only held in check by disgust. Going back to the bread, he gathered a little heap of crumbs and scooped them into the remainder of the yellowish, turbid water in the mug. The mixture stirred with a fingertip became a thin pap which he swallowed in two gulps, but the only effect was to increase his hunger. Three days had passed since they had put him in this cell, and this was the first food he had eaten. He wondered how long it would be before he began to starve to death, and what the symptoms would be. Would he become too weak to walk, too weak to carry the latrine bucket to empty it, too weak to get off the bed or to hunt for the fleas whose bites had covered his flesh with weals?

Two full days had passed since Craker's visit. Craker had gone to the asylum on the morning after his visit to Prieto, written Dick's name on a slip as before and handed it in at the reception office, where the official had glanced at it, consulted a list, shaken his head, and said, 'Is politico. Politicos no have right of visitation.'

'You're mistaken. I saw him yesterday.'

The man shrugged and turned his back, and Craker wondered in bewilderment and agitation whether this was not another of the awful mistakes they made in prisons, where, as he had heard, it was not unusual for one prisoner's records to be muddled with another, or a prisoner himself to be lost for days or weeks on end. And then, remembering Prieto's warning, he asked himself could this be the unexpected solution? He went off, still perturbed, to confer with Hollingdale on this surprise development.

That same morning, following the warder back to his cell from emptying the latrine bucket, Dick noticed that the letter 'C' fixed to his door had been replaced by a letter 'P'. A

179

half-hour later the man in charge of stores came in with his own clothes and gestured to him to change into them. He picked up Dick's prison pyjamas and went off.

Dick turned his attention to the bread again, trying to recover a few more untainted fragments from the areas colonized by the flies. There were footsteps in the passage, the key turned in the door lock and the warder came in followed by a second uniformed man, who was fat, smooth and dimpled, with hairy hands and a woman's pink mouth in the grey, *papier-mâché*, light-starved face of an official who had spent his working life in the perpetual twilight of prisons. A snail had left its tracks across his flies.

The warder said something to his fat friend and they both laughed shrilly – a sudden concerted high-pitched sound like the alarm of jungle birds. The fat man waddled over and picked up a piece of bread. He held it for inspection, the pink mouth turned down at the corners, in a fat-padded palm, prodding at it with a forefinger. 'Insectos,' he said, shaking his head in abhorrence. 'Here,' he said to Dick, 'food is bad. Is not our blame, but is no money to buy food. Is stealing everybody. Food they steal, blankets they steal. They don't leave nothing.' He seemed full of conciliation and reason; anxious to explain why things should be so bad.

He flicked at the meat again, turning it over on the platter, then hissing with disgust. 'Is very bad,' he said. 'You know what is this meat?'

Dick shook his head.

The fat man said, 'This meat is from a dead cow. No has been killed. Is dead from enfermedad – ulceros. Tuberculosis. Maybe putrefaction of the testas from which comes the milk. You like how this meat tastes?'

'I haven't eaten any.'

'That is good for you. Maybe this is from aborto. You comprehend what is aborto?'

'No.'

'Aborto is when young cow is dead in mother's tripas. This meat is making you shit. Is making you shit all the time. Is better you not eat this goddam stuff, huh?'

'I'm starving,' Dick said. 'I've got to eat something.'

The fat man took Dick by the elbow and steered him no further than two steps away into the token privacy essential to confidential discussion. He dropped his voice to a whisper, his mouth close to Dick's ear. 'You like this man?' he asked. He breathed out a gust of sourness, an essence of stomach juices in fermentation, and gave Dick's arm a persuasive squeeze.

'No, I don't like him.'

'Please you must not say that. This man like you very much, he say me to say you this. You go with this man for be his friend and he will be a friend for you. You want eat good steak cut from cow's ass? No abortos, no abscesos, huh? Steak meat maybe with batatas fritas and jew-beans. You like eat that?'

'Yes.'

'This man will bring you steak meat every day if you will go with him to be his friend.'

'I don't understand,' Dick said. 'I don't know what you mean.' But he understood only too well, and he felt the panic twisting in his stomach, and looked down at the sweat on his hands.

'This celda – what you call it, room? – no is good for you. It stinks bad, no? No have light, have spiders going to give you poison of the blood. Listen, they say me about you. What you do to this guy you kill?' There was admiration as well as cajolery in his voice. 'You pretty good asesino, no? You chop his head, maybe? You cut him in the neck with hacha?'

'It was an accident. I shot him by accident.'

The fat man seemed disappointed. 'For me is equal. For me has no importance, but maybe you have to stay here a year, two years. This man, he says can find you a better celda, maybe with a window, and pot with flores, and a picture of a woman with a big fat ass on the wall. How you like that? Good, huh?' The fat man's eyes took in all the drab details of the cell, and he shook his head in revulsion. 'Is better to change,' he said. 'Here it stinks and there are too many insectos.'

A low bird-like chirping sound at their backs recalled their attention, and the fat man placed his hands on Dick's shoulders and twisted him round to the spectacle of the warder holding a pair of filigree earrings to the lobes of his ears. He suddenly began an obscene rotation of the hips, and the fat man whispered an explanation. 'A present for you for wear. For show you are his friend. Is gold, no? No is imitation. You put them now, okay?'

The warder hovered expectantly, an earring held high in each hand like a bullfighter preparing to place the banderillas. He shifted a little closer, hips bouncing, his face set in an ingratiating smirk that contained an element of wariness.

'You take the pendientes – danglers you call them, no?' the fat man said. 'You put them. Are for you.'

Dick shook his head. 'Men don't wear things like that. Please go away and leave me alone.'

The fat man put a consoling arm round his friend's shoulder and translated Dick's objection and the warder's smile collapsed. He seemed to be on the verge of tears. The two men confabulated in low tones, heads close together. The fat man left his friend and returned to Dick. 'Okay, then. You no wear pendientes. You want brazalete for the arm, a finger ring, stockings from silk, maybe?'

'No, I don't want any of those things. Go away. Just go away.'

'Shoes with acute heels, a hand-sack of cocodrilo, a sustain for the chest – a buster, how you say? – a smart nice dress for wear, cosmeticos maybe you want?'

'No, no, no, I don't want anything. All I want is something to eat.'

'A shneak-feel pantie for you, a fur-paw, tit-cups, a no-shmell spray?'

'No, no, no, no.'

'*No quiere nada*,' the fat man said disgustedly to the warder. '*Absolutamente nada. Quiere carne.*' To Dick he said, 'This man is sad you no take anything for show you his friend. What you want for eat, huh? You want for eat cotlets from young sheeps? A puerco-snout, a bull-pic in green salsa, bloody sausages, lamps' bollix? A sweat-breed, a scrog, fish-farce, pigs' hands en rice, fried chicken, maybe?'

'Fried chicken,' Dick said.

The two men drew away for another conference, and the fat man reported back.

'Fried chicken no is prison food. Is from restaurante. Tomorrow he will go to restaurante and buy for you the fried chicken, if you will go with him to be his friend.'

'Tell him to go away and leave me alone,' Dick said. 'I don't want anything to do with him. I don't want the chicken either.'

Dick's rejection set off an outburst of fury in the warder, who raced up and down the cell waving his arms and chattering like an enraged monkey. The affability had suddenly drained, too, from the fat man, whose woman's mouth was set in an angry pout as he wagged a fur-backed finger in Dick's face.

'You Communista? You espia, no?' he said. 'This celda is only for regular criminales. Tomorrow you must go to celda with three crazy Communista espias. Is one big crazy Negro guy going to take you for his friend. Maybe you going to be friend for all of them.'

'I won't be here tomorrow,' Dick shouted. 'A lawyer is coming to fetch me today. He's the lawyer for our embassy. He's been to see the Ambassador about me already.'

The fat man jabbered his translation and the pair broke into their shrilling, tropical bird laughter again. 'No man is coming,' the fat man said. 'You are a politico, and a Communista espia, and for you no is visitation. My friend say me this is last oportunidad for you to be his friend. He say me you must not go with him too much. Maybe one time, two times every day, three times maximum. First you eat fried chicken from the restaurante, no. You give him now one kiss, he brings you fried chicken from restaurante.'

Dick had backed away, but the table cut off further retreat.

'*Venga*,' the fat man said in soft encouragement to his friend, and then to Dick, a simper breaking through the pout, 'He has shame. Shy, you say, no?' The warder moving stealthily forward, had pursed his lips hideously, and was sucking drops of salivated air like an infant suddenly deprived of the teat of its feeding bottle. 'One beso,' he pleaded in a phlegm-encrusted whisper. 'One kees for me, blease.'

He came closer, clutching with chubby fingers, jabbing and feinting as if trying for a hold in a wrestling match, then suddenly he caught at the waistband of Dick's trousers, and Dick tore his hand away, reached behind him to find his mug, and smashed it in the man's face. The warder's nose flattened under the impact and he backed off with blood showing at the nostrils. At this moment the fat man joined the struggle and, bending suddenly to butt Dick in the solar plexus with his head, he next seized him by the legs and jerked him off his feet.

Dick went over backwards, and both men fell on him. They dragged him by his arms and legs screaming to the bed and threw him face down on it. The fat man wound both arms round his legs and the warder, lying across Dick's back, had for the moment imprisoned Dick's arms in a way that left his own right arm free, and he was nuzzling into the nape of Dick's neck, and wrenching at the buttons on his trousers.

Dick tore himself free. He clawed at flesh and bit into muscle where he found it, and kicked out at kneecaps, shinbones and groins. He reached the door and began to bang on it with his fists, and almost immediately, before he could be torn away, it was opened and a third warder stood there in the door opening. He was young with an almost fleshless face, a close-cropped stubble of hair and pale, flat eyes. He spoke, and when he stopped speaking his lips disappeared. 'You Frazer, huh?' he asked.

'Yes, I am. Those men were attacking me.'

The third warder waved to the two others across Dick's shoulder, then he put his hand on Dick's chest, pushed him back into the cell and walked in after him. 'OK, Frazer, so they were attacking you.' To the others he said with a polite smile and a nod, '*Perdonen la molestia.* I was telling those

184

guys sorry to spoil something for them,' he explained to Dick.

He pushed Dick back another step then chucked him under the chin. 'Why you a bastard Communista, Frazer?'

'I'm not a Communist.'

The man's mouth was a line ruled under the long thin nose. 'Turn round,' he said.

Dick turned and the man struck him with his fist over a kidney. Dick doubled up as agony shafted through every nerve in his body.

The warder's mouth had reappeared. 'You Communista, Frazer?'

'Yes, I am,' Dick groaned.

'So OK, Communista, grab your things and let's get going.' He picked up Dick's mug, his spoon and his plate and thrust them into his hands. 'Know where you're going, Communista, now?' he asked him.

'No.'

'Well, lemme tell you. You're going for a ride. They're clearing all the Communista bastards out of this prison, and taking them for a nice long ride.'

He held a finger pointed to his temple, clicked his tongue in mock sorrow, and struck Dick again, this time a light, contemptuous blow on the cheek.

They all laughed, the new arrival contributing his high-pitched mirthless screech to the chorus of jungle birds, before, with a sudden violent shove, he sent Dick staggering towards the door.

Chapter Ten

In a mere forty-eight hours there had been radical alterations in the complexion and the pulse-rate of the city.

Quite suddenly the population, sensing profound changes that lay ahead, fell into a mood of self-examination. People prepared arguments in justification of past actions, tested the respectability of their present way of life, and peered with troubled eyes into the gathering murk of the future. An unsuspected sympathy of the better placed citizenry for the productive classes supporting them showed itself in small ways, such as the hastily introduced fashion for fishermen's smocks, and roughly plaited straw hats worn by the peasant in the fields. Guests at the Tropicana nightclub owned by a crime syndicate from New Jersey, danced under its advertised thousand artificial stars to old revolutionary songs about freedom and justice cobbled into new Samba rhythms. Beards of the kind sported by soldiers of the rebel army were being grown as fast as chins could grow them, and the leading sugar baron, announcing himself a convert to socialism, dismissed his servants without notice, locked his nine cars away, and showed himself at the races in a cotton shirt and rope-soled shoes, at the reins of a farmcart. The prostitutes of Havana united to protest against US support for the failing dictatorship by doubling their charge to US soldiers from the Guantánamo base. The popular swing to the left was resisted by the police in a new campaign against defeatism during which, in a raid on Woolworth's stores, they confiscated the whole stock of ornaments in the form of Statues of Liberty, amounting to over a thousand items in several sizes and qualities of production.

Craker decided as a precaution to have a Union Jack fitted to the wing of his Thunderbird, and picked up an old copy of the *Post* at the garage where the job was being done.

He scanned the personal columns and then turned to the back page where the news snippets could be extraordinary. The name Anna Reyes caught his eye. The famous Anna, he thought. It can't be anybody else. He read on.

> Anna Reyes, the clairvoyant much in vogue among leading members of society in her palmy days before falling from sight after her involvement in a notorious poisoning case, was in the news again today. Reyes claimed to newsmen to have been visited by the spirit of Juan Stilson whose death in a hunting accident we reported last week. Communicating through a 'direct voice trumpet' he told her that he had been murdered, gave details of the crime, and named the murderer. He told her that he would continue 'to haunt this world' until justice was done.

Checking the date of the paper, Craker found that it had been printed on the day before Dick's arrest. Preposterous, he thought. Where else in the world could stuff like this actually be presented as news, in the certain knowledge that not an eyebrow would be raised?

Suddenly he shivered, and the shiver took him by surprise. What's the matter with me? he asked himself. Surely I'm not superstitious after all. What is it – weakness? Old age? Could a faulty heart have anything to do with it?

The mechanic finished adjusting the flag. Craker got into the car and drove over to see Caryl at the Presidente.

'I had a brief meeting with my contact in the Ministry this morning,' he told her. 'Things are coming to a head sooner than expected.'

'Tell me quickly,' she implored him. 'Is it good news, or bad news?'

'Good,' he said. 'I would say so.'

She took a deep breath, then released it, her hand held between her breasts. 'Thank God,' she said. And smiled.

'I'm afraid its been a time of terrible tension for you,' Craker said. 'And for me. This has become a sort of personal crusade. I wanted to report to you now because I think it's essential for you to know exactly what's happening. It would appear that your beautiful ring may have done the trick, which is to say that all that wretched business with plea-bargaining is out, for which I'm profoundly relieved.'

'I am too,' she said. 'I can't tell you how much. It all sounded so terribly risky.'

'What is envisaged now is a clean-cut operation. If all goes well Dick should be free by this time tomorrow. My friend tells me everything's been arranged.'

'How marvellous. How truly marvellous. And you can trust him?'

'In matters like this, absolutely. Crooked men are often very trustworthy in certain ways. Possibly they need to think well of themselves more than most of us do. He seems to have hit on a brilliantly simple solution. He's managed to doctor the register at the Remand Centre to have Dick reinscribed as a political prisoner.'

A flash of alarm seemed to widen her already enormous eyes. The expression aroused in Craker a kind of protective frenzy. 'It was the one certain way of getting him out of the place,' he explained.

'I read in the *Post* about political prisoners being shot while attempting to escape. It said the guards lost their heads.'

'No fear of Dick attempting to escape. It won't be necessary. Let me tell you how the plan works. They shift political prisoners out of Havana every few days. Our friend, who's by way of being a pretty influential man, will be down waiting at the Remand Centre when the convoy's made up. As I understand it, he's been able to bribe the officer in charge of the convoy to allow him to smuggle Dick away.'

'I almost can't believe it,' she said. 'After all this awful suspense.'

'We have to be there exactly at three to collect him. No earlier and no later. For some reason the timing's of great importance. We've synchronized watches.'

'The waiting is going to be unbearable,' she said. 'Are you sure nothing can go wrong?'

'It's an intricate manœuvre. A sort of three-card trick played with people, but I'm quite certain everything is going to be all right if we do our part. All we have to do is be there to get Dick off the scene quickly when the moment comes.'

'And once he's with us he'll be safe? All this terrible business will be over?'

'As soon as we get him away Dick will have ceased to exist as far as the Department of Justice is concerned. All the records will vanish, and he'll have vanished, too. My friend will kiss your hand and give you back your passport, and that will be the end of the thing.'

She shook her head in wonder and delight. 'And we'll actually be able to go home?'

'Why not? As soon as you please.'

She jumped up from her chair. 'I'll tell you a most extraordinary thing. In the excitement of it all I'd actually forgotten Andrew gets in at midday.'

'Of course he does,' Craker said. 'I'd forgotten, too. Of course, it's tomorrow.'

'He rang me from New York,' she said. 'We had a long talk. Isn't it wonderful?'

'Yes,' he said. 'It's all worked out very well. He'll be able to go with us.' He experienced the smallest twinge of jealousy. What he had done for her had nothing to do with the fulfilment of duty. It had been an act of self-abnegation and devotion worthy of its rewards. But now this stranger, this lantern-jawed Calvinist from the glens, would arrive to thrust him aside. His spirits sagged, and he felt soured and pessimistic. 'Let's hope the plane isn't delayed,' he said.

Her alarm showed pitifully, and Craker was instantly repentant. 'It's unlikely to be,' he said, 'not seriously, anyway. Things are so chaotic at the moment, you can never be sure, but it's normally on time.'

'I couldn't bear not to be there to meet him, but wouldn't it be safer to leave a message and tell him to come to the hotel?'

Optimism, and with it generosity, returned. 'I don't think it's necessary. After all, we've hours in hand. I can check with the airline in the morning on the probable time of arrival. And the Remand Centre's only a half-hour from the airport. We've all the time in the world.'

189

She leaned across on impulse to throw her arms round his neck. 'You've made me the happiest person in the world,' she said.

'Could almost be a holiday, couldn't it?' Craker said to Caryl, and she agreed. The streets on their way to the airport were full of people dressed in their best talking excitedly and accosting one another with wild affability as they paraded up and down past closed shops and banks, as if constant, aimless motion and sheer noise were accepted as antidotes to anxiety. Craker noted that bands of dogs abandoned by their owners had formed under chosen leaders to forage for food. The traffic lights had ceased to work, and the traffic policemen lounged at street corners, ready with sheepish apologetic grins to wave cars on in any direction they might feel like going.

There was streaming confusion at the airport, and once again he observed that even in this atmosphere of near hysteria Caryl's nordic appeal was the passport to a tiny success, for where the way was barred to other cars, the police waved them through.

Within the building the arrival and departure areas were divided only by a chain, separating the anxiety of the crowd that were here to make their escape from the calm of the few awaiting the handful of hard-core travellers who would shortly fly in from New York.

Craker savoured a moment of depression. Among these fugitives there were a few hatchet-faced, narrow-eyed, taciturn men looking like George Raft who had taken their profit of this city and decided that it was time to go, but there were others whose prospective loss saddened him. He noticed with regret, her boarding-card in hand, the madame of a bordello he believed to be the most civilized in the world. There was an enchanting actress, and a brace of great harlots – always beyond his reach – who had spun themselves cocoons of poetry, even legend. These he would see no more, and each one with her going was smuggling away a little contraband of gaiety and grace. Sorrow struck at him.

190

Beauty and music were draining from the city, like life-blood from a severed artery.

'Perhaps I'd better find out what's happening,' Craker said.

He went to the enquiries desk and returned. 'The plane left on time,' he said. 'It's run into headwinds which will slow it down. It could be fifteen minutes late. No more. Let's go and have a drink.'

They went into the bar where they found two close-cropped men in flowered shirts drinking and shooting dice at the counter. Both Caryl and Craker recognized them, and Caryl remembered that she had met them both at a party at the American Embassy, and that one was called Howard, and the other Vin.

Howard looked up from his dice and saw them, and Caryl waved and they went over.

'Not leaving us, ma'm?' Howard asked.

'No, I'm meeting my husband,' she said. 'He's on the plane from New York.'

Vin glanced at his watch. 'Forty-three minutes to go,' he said. 'Why doncha have a seat?'

They pulled up stools and sat down and Craker ordered dry sherries. He studied the two young men curiously but with discretion. They were rumoured to be members of an intelligence organization working under cover as clerks in the Embassy. There was a certain similarity between the two. Both had young, lean, unlined faces charged with assurance and belief. Back in England they might have been young clergymen of the dedicated sort. 'Travelling, gentlemen?' he asked politely.

'No, we're just here,' Howard said.

'Keeping an eye on things,' Vin added.

'Rather a tense situation, eh?' Craker said. 'Do you think there's truth in the rumour the President may be departing?'

Howard got down from his stool. He led Craker to the window at the end of the bar. Through it Craker saw an acre of sun-whitened airfield in which stood three elderly DC 4s parked abreast. They were guarded by sub-machine-gun-armed police. 'Waiting for the big feller,' Howard explained.

'So he is on his way out?'

'That's what they tell us. When he takes off a coupla hundred million dollars are going with him in those planes.'

'Does this mean the government's throwing its hand in?'

'No, sir. This guy was a reactionary and he has to go. The fight will go on under democratic leadership.'

'That's very heartening news,' Craker said. 'I was beginning to despair.'

'No cause to do that, sir. Everything's going to be OK. This guy had to go and this is the way it had to be done.'

'Well, I'm sure if you don't know what's going on behind the scenes, nobody does,' Craker said.

He went back to Caryl. 'Howard's just been showing me the President's plane,' he said. 'It seems he'll be leaving us.'

Occupied by her thoughts in the shadow of coming events, she seemed not to hear him. 'Why don't we go up on the terrace and watch the plane come in?' he suggested.

They climbed the stairs to the roof garden and stood against the rail together looking across the plain towards the north. She placed her hand over his on the rail and he felt a boyish thrill at the contact.

'The plane seems to be earlier than expected,' he said. 'Surely that's it over there, over the clump of palms.'

'Where?' she asked. Then she saw the Eastern Airlines Flight 438 from New York slide up, starred with sunshine, from the wind-marbled backdrop of the Gulf into the lagoon of the Havana sky. It lowered itself to breast the mirage sheeting the end of the runway, wavered in semi-solution, then took on solid shape to charge towards them and stop, barely fifty yards from where they stood looking down.

Holding Caryl's arm, Craker caught the vibration of her excitement, then glimpsed in the quickest side-glance the glistening of her eyes. Five passengers came through the cabin door, four of them short, ordinary men with the bewilderment of air travel in their faces. The fifth was tall, equipped with overcoat over his arm for the dignity of a cold climate left behind, and serene of expression and manner even at this distance. Standing there in the press of small men, he took stock of the situation before moving on.

192

'That's Andrew,' she said. She waved with both hands.

Yes, he said to himself, that's Andrew. There's no mistaking that. How solid, splendid almost, he was in this environment of excited, fussy movement. A moment later he was at the bottom of the gangway, overtaking in a few of his long, loping strides the passengers who had been ahead of him. Caryl was waving and calling, but he neither saw nor heard, and passed below, looking straight ahead and leading the crocodile of passengers out of sight into the airport building.

They went down, stopping at the foot of the stairs to glance through the door in the partition closing off the Customs Hall. It was empty apart from a single official slumped dejectedly behind the long table. 'Will you excuse me for just two minutes?' Craker asked Caryl. 'I feel I ought to phone the Embassy.'

He patted her arm and left her standing well-placed to see the passengers as they came through Immigration into Customs. He found a phone-box, but automatic dialling produced no result, and the operator told him the number was engaged and promised to ring back. Craker went to the bookstall and bought a copy of the influential and conservative *Diario de la Marina*, and glanced at an article that was meant to be humorous but was also worrying. It was headed *Is Voodoo a Reality?* and referred to the growing belief held by certain elements of the population that the rebels' astonishing successes were to be ascribed to supernatural causes. Mentioning that bullets claimed to have bounced off rebel bodies were on offer for use in magic rites for ten dollars apiece, the paper sorrowfully concluded that voodoo *was* a reality if enough people could be induced to believe in it.

The telephone rang and Hollingdale was on the line.

'I'm at the airport,' Craker said. 'I thought you ought to know the Big Chief is leaving.'

'Now? Immediately?'

'Sometime soon. The planes are waiting to take off.'

'We've been expecting it for days,' Hollingdale said. 'One of the generals is taking over.'

193

'I thought you'd like to know.'

'Nice of you to ring.'

Hollingdale sounded harassed, eager to get rid of him. He hung up and wandered back towards the Customs Hall, turning a corner to bring Caryl into view just as the loudspeakers started a roaring announcement, not a word of which he could understand. Then the first of the passengers from New York came through the glass door of the Customs, to be instantly engulfed in a surging mob of relatives and friends, materializing from nowhere to meet them. A moment later Andrew Frazer was carried into sight by a rush of bodies, an arm outstretched towards Caryl, who had been forced by this time to the back of the crowd.

Craker preferred not to be present in the first moments of their reunion and, backing quickly away, he took refuge behind a shuttered cigar kiosk, waiting some ten minutes for the joyful outcry outside the Customs Hall to fall silent before coming out of his cover again. Caryl and Andrew Frazer stood facing him, now alone. Andrew Frazer had his arm round his wife's shoulder, and he flung up a hand as if in salutation of a friend of lifelong standing as Craker approached. Craker chided himself for the poverty of his imagination, which had created the expectation of nothing better than a stereotype of an old husband with a young wife. He had seen so often in his mind's eye a face that was patient, spartan and long-suffering. The reality suggested more spirited qualities. Craker knew that Frazer was fifty-five, but he looked ten years younger, a man with bold, dark eyes, a ready smile, and a touch of merchant-adventuring swagger about him. It's I'm the old crock, he thought sorrowfully.

They shook hands and at that moment the loudspeakers began their outcry again, and they shouted greetings at each other that neither heard and then gave in to laughter. Frazer poured his gratitude into the static-filled pauses as the speakers drew breath, and Craker hastened to put him at ease. 'I've done my best. We've all done our best. We're very, very fond of Dick. Caryl will have told you. Yes – all set for three. I'm sure it's going to be all right.'

194

Caryl had taken Craker's hand to praise him to her husband, and Craker feeling a twinge of embarrassment was saved from graceful speech-making by a fresh blaring interruption. Frazer pretended to beat the sound away as if wasps were circling his head. 'Why are they telling us to keep calm?' he shouted.

'That's all I can make out myself,' Craker said. 'You've arrived at rather a critical time. The President's just about to pull out. Perhaps it's something to do with that.' He could not be sure how much Frazer had heard.

People were beginning to scamper in all directions. A ground-hostess in trim grey broke through the disorder to reach them. Her lacquered smile was schooled in the routines of frustration and calamity. 'Cubana Air Lines – ' she began, and the loudspeakers gagged her. Her lips moved, and the big, vacant eyes scanned their faces without commitment. She put her mouth to Craker's ear. 'Please proceed to the bar,' she screamed, 'where complimentary refreshments will be served.'

Frazer caught her by the arm. 'Can you tell us what's happening?' he bellowed.

' – Ron Bacardi, h-whiskay, Cuba libres, or h-what you like,' the girl said. 'All with the compliments of Cubana.'

'But I don't want a drink. My luggage hasn't turned up yet. I want to collect my luggage and get away.'

'OK,' the girl shouted back. 'I see you at the bar.' She backed away, and disappeared instantly from sight among the crowd. Then in a moment when the loudspeakers had spluttered into silence they heard a new, more urgent sound.

'What on earth's that?' Caryl asked.

'Possibly shooting,' Andrew Frazer said. 'I suppose that's why we were asked to keep calm.' They were caught up momentarily in a stampede largely composed of peasant women carrying bundles of chickens tied by the feet. A large, jagged hole opened suddenly in a wall of frosted glass to show most of two of the three DC 4s on the tarmac, and ribbons of smoke flung from a clump of palms, falling among the planes like the streamers tossed shorewards from a departing cruise ship. They heard the splutter and snap of

195

squibs exploding distantly, taking into their lungs a whiff of cordite mixed with the running crowd's sweaty odour of fear. A child dodging past them splashed the floor with a trail of piddle. They saw through the jagged icicles of glass that one of the planes was now burning gustily, and that two uniformed men were dragging a third by the heels from the crimson smudge where he had lain on the tarmac.

Frazer gestured towards the bar. 'Perhaps we should proceed as suggested. Looks a little quieter in there.' They struggled through to the bar's little oasis of tranquillity. Only the American called Vin remained at the bar. He had just called over the Negro barman to order a dry martini, giving the most precise instructions as to its composition. He turned to grin and flap a hand in mock exasperation as they sat down at a table.

'What's going on out there?' Craker called to him.

'Bunch of wild guys tried to shoot up the place, I guess,' Vin said. 'Howard's gone to find out.'

'I wonder how long this is going on?' Frazer asked.

'My guess is it's as good as over now,' Craker told him. 'One of these hit-and-run affairs they seem to specialize in.'

In fact the distant explosions had ceased. They heard a wail of a police car siren, then ambulance bells jingling, and then these stopped too.

'I think we can relax,' Craker said. 'I hope you weren't too frightened,' he said to Caryl.

'I wasn't frightened in the slightest,' she said.

The loudspeakers gave tongue again, but with the return of relative calm, they were lucid and persuasive. 'What are they saying now?' Caryl asked.

'Arriving passengers' luggage will be transferred direct to the air terminal bus,' Craker translated. 'There may be some delay. Another announcement will be made soon.'

'What do you think they mean by some delay?' Frazer asked.

'I'm going to find out,' Craker asked. Knowing the ropes, he went to find the Duty Officer. 'An hour, two hours, maybe,' the man told him. 'There is still some trouble. We do not know ourselves what is happening.'

196

Craker found the doors guarded by soldiers. Through them he saw the sunflower-yellow cars of the secret police come and go, and inert, sheeted forms being carried by on stretchers to be loaded into ambulances. In the background a grey filament of smoke rising behind an immense 7-UP advertisement denoted the spot where all that was combustible of an aeroplane was turning to ashes. He made an effort to slip through the doors, and a soldier pushed him back. '*No puede pasar.*'

An officer came strutting up, stern-faced under his gold-braided hat. '*Qué desea?* What can I do for you, please?'

'We have to get down to town. It's a matter of urgency.'

'I'm sorry. All the people must wait here for permission to go. It is not permitted now to pass by the streets.'

Craker went back to the bar where he found Caryl and Frazer sitting, cheeks together. They moved apart almost guiltily as he came in. 'Rather unfortunately,' he said, 'they're not letting anyone out of the building. I have a feeling we could be here for a long time.'

'What are we going to do?' Caryl said.

Craker saw Howard come into the bar. 'Hold on a moment,' he said. 'I think perhaps I'd better see if our friends over there have anything to suggest.'

He caught up with Howard at the bar. 'What's the story?' he asked.

'The story,' Howard said, 'is that three beards with a heavy machine-gun managed to get over the perimeter fence last night and hide out in some bushes. The idea was to knock the President off whenever he showed. What happened was one of the guard dogs sniffed them out so the action turned out to be kind of premature.'

'How much longer do you think they're likely to keep us here?' Craker asked.

'*Quién sabe?* It takes these guys quite a while to adjust to any new situation. They specialize in shutting the stable door when the horse is gone.'

'They tell me,' Craker said, 'that you people are the real powers that be in this country. We're in a great hurry to get away. Could you get us out of here?'

'It might be possible. Where do you want to go?'

'Down town, as fast as we can. I have a car in the park.'

'Come with me, my friend, and let's go see what can be done,' Howard said.

Craker waved to the others to come over. 'Howard's going to have a try at getting us out of this building,' he said. 'I think we should go now, if and while we can. We've still got some time in hand, but we'll go and sit and wait in a café if needs be. The thing is to get out of here.'

'Where did you say you were going?' Howard asked.

'The Asylum. The old Manicomio. Near the Stadium.'

'Leave yourselves plenty of time. That's my advice,' Howard said. 'I just heard they put up barricades and closed off half the streets. These Cubans live on their nerves.'

Howard led the way through the Customs Hall and then past the Immigration booths, where no officials were to be seen. They followed him along a passage leading to the Arrivals entrance door which was guarded by a small soldier, rifle slung, in the act of picking his teeth. Howard showed his pass. '*Diplomaticos*,' he said, and the soldier stood aside. Stepping out into the open they were confronted with the aftermath of a small disaster. A firestorm had raged here briefly over and around the stricken plane, of which nothing remained but an effigy in wires, ribs and buckled plates. Firemen, coughing in the air fuming with scorched shellac, resin, rubber and carbonized oil, were sluicing the tarmac with their hoses. No one glanced in their direction as they made their way round charred debris to the gate in the fence leading to the car park. Here Howard left them.

They found the Thunderbird parked close to the gate, instantly located by the Union Jack protruding a foot high from the wing. The sight of the flag, and the gentle unassuming authority – perhaps even the stolidity – for which it stood, had the effect of a tot of whisky on Craker's nerves after the untidy emotionalism of the past hour.

He held the door open for Caryl, just as one of Batista's new British planes came sneaking in from the sea, to sheer off suddenly, turn back and make a bolt for the sheltering horizon. Looking up at it, he shook his head reproachfully. A matter of temperament, he thought.

'I have a feeling the worst of our troubles are over,' he told them. 'If nothing holds us up we shall be there nicely on time.'

Chapter Eleven

They left the Rancho Boyeros Airport ring road at the 16th Avenue and were immediately stopped by a motor-cycle patrolman, who waved them in to the roadside. 'What's wrong?' Craker asked.

'Is coming the Presidente.'

'How long do we have to wait?'

'A short time. Is coming now.'

'Which can mean anything,' Frazer said. 'Five minutes, an hour. It's all the same to them.'

'I don't think we need worry,' Craker told him.

Caryl, at Craker's side, had covered her face with her hands.

'We've all the time in the world,' Craker assured her, and she took her hands away and smiled.

Fifteen minutes passed, then a flashing of reflection showed through the trees ahead, and the patrolman ran to his machine to pick up his radio. The white doves went clattering up from the road, and in the same instant the front rank of six riders of the President's escort came into view, on their glittering Harley-Davidsons, and a surge of excitement left Craker short of breath.

The Harley-Davidsons passed in a roll of thunder, pennants flying, to be followed by two gaily-coloured cars carrying officers of the secret police and the benign-looking American adviser from whom it was said they took their orders. Then came the President and his family in their bullet-proof Cadillac, and Craker strained his eyes with huge curiosity to catch a glimpse of all that was left of the brave ex-sergeant, the witty, generous half-breed who had ruled the country first well, and then badly, for so many years.

More cars passed, crammed with the sports, the jokers, the bladder-men and the canasta players of the President's personal circus, all of whom – since the President was never a man to leave a friend in the lurch – would go into exile with him. Another dozen outriders brought up the rear of the procession, and the spectacle was at an end.

'I think we're being allowed to go,' Craker heard Frazer say. He turned his head to see the patrolman signal to them.

Tenth Avenue was empty, and Craker reached 80 m.p.h., badly slowed thereafter in the narrow streets of La Sierra suburb on its hill. He avoided a procession with banners, dodged wandering drunks, slowed for frantic devotees carrying their saint from a church, and stopped for a road-block where they were questioned with agonizing slowness, and most meticulously searched.

They started off again, reaching the Remand Centre with five minutes to spare. The road seemed strangely empty.

'I wonder what's happened to the convoy?' Craker said. His instinct warned him that something had gone wrong. He changed down, and slowed to a crawl.

'What do you think we should do?' Frazer asked.

'I think I might risk a discreet enquiry. If anyone starts to show too much interest just wave your hands about and talk English to them.'

Craker pulled up a few yards ahead of the asylum's entrance, got out and walked back, imagining as he came closer to it that he caught a whiff of the sad, stale odour of decomposing lives. He had never quite accustomed himself to the way in which the Latins could overlook the presence of pain and grief – an indifference as characteristic of them as the curved nose of the Semite or the Mongol's slanted eye.

There was nobody about, not even the handful of harmless and continent imbeciles sometimes temporarily deported to the steps leading up to the building when a ward had to be cleaned and disinfected. A small courtyard with a spinney of slender columns supporting Moorish arches had been built by a long-vanished original millionaire to screen the main doors, and as Craker explored this shadowy area he noticed a movement behind one of the columns, and Prieto came into sight. There was something fugitive in his manner, and his expression was twisted and grimacing. Craker went to him, and Prieto, his jaw shivering, caught him by the sleeve.

'Carlos, whatever's the matter?'

'The van has already gone with the prisoners.'

'I don't understand. Gone where? Why? You told me to come at three. It's exactly three now.' Craker held up his wrist to show his watch. 'Three to the minute.'

Prieto wrung his hands. 'There's been a calamity. News came through that a rebel column was moving to cut the road to the coast at San José. The convoy was cancelled and the officer in charge of the van taking the prisoners from this place was ordered to leave immediately and to make a detour via San Antonio. They left an hour ago. There was no way of reaching you.'

Craker took two quick breaths. 'So that's the end. So there's nothing more to be done. The father and mother are out there in the car. How am I going to break it to them?'

'It's not only that, Pelham. There's something else I'm obliged to tell you. Extremely violent, unpleasant things can happen at a time like this, especially when there's been a breakdown in morale.' He faltered.

'What are you trying to tell me?'

'I think it is better to come clean, as they say. I questioned the Governor closely and he tells me that the orders to the guards were that any attempt on the part of the prisoners to mutiny was to be ruthlessly suppressed. Do you know what that means?'

'Yes, it means an invitation to murder.'

'Exactly that. It's left to the guards. They're not ordered to kill prisoners. They're ordered to suppress mutinies. The prison officer in charge knows what's expected of him. It's what happened last week.'

201

'Is there anything *at all* to be done now?'

'There's a one in a hundred chance,' Prieto said. 'Perhaps it's less than one in a hundred, but it still ought to be considered.' He glanced over his shoulder. There was an aperture like an old-fashioned post-office window in the wall behind them, close to the great steel-reinforced doors, and through this the gate-keeper watched them moodily over the rim of a coffee cup, from which he took slow sips. Prieto steered Craker with the slightest of gestures, as if directing a radio-controlled toy, back towards the top of the steps and the street.

'I've experienced a conversion,' he said in a conspiratorial whisper. 'That is to say, spiritually. I've seen the error of my ways and changed sides.'

'It's something I thought might happen,' Craker told him. They were out of all possible earshot of the man at the window. 'There are seventeen prisoners in that van,' Prieto said. 'Several of them are of great value to the rebel cause. What I'm thinking of is a rescue attempt. I believe it could be brought off.'

'By whom?'

'Naturally by the rebels.'

'It's three now,' Craker said. 'How long does it take to get to Batabanó for embarkation, even allowing for the roundabout route via San Antonio? Four hours? Certainly no more. The mutiny could happen in the next hour. It could have happened already.'

'It couldn't. It won't today. They can't get any further than Rincón this afternoon because the bridge over the Govea is under repair. The arrangements are that they're to be kept in the barracks at Rincón tonight. Whatever's planned will be for tomorrow morning on the road between Rincón and Melena. It's been chosen because it's completely deserted, so there's no fear of witnesses.'

'Why not tell me just what you have in mind, Carlos?'

'I've been informed of the exact route the van will follow, and it can be worked out roughly where it should be at any given time. What we have to discover is some way of getting this information to the rebels.'

'Exactly where are they?'

'They were reported to be on the point of entering San José about two hours ago.'

'In force?' Craker asked.

'A column of them, whatever that means. Numbers don't count in this war. Reputation's all that matters. You heard about the armoured train at Santa Clara surrendering to three men on bicycles?'

'I heard several versions of the story,' Craker said. 'The main thing is it surrendered. How many miles is San Antonio from Havana?'

'Say twenty.'

'And let's suppose a rescue attempt could be staged, how far is San Antonio across country from, say, Rincón?'

'Another twenty miles. It would be rough going. Most of it over cart tracks.'

'I wish I could go to them,' Craker said. 'And I say it most sincerely. But, I have to face the fact, I'm not so young as I was.'

'I'm sorry to say so, Pelham, but you wouldn't be any use if you did. Nor, I have to admit, would I. I'm too compromised, and they'd take you for a foreign spy in government pay. They'd see it as no more than a trick to lead them into a trap. For this we need to find someone who is acceptable to them.'

'Do you know of anyone, Carlos?'

'I don't know any rebel sympathizers. If ever I did, it was unwittingly. Nobody would ever have believed that a man in my position would hold the views I held.'

'There's a young American I got to know, lives down on the wharf,' Craker said. 'I've some reason to suspect he has the right connections for this kind of thing. I wonder. I wonder what the chances are . . .?'

Chapter Twelve

They discussed their predicament in the wilderness of the Presidente's deserted lounge, while Havana's defences crumbled. In the very moment when Andrew advanced a cautious optimism which Caryl swept firmly aside, the Cuban general's redoubt was breached, and soldiers rounded up for a do-or-die stand were quietly slipping away, to be seen no more. At precisely this time a body of urban police eager to surrender to any unfamiliar uniform gave themselves up to a bewildered municipal health inspector as he emerged from a drain. Sanger, sent by Hollingdale to reconnoitre along the coast road, had reached a holiday hotel three miles out of town, where he put through almost the last phone call to be made in Havana before all the lines went dead. 'It's incredible. I'm at the Delfin in Punta Blanca. A rebel column's just gone through. I was up on the balcony with the manager, and they were waving to us.'

'What did you do?'

'Waved back.'

'Without enthusiasm, I hope.'

In the lounge of the Presidente the grim rearguard action against despair continued. 'Of course it's a setback. Of course it's a disappointment,' Andrew Frazer said. 'These things never happen as planned. It was all too simple. Hard as it is to do so, we may have to resign ourselves to a day or two's enforced inactivity while the dust settles and things begin to sort themselves out. At least we know by past form that the first thing the rebels do when they take any town is throw open the prisons.'

Hope filled the room like a thin, badly laid smokescreen for fear, and Craker preferred not to dissipate it by revealing the true facts of the peril threatening their son.

204

'But there must be *something* we can do.' Caryl made little combative gestures. In a way Craker found her a stronger figure in this emergency than her husband – less prepared to comfort herself with the ensnaring belief that time and chance were on their side.

'Carlos Prieto's suggestion was that we should try to contact the rebels,' Craker said. 'I think it's a good one, and we ought to do so.'

'But how?' Andrew asked.

'Caryl – you remember young Carmichael, don't you?' Craker asked. 'The American boy who lives on the wharf. I've good reason to believe he has the right connections as far as we're concerned. Anyway there's nothing to be lost in seeing him and finding out if anything can be done.'

Craker knew that Caryl would want to be included in the mission, but he was ready with reasonable objections, and succeeded in putting her off. 'He's not an easy boy to talk to. Perhaps it might be better if I saw him by myself? Andrew might care to act as my chauffeur for once.'

They pulled up at the wharf gates, where Craker left Andrew Frazer, and went in alone. He found Jerry standing at the edge of a pier dangling a line in the water.

'Still here, Craker?'

'Why shouldn't I be? It's a very exciting time to be in Havana.'

'Ya mind not moving around? You're frightening the fish.'

'Sorry,' Craker said. 'I wanted to talk to you about poor old Dick. They're shipping him off down to the Island. I expect you know what that can mean?'

'Yeah, ending up in a ditch with a slug in your head.'

'Something you told me at our last meeting made me think you might have contacts with the rebels.'

A fish bumped the bait with its nose but refused to be tempted. 'Go on,' Jerry said.

'I hear they were in San José this morning.'

Jerry pulled in his line and began to change the bait. 'Why don't you tell me what you have in mind, Craker?'

'I'm looking for someone to go to San José with a message for the rebel commander there.'

'Someone meaning me.'

'Yes.'

'What's the message?'

'It's to tell them that seventeen prisoners have been moved out of the Remand Centre today to be taken to the Isle of Pines. The plan is to hold them overnight at Rincón, then stage a fake mutiny and massacre them somewhere along the road to Batabanó. Dick's on the convoy.'

'You think the rebels might try to spring them?'

'That's the idea. It would be quite an adventure, if you felt like taking it on.'

'Yes, it would, wouldn't it?'

'And it might save your friend's life.'

'That's something to think about.'

He pulled in his line again and began to wind it round a piece of cork. 'Do you have a half-hour to spare, Craker?' he asked.

'I've all the time in the world.'

'You come in that dream car of yours?'

'I left it at the gates.'

'Why don't we take a little ride together? See if something can be done?'

'Very good idea. Would we be going to San José?'

'No. The war has come a little nearer than that. We'll be going just across town.'

They walked together to the car. 'Dick's father will be with us,' Craker said. 'He just got in. He knows they're taking Dick to the Island, but he doesn't know what could happen before he gets there. Couldn't bring myself to tell him. Didn't see any point.'

'I get you,' Jerry said.

They reached the car. Jerry shook hands with Frazer and they got in.

Craker started up. 'Straight ahead,' Jerry said. 'All the way up the avenue, past the ministries. Make for the Cathedral.'

At the Calle Obrapia they turned left, passing immediately into the narrow streets and the tall, grey buildings of the old town. They nosed their way through secret alleyways shaded by roofs of trellised vines, and tiny squares compressed among the buildings. Half-completed barricades had been thrown up in the side-streets.

Jerry signalled to Craker to pull in. 'Better drive up on the sidewalk,' he said. 'Get as close as you can to the wall.'

Craker manœuvred the car into position, and they stopped.

'Kind of quiet, isn't it?' Jerry said.

'Where have all the people gone?' Frazer asked.

'A lot of them are down the cellars. A few of them went up on the roofs. When they see a cop they shoot him. You could call this rebel territory. You guys stay where you are. I'm going to have a word with a friend.'

Jerry got out and began to walk back. He turned into the first alleyway, walked on fifty yards, then turned again. He stopped outside the double gates of a firm advertising itself on its fascia board as car body-builders, opened a small door in the gate and went through into a nerve-shattering inferno of metal being hammered flat, riveted, and sawn, in the flicker and flare of welders at their work. At that moment a metal shell was being lowered on chains over a car chassis, watched by a bearded young man in a tartan shirt, who was smoking a 9-inch cigar.

Jerry went up and slapped the bearded man on the back, and the man turned and gave him a long, slow stare.

'Capitano,' Jerry said.

'Good day, my friend,' the Captain said. '*Qué hay*? Any noticias for me?'

'Nothing much,' Jerry said. 'Looks like everything is pretty quiet. That frigate just pulled out about a mile and dropped anchor again. A guy went out in a crab-boat. He said they were playing cards and listening to sweet music on a phonograph.'

'The sailors are tired of this war, too,' the Captain said. 'There were no SIM cars in the streets?'

'Not a trace of them. Those guys are all down their bunkers.'

'The people will revenge themselves very soon,' the Captain said.

Jerry noticed that he never smiled; he must have worn out his capacity for mirth.

'Were you able to get noticias about the Estado Mayor of the Marina of War?'

'I had success there, Capitano. We sent a blind guy to talk to them. We figured he could ask questions without anyone wanting to know why. One of the matelots told him they were running out of shells. They've called in their patrols. I guess they've had all they can take.'

'But their road-block is still there?'

'It's still there.'

'We are making an iron-clad that does not pass by these narrow streets. It must pass by the port.'

'My friends and I can take care of the block when the time comes.'

'And the boat to take our soldiers to La Cabaña?'

'It's all been fixed. An old smuggler friend is ready whenever you are. Be a nice change from smuggling in hogs.'

'All this is good noticias,' the Captain said. 'You have worked very much. What do you ask in return?'

'Well, there was one small matter you might be able to help out with.'

'What is that?'

'A buddy of mine is in the can. They put him with the Politicos, and the news is they're being shipped off to the Island.'

The Captain spat out the chewed end of his cigar. '*Puta!* Where from are they sent? How many is it?'

'Seventeen from the asylum – the Manicomio, no? They're all set up to be knocked off in the morning, somewhere along the road. There's a guy out there in the car from the British Embassy. They told him about it.'

'*Asesinados, todos*,' the Captain said.

'Sure, the lot. Some of these guys have seen some pretty bad things. They've had bad things done to them. The Batista pigs want to shut their mouths.'

'A crimen of war,' the Captain said. 'Very bad.

Horroroso. We must find some way to stop this, but how can we do? Where is these men?'

'Tonight they'll be in the can at Rincón.'

'Ah, if only we could go there to take them.'

'What's to stop you, Capitano?'

'We have a plan. Rincón is for four days more. Three days, minimo. For me, I would go now, but I have no order to do this.'

'Well then, you have to get an order, don't you? Besides my own buddy, how many of your own guys are going to get their asses shot off if you don't do something about this?'

'Is still a big problema.'

Jerry took out the silver bullet and put it in the rebel captain's hand. 'Know what this is?'

'Sure. Is one bala for suicidio. I have one also.' He looked more closely at the bullet. 'This belongs to Commandante Abel. Is engraved here.'

'Is he big enough to give you the order you need?'

'Oh yes. A Commandante is the highest grade in our army. Is OK for him to give any orders.'

'Commandante Abel gave me this bullet a coupla weeks back when he was still capitano. My friend and I helped him to get back after they pulled him out of the water with a hole in his neck and I guess it was the only way he could say thanks. Any way you can talk to him?'

'I don't know. First I have to find where is. Maybe is in San José. Maybe is in Matanzas. I will try.'

'How long will it take?'

'I don't know. We have radio communication with San José. If he has come there already it will be very quick.'

'A half-hour maybe?'

'Less.'

'What if he says it's all right to go to Rincón?'

'Then we go.'

'Right away?'

'Not right away, no. The iron-clad car is not yet prepared. In the moment of being prepared we can go. But there is much work to be done.'

'Capitano, I have a favour to ask. If there's any room in the car could I be included in this trip?'

'That, too, I must ask. But if permission is given there is room.'

Jerry went back to the car. 'I saw my friend,' he said.

'And what did he say?' Craker asked.

'What I hoped he'd say.'

'And they think they can do something?' Frazer said.

'He'll do what he can. That's about all I can tell you.'

'Does he think there's a possibility of bringing off a rescue?'

'Sorry, Frazer, I guess you know there's such a thing as security.'

'Of course. Of course. I understand. I'd like to have a hand in anything that might be proposed, should that be at all possible.'

'It's out of the question,' Jerry said. 'All you and Mr Craker can do, is take the train down to Rincón and wait. That's if you find anyone in the Gubernación to give you a pass. Get down there tonight and stay at the Comercio Hotel. He told me to say you'll be contacted. That's all he said.'

Chapter Thirteen

Three of the political prisoners Dick found himself with in the much larger and cleaner cell to which he was taken were serious-minded young men from a solid bourgeois background who had been spirited away from their homes, and brought here in the dead of the night. No charges had been made. They had simply disappeared, and they admitted to a sorrowful suspicion that their disappearance might prove final. The other two had been captured fighting with the rebels. One was an enormous Negro, who spoke English, having worked in a US army mess on the Guantánamo Base. The other was a young American romantic who had been attracted to the rebel cause. There was something a little strange about this young man; he was troubled by a spasmodic trembling of the chin and a twitching smile, sometimes followed by a quick spate of words that dried up suddenly like a trickle of water in a desert. His hands and arms were heavily bandaged.

Dick's five cell-mates accepted him with indifference. The Negro, who had assumed leadership, warned him to share in the cleaning-up, and to have no more truck with the warders than to answer as briefly as possible when spoken to. This man had a mania for hygiene and, apart from the American who could not use his arms, he kept the inmates of the cell incessantly at work scrubbing and scouring the walls and floor.

The American sat for hours on end nursing his damaged arms and moaning softly. He was believed by the other prisoners to have been subjected to torture, but this he indignantly denied. Dick learned that the knowledge that a man had been tortured lessened rather than increased him in the eyes of his fellows, who were convinced that he was certain to have been broken and changed by the experience.

'They gave the guy mazeppa,' the Negro told Dick. In speaking he displayed his empty gums and the rippling pink serration of scar-tissue where the teeth had once been, before they had been knocked out in the course of the interrogation.

He had explained that mazeppa was the traditional Cuban method of dealing with prisoners who were exceptionally stubborn in their refusal to talk. The victim was dragged by the wrists at high speed over an uneven surface, in the old days behind galloping horses, nowadays tied to the bumper of a car. Two minutes of this treatment meant the loss of the use of the arms for ever, and occasionally the hands were wrenched clean away. It was a torture, the Negro said, that no man ever born could withstand, and saying this, he looked accusingly in the

American's direction. He was enraged that the American should have to be assisted in the performance of his natural functions, a fatigue he assigned to the three Cuban civilian detainees, who did whatever they were obliged to do with ill-concealed disgust.

Dick got on well with the Negro and had no objection to carrying out the small tasks he assigned to him, but there was something about the American, in particular his over-friendliness, that made him nervous and suspicious.

When the Negro dozed off the American took Dick aside and held up the bandaged arms. 'Burns,' he said. 'They surrounded us in a barn and set fire to it. Don't pay any attention to what that black cocksucker says ... Listen, Bud, they're taking us to the Island tomorrow. I guess you know what that means?'

'Is it worse than this?' Dick asked.

'Worse than this? Are you kidding? All the hacks are psychos. You get up their nose and they make you drink piss out of some poor guy's skull.'

'Did you ever come across an American from Paris, Missouri, who was supposed to be fighting with the rebels?'

'No, why should I?'

'I wondered, that's all. A friend of mine used to know him.'

'Never knew anybody from Paris, Missouri. Ever heard of Plum Creek, Nebraska? That's where I was born and raised. Went to Plum Creek High.' His lower jaw began to shake, and the persuasive smile became a little crazed.

The Negro woke up. 'What's that man over there talking to you about, Limey? What's he telling you? Don't listen to that asshole. Nothing he's going to tell you's good for you to know.' He sniffed at the air and let out a furious bellow. 'Listen, you guys been farting again. How many times am I going to tell you to stop farting. You don't stop that farting and I'm sure going to tear the linings out of your boots and use them to plug your asses.'

The American shuffled closer, primed with confidences, and Dick smelt the prison rice and beans churning in stomach acids.

'They're going to pretend the van's broken down. Maybe it's bust a spring or a shock-absorber or something. One of the guys with us is a trained mechanic, worked in a service station. They're going to have to let him out to work on the car, and as soon as they unlock the door and open up the back that's our chance. This time we won't be padlocked up the way they usually do. The plan is to stop where there's cane growing on both sides of the road. All we do is run into the cane and we're OK.'

'What about the guards? We have guards with us, don't we?'

'They're OK. They won't shoot. It's all been fixed. These guys want to keep their noses clean for what's coming. They want to come out of this smelling like roses. They know if they knock anyone off, they're going to get whacked out themselves when the time comes. Revolutionary justice, man. You heard about the big wall in La Cabaña? I guess none of those guys want to finish up in the ditch they have up there.'

'How do you come to know all this?' Dick asked.

'One of the hacks is on our side. He tells me what the score is. The hack that brought you in. I know he hit you but that was to make it look right. He'll treat you like he was your twin brother from now on.'

This seemed possible to Dick. The warder had just brought him a solid helping of food which he had eaten ravenously.

'What about the Cuban fellows? Are they going to run for it, too?'

'They sure are. It's their only hope, man. They know what's waiting for them on the Isle of Pines.'

The American's chin began to tremble again, and he clamped his jaws together and thrust his bandaged hands under his armpits.

The Negro kept up with the news through a contact among the prisoners on remand he met every morning while slopping out in the latrine, and whom he rewarded with a daily cigarette.

Next morning he came back in a state of depression. He sat on the edge of Dick's bunk rocking his head from side to side. 'I got news you ain't going to like, kid,' he said. 'Guy back there just told me half our fellers got shot on the last convoy down to the Island. They made them run, then they shot them.'

'Do you believe him?' Dick asked.

'I have to. That's the way it is in this war.'

'I don't,' Dick said. 'One person says one thing, and another, another. All you hear is rumours. They make them up as they go along.'

'Aren't you afraid, boy?' the Negro asked.

'No, not really. Anyway, I don't think I am.'

'Even if we finally get there, you heard all about the Island?'

'I know what the American told me.'

'Didn't that make you scared any?'

'I think he wanted to make a sensation. It's probably not like that at all.'

'I wish I could feel the way you do, boy. You certainly got cojones. When's the last time you were afraid?'

'I was alone with a man in a wood at night,' Dick said. 'It's like something you dream, but I know I didn't dream it. I had to do everything this man told me. He got inside me and moved my arms and my legs.'

The Negro nodded his sympathy, and his absolute belief.

'Whenever I spoke, it wasn't me,' Dick said. 'It was this man speaking through my mouth. I couldn't get away. You've seen the way one of those ventriloquists has his doll sitting on his lap and makes him talk and act in any way he wants him to do. It was like that.'

'One of those houngan guys, was he? That was bad, son. You hear about those things.'

In the background the American began to moan. 'Listen, fellers, I need to shit. Will one of you guys help me to shit?'

'Shall I go and help him?' Dick asked.

'Go on with your story. Let him wait.'

'That's all there is to it,' Dick said. 'I got away somehow. He must have let me go.'

'He broke the spell,' the Negro said. 'Lucky for you he did, huh? You could have stayed that way. Some poor guys do all their lives.'

'After that I don't think I could be really afraid any more again. When I was in the other cell where I was before they brought me here two pansy warders got hold of me and got me on the bed, but I wasn't frightened, I was angry.'

'You were alone. You been alone too long, that's the trouble. We're together now. That's something.'

The American had begun his pleadings again, and the Negro jerked his head in his direction. 'OK,' he said, 'if you wanna go look after him.'

At about mid-morning on this day a young trainee warder asked for an interview with the Governor and told him that he had been offered a bribe to become a party to a plot by which an important political detainee was to be allowed to escape during the transfer of prisoners to the Isle of Pines. He believed there might even have been several prisoners involved. He implicated the senior officer in charge of the transfer, who indignantly repudiated the charge, but was none the less suspended from his duties by the Governor while investigations were made. The Governor sent for the papers of all the prisoners to be transferred, and immediately, and to his consternation, noted that he had not one but three important prisoners in his charge, a fact that the many distractions he had been exposed to in these days of crisis had caused him to overlook.

The names of the three important politicals on his list were prefixed by the letters DE, indicating their membership of the secret and powerful students' organization, the Directorio Estudantil, now in alliance with the rebellion. A red asterisk against each name meant that they were to have been held incommunicado, in maximum security. The Governor learned that they had been put in a cell with three other prisoners, and that no extra precautions of any kind had been taken. It was while he was gloomily pondering this matter that a telephone call came through from Security Headquarters informing him that the rebels were on the point of cutting the main road from Havana to Batabanó. The Governor then gave orders for the route to be changed, and for the prisoners to be got ready to leave without delay.

The Governor was a lazy man, subject in consequence both to guilt and panic, producing a gross inflation of whatever problem happened to be troubling him. He saw his career imperilled by three dangerous revolutionaries who had passed unnoticed through his hands, and who might even now, while they remained his responsibility, find some way of effecting their escape. His reaction was to telephone a friend of long standing who had just become Chief of Staff to the general who would take over as soon as it was announced that the President had gone.

This man, disturbed in conference with the General at a moment of some emergency, showed impatience at being requested to send an armoured vehicle to act as escort for a prison van transporting political prisoners, even when the Governor assured him that they were seventeen of the most important and dangerous political detainees in the country. Why not get rid of them? the Chief of Staff asked. Repercussions, the Governor told him, then confided that something could happen to ease the problem in the latter stages of the journey. Unfortunately the Chief of Staff had been for some time involved with the Governor's sister so, more to get rid of the man than anything else, he finally allowed himself to be persuaded to send a platoon of infantrymen in a truck.

All this happened at a time when a new strategy for the conduct and successful conclusion of the war was being devised almost every day, and the Governor chanced to have telephoned precisely at the moment when the General and his staff were discussing the latest of such plans. These men saw themselves as realists. Things were bad. Only the Province of Pinar del Rio and a quarter of that of Havana, constituting in all about one-eighth of the country's total area, remained firmly in Government hands, but agreement was reached on the feasibility of creating a redoubt here to be protected by a chain of strongpoints built from Havana to the south coast, at a point where the island was little more

216

than thirty miles across. The General pointed out once again that the rebel forces remained numerically small, that they had over-extended themselves and run out of fuel in their drive on San José de las Lajas, that they were without air cover, and that their armour consisted of no more than a handful of cannibalized tanks. The US adviser present assured the military men that the creation of a viable redoubt would find favour with his government. But, he said, there could be no more falling back, and no more mistakes.

He took the opportunity to tell them that what had been almost lost here was not so much the shooting war but the battle for men's minds. The rebels had created a legend that had to be broken at all costs. Something had to be done to put an end to the wild exploits, the outrageous coups, and the prestige they bred. Some way had to be found to eradicate the brand of defeatism which had permitted a certain ex-Argentine doctor to lead 148 men to the capture of a whole province; which had caused an armoured train to surrender to a man on a bicycle; and a mulatto singer and his friends, who fought with their guitars slung on their backs, to surround and cut off the town of Guantánamo. It was this kind of thing that fired the peasant imagination, and it must never be allowed to happen again.

The meeting broke up with guarded optimism and enthusiasm. As at Verdun and Madrid, the watchword at San José was to be, 'They shall not pass.' So far, and not an inch farther. The adviser, impressed by their resolution, promised helicopter gunships. It was decided there and then to carry out air attacks on any unidentified movement of men or vehicles into a ten-mile-wide strip of territory to the west of San José, joining the north and south coasts. There were no mountains here where the rebels could hide from the planes, no jungles, no swamps. In this free-fire zone, not a cow, not a dog could move unseen. Here the rebels would be confronted, brought to a halt, defeated and thrown back. The enemy had been contained at last, to the satisfaction of all. At least on paper.

*

At midday the prisoners were stripped and searched, given papers to sign acknowledging that their treatment while in prison had been exemplary, and then taken down to be loaded into the van. The prison van was a gift, said a plaque fixed to its side, to the people of Cuba from those of the United States, and it was powerful and impressive, with air-conditioning and interior fittings in stainless steel that might have been produced by a Swedish designer. The prisoners sat facing each other on comfortably padded benches, nine on one side and eight on the other. According to the regulations they should have been manacled to rings fixed to the body of the vehicle, but it seemed in the atmosphere of despondency and confusion that the precaution had been overlooked.

At the last minute the Negro, clutching his stomach suddenly in pretended anguish, asked and was given permission to go to the latrine. A guard should have been sent with him, but this regulation too was ignored, so he was able to recover from a sewer pipe a knife with a 3-inch blade he had made from a scrap of iron wrenched from a bedstead. This he hid in his boot.

The journey to Rincón, reached in less than two hours, passed off without incident. The prisoners were locked up for the rest of the day and the night in the punishment cells in the empty barracks. The Negro found himself alone with the American and took him by the throat. 'You been a good fighter in your time, Gringo, but I have to kill you. You got five minutes to live. They gave you mazeppa, din they?'

The American's eyes began to bulge. Pink stains spread into the whites as the blood vessels began to burst. The Negro released the pressure. 'Well, did they? You got four minutes to go.'

'Yes, they did,' the American said. He wept.

'And they told you you'd be sent back for a second treatment if you din sell us down the river, huh?'

'What difference did it make? They were going to knock you guys off whatever happened. The way I figured it, you had some chance if you made a run for it.'

'The hack in charge of this outfit said anything to you yet?'

'No.'

218

'Well, tell him if he does it's all set up. Just tell him that. What was it you told the boy they were planning to do? I want to hear it in your own words.'

'They were going to make it seem like they had trouble with the van. One of these guys is a mechanic. They'd say they needed his help, and open the doors to let him out.'

'And you were going to yell out, "OK, guys, this is it. Let's make a break for it." Am I right?'

'Yeah, I guess that's it.'

'The only real difference being you told him nobody was going to get shot, huh?'

'I don't think they would of. One or two maybe. All these screws want to do is pull out of this and get back home. They got their own lives.'

'Where exactly was this supposed to happen?'

'They never told me.'

'There was going to be a guy with a machine-gun behind a hedge or something, wasn't there?'

'I told you they didn't tell me. Why should they tell me things like that? Maybe that's the way it was going to be.'

'I ought to finish you off now,' the Negro said, 'but I figure it's going to be worse for you to stay alive.'

Work on the bridge outside the town was finished by six in the morning, and at six-thirty the prisoners were taken down to be locked in the van, and a start was made. They passed the last sizeable town, San Antonio de los Baños, once famous for its curative waters, and then rattled into flat country, with clearings here and there in marshy scrublands where cane and a few pineapples were planted and harvested by peasants from distant villages. The seventeen prisoners were seated as before, talking and joking in a dispirited way. Two guards armed with Thompson sub-machine-guns sat with the driver, and the senior prison officer in charge of the transfer squatted on a stool fitted at the rear of the van with his back to the door. He was the last-minute replacement for the officer who had been suspended from duty; a cruel, ambitious man with the face of a mild sort of dog, very

219

smartly turned out, his 9 mm. German pistol in a highly polished holster. Once again a regulation had been broken, because his proper place was in front with the others. No officer was allowed to travel with the prisoners unless they were properly shackled. But in this case there was a good reason for not shackling them, and he preferred not to ride in front as this was considered hostile country and he was afraid of his uniform attracting a sniper's bullet.

The Negro sat next to him and Dick sat next to the Negro. A little of the sun-washed landscape could be seen through an armoured glass window roughly a foot square in the back of the van. There was a similar window with a microphone set in the glass in the steel partition separating them from the driver's cabin. By craning his neck the Negro could just see the truck bouncing and rattling along behind them, with its twelve dejected-looking riflemen and one corporal, all of them either boys in their late teens or men in their forties, who were the best that could be spared from the real fighting for missions of this kind. The truck was the most decrepit Ford the Negro had ever seen.

Half an hour after they had left Rincón they stopped and the driver conferred with the Chief Officer through the partition. A radio message had just come through from HQ with the warning to all military units that an unidentified armoured vehicle had been spotted by a helicopter moving across country in a westerly direction near Durán, where it had used a railway bridge to cross a river. Durán was a village of no consequence hidden like a flea somewhere in the yellow hide of the cane country at least fifteen miles from their present position. The officer told the driver to record the message in his log, and to stay tuned in for further news of the intruder, if such it was.

Watching through the rear window, the Negro noted that the old Ford had fallen well back, and he estimated that two minutes passed before it came limping up, fizzing and popping, to pull in behind them. He decided on a plan of action.

They started off again, and he spoke slowly in English, certain that the officer did not understand, although he believed that at least one man in three of the prisoners would.

'Listen, you guys, we have about ten minutes to live unless I can jump this man. Start a fight up the front. Kick the American's teeth in or something. I'm going for the gun.'

For a moment there was no response, then there were shouts and screams with the American rolling on the floor with one of the civilian suspects on top of him, tearing at his mangled arms. The officer half got up, his hand dropping to his holster, and as he did so the Negro drew the knife hidden now in his sleeve, caught the officer by the wrist, spun him round and held the point of the knife to his neck. He pushed the point a quarter of an inch into the muscle and turned it, and the man screwed up his eyes and sucked his lips together, then let out a small groan.

The Negro snapped open the officer's holster flap, took out the pistol, and jammed the barrel into his side, choosing the small, soft corridor of flesh between ribs and hip. He pricked gently once more with the knife point, causing the officer to open his eyes wide in panic, and swivel them sideways without moving his head. '*Te voy a matar*,' the Negro whispered. 'Going to blow your head off.' He dodged behind the man, knife in one hand, prodding at the base of his skull with the pistol in the other, and hustled him to the front of the van.

He drove and manœuvred the officer to the microphone in the glass. '*Habla normalmente, pendejo de mierda*. Speak like you always do, cunt-hair. *Diles que vayan a toda velocidad*. Tell them to get this clunk going as fast as they can.'

The officer spoke into the microphone, and the driver turned his head sideways, to glance as if for confirmation at the terrified face he saw through the window. Then he pressed down the accelerator and the van began to pick up speed.

'*Más rapido*,' the Negro said. He jabbed in emphasis with the pistol into the conjunction of vertebrae and skull, and the officer gasped for breath, then passed on the order.

As the speedometer needle climbed past the 80 m.p.h. the

221

Negro called back to Dick. 'How about that truck back there, boy? We lost it yet?'

Dick looked out of the rear window. The red laterite road snaked away into a pall of dust, half enshrouding the small pink kernel that was the truck. 'It's quite a way back now.'

'A mile, huh?'

'Could be. Could be more.'

'Tell me when it's out of sight.'

The van lurching into a fast bend threw Dick off his balance. He fell across the bench, then picked himself up.

'Still there, is it?' the Negro called to him.

'Hard to say. You can't see anything much for the dust.'

'What sort of country we in now?'

'Cane-fields all the time. We just passed a windmill.'

The Negro had detected a slight movement in the prison officer that warned of a preparatory tensing of the muscles. Still holding the pistol, he brought up the elbow of the right arm to smash the man's face against the glass. A bubble of blood formed at each of his nostrils. '*Quando de la señal,*' the Negro said, '*dile que frene y pare en seco.* When I give the word, tell him to stop dead, OK? *Comprendes?*'

'*Comprendo,*' the officer said, the blood now beginning to drip from his moustache.

'You guys all ready? *Listos, muchachos?*' the Negro shouted to the prisoners. Then to the officer, '*En el momento de parar, diles que abran la puerta.* As soon as we stop, get the doors unlocked, or you're finished.' He called to Dick again. 'Any sign of that motherfucking truck?'

'None, it's gone.'

'Right then, here we go.'

'*Ahora,*' he told the officer. 'Now, you bastard.'

The officer poured a stream of orders into the microphone and the brakes went on, throwing the prisoners all over the van.

Both the officer and the Negro sprawled and recovered themselves. '*Rapido, o te mato,*' the Negro said. 'Tell them to move fast or I'll blow you apart.'

They heard the cabin door open, the rush of footsteps to the rear, then the metallic chuckle of the key in the complex lock. As the door swung open the guards behind it ducked for cover, but the prisoners hung back in terror.

'Get the hell out of this. Run for it. *Corren*,' the Negro was yelling. 'They can't shoot you. *No os pueden asesinar*. They know I'm going to cut this clown's head off his neck if anything goes wrong.' He drove the officer into a corner where he slumped down on the bench, while the Negro, lips edged with froth, slashed with his knife at the air a few inches from his face.

They were all through the door now, and the Negro backed away, keeping the prison officer covered with the pistol, then dropped to the ground and slammed the door. He edged round the back of the van and, seeing that the guards and the driver had taken refuge in the cabin, he levelled the pistol at the window, and fired a single shot. He turned, satisfying himself that all the prisoners had escaped into the cane, with the exception of Dick who still stood waving his arms and beckoning to him at the side of the road, and the American, who had made no attempt to get away.

'Run,' the Negro said. 'Get the fuck.'

The American shook his head, his jaw sagging and all his features loose in his face. He dodged round to the side of the van, throwing up his arms in surrender, but as he did so a bullet from the window brought him down. Dick was urging and imploring the Negro, who stood for a second, pistol in hand, his thoughts jumbled in the emergency, then alerted by the dry skid of locked wheels in the dust as the truck pulled up only fifty yards away and the soldiers began to jump down from its sides. He ran to the roadside to hustle Dick back out of sight, then dived after him into the cane.

They were at the bottom of a low hillock with a ruined windmill on the top. 'Let's get up there. See what there is to see,' the Negro said. The cane grew in dense clumps reaching twice their height. They squeezed their bodies through the narrow openings between the stems and fought and struggled their way up to the small cleared space round the mill.

They threw themselves down, breathless and panting

among the rank weeds that had grown where the cane had been cleared. 'Safe enough up here,' the Negro said. He laughed with relief. 'Never find us in this.' But an infantryman had spotted them in the two seconds in which they had been visible from the road as they reached the top, and he called excitedly to his corporal and pointed to the spot where they had been.

'What do we do now?' Dick asked. He lay back filling and emptying his lungs luxuriously, a little dizzy with the overwhelming delight of freedom regained.

'We stay here and wait. They got about a thousand miles of cane growing round here. Sometime those guys are going to get tired of hanging around, and they'll go away.'

'Did you see what happened to the American?'

'I saw what happened to him, and I knew it would happen.'

'I was sorry for him.'

'Yeah, he had a raw deal all the way through. It was better for him to go that way.'

'Quiet, isn't it?' Dick said.

'It sure is, too quiet for my liking. Don't hear anything cooking down there, do you? They're still around, though. Wonder what in hell is going on?'

'Do you think we could risk going down part of the way to take a look?'

'You wouldn't see anything. You can't see a foot in front of your face till you get to the road. What's the point? Just content yourself and stay where you are and wait. Christ, we've got all the time. They want to stick around and waste their time, let them.'

A sail torn from the mill had fallen close by. 'Ain't been no one here for quite a while,' the Negro said.

'No.'

'Did you hear anything just then?'

'I heard a bird,' Dick said.

'I heard a dog just now. Long way away. Not too many people in these parts.'

'Do you smell anything?' Dick asked.

'Like what?'

'I thought I smelt smoke.'

The Negro sniffed at the air. 'Yeah. I smell it too. I have to tell you something. I gotta hunch they set fire to the cane.'

'You mean they're going to try to smoke us out?'

'Roast us out is more like it. Listen, be quiet. Can you hear anything now?'

'I think I can hear a fire going on somewhere. Flames crackling.'

'Well, that's it,' the Negro said. 'It was to be expected. It's what they always do. If you go into the cane, they put a match to it. Lucky for us we're where we are. They've checked on the wind and lit the fire so it gets carried in our direction. The way they figure it we're going to have to make a run for it, and they'll be strung out in a line down there waiting for us when we do. What they don't know is we've found ourselves this little spot where the cane don't grow.'

The noise of the fire moving towards them strengthened as the sap trapped in the thick cane-stems boiled and the stems exploded, and the flames began to race through the sun-dried foliage across the top of the field. Swirling air-currents snatched up bunches of flaming leaves and dropped them at random to start new fires. Tendrils of blue smoke began to curl into the open space where Dick and the Negro crouched among the weeds, and ash floated down softly like great black moths about to settle.

'Listen, boy, what's your name?' the Negro asked.

'Dick.'

'Well, don't you worry, Dick, huh? Everything is going to be OK.'

'I know.'

'My name's Sansó. That's like Samson in English. Call me Samson if you want.'

'All right, Samson.'

'The Lord got us out of the prison. He got us as far as this. He's going to see us through.'

'I'm not worried. Not yet anyway.'

The fire came up through the cane leaping from clump to clump. The smoke thickened and the Negro began to cough. 'Know what you have to do, Dick? You have to take off

225

your shirt and you have to soak it in piss the way I'm going to do mine, and then you have to wrap it round your head, so as the smoke don't choke you. Go ahead and do that.'

Dick stripped off his shirt, bunching it in his hands before urinating on it.

'Get it soaked,' the Negro said. 'But don't use any more piss than you have to, because it's going to dry out fast and you're going to need all you got. Gimme a hand to fix this in position.'

Dick tied the Negro's shirt behind his head.

'You breathe all right through that, Dick?' The voice came muffled through the wet cotton.

'Just about. It's not easy.'

'That's the way it has to be if it's going to keep the smoke out. You don't feel like you got to cough any more, do you?'

'No, it's better now.'

'You gotta keep it wet, that's all. It's going to dry quickly in this heat.'

'It's not as hot as it was.'

'You're right. It's cooling off fast,' the Negro said.

He turned on his side to lift the corner of the shirt and study the frontier of blackened cane curving round them, seeing that the active fire had passed them on both sides and gone on down the slope of the hill. Smoke hung over them in gauzy, thinning clouds, with the sun breaking through. He pulled the wet shirt from his mouth and took a breath, this time without coughing, then drew his hand over his face to wipe away the ammonia-saturated grime. 'I guess we made it,' he said.

Dick sat up and unwrapped the shirt from his head. 'Out of the valley, huh?' the Negro said. 'We made it, Dick. We ain't neither of us going to burn after all. That's a cane fire, it burns and then it's finished. Those guys down there are sure going to think they fried our asses. Wonder how long they're going to stick around down there before they give up and go home?'

As he spoke they heard the crackle of firing from the direction of the road. A pause, two explosions, cries, more sporadic shots, then silence.

'Now what you suppose that could have been?' the Negro said.

'Maybe they caught some of the fellows we were with,' Dick said.

'And whacked them out, you mean? Maybe that's what happened, tied them up and tossed grenades at them. These are the things they do.'

'How long are we going to stay here?' Dick asked.

The Negro stood up to take cautious stock of their surroundings. He wrung out his shirt and put it on, looking down over a meadow of white ash, spiked with the blackened and still smouldering stumps where the densest growths of cane had resisted the inferno for a while. There was a view of a hundred yards of road with distant unrecognizable figures trotting along it.

He ducked down quickly, then squatted at Dick's side. 'We lost our cover. Too hot down there to make a move now, but as soon as this ash cools maybe we should take off.'

The Negro pressed the release catch on the pistol and slipped out the cartridge clip. 'Five more bullets,' he said. 'I got a feeling that any minute now those guys are going to start moving up here.'

Chapter Fourteen

Jerry went back to the backstreet workshop, as instructed, at four in the morning, the hour when, even in these turbulent times, the city snatched a little sleep. Work on the strange vehicle Jerry had seen in course of preparation was complete, and it waited, reminding him of a rhinoceros without its horn, with its hooded snout pointed close to the gates. In the twelve hours that had passed a form of turret had been added, which seemed absurdly high in proportion to the rest of the car, and its raised cover gave it the effect of an opened meat can.

The Captain spoke of the machine with a kind of mistrustful pride. 'There are troubles,' he said. 'Is hot. Is very slow. The weight is so great is only possible first and second gears. For propaganda is good. For moral-effect.' Jerry clambered through the only door, which snapped behind him like a steel trap. He sat cramped behind the Captain at the wheel with a small, bearded soldier wedged into an angle in the metal to his right, and a sort of infant's high chair, into which the machine-gunner was safety-belted, between them. The only light filtering into this iron cavern was through two narrow foot-long slits in the sides of the body, and the louvred visor replacing the windscreen of the original car. When the engine started Jerry felt as though he was seated over a metal box in which thousands of nails were being violently rattled.

They drove slowly, squeezing their way through the narrow streets down to the Avenida del Puerto, then turning in the direction of the Calzada Jesus del Monte which carried all the traffic to the south. The Naval authorities had left the last of their road-blocks manned, where the road was narrowed to a bottleneck by a dry dock running across the base of the piers along which the ocean-going liners tied up.

The operation at the road-block was a carefully timed one. A chain hanging from hooks on iron posts closed the road. A petty officer and an ordinary seaman, stupefied with boredom and sleep, lolled back in chairs at one end, while at the other a Marine Corps gunner squatted to smoke a clandestine cigar encircled by the sand-bagged enclosure for his machine-gun. Five minutes before the armoured car was due a pimp of some standing from the wharf came up into the lamplight with a bedraggled girl in tow and a proposition involving the barter of love for food. The two sailors allowed themselves to be enticed away into the shadows just as a staggering wino moving in from the other direction called the gunner's attention to the bottle he was carrying. The gunner took the bottle from him and raised it to his lips and the wino skipped behind him with a cosh made up from materials to hand – lead from the nets, cushioned in a thick cuttlefish sleeve. He then unhooked the chain, and within seconds the armoured car came rumbling up and passed through.

There were more manned blocks to be passed in the city's suburbs. The Captain used side roads to by-pass one, and bluffed his way with false papers through the second, but at the third a couple of shots were exchanged before the men at the barrier threw down their guns and decamped. 'Is a pity,' the Captain said. 'Now they will look for us for sure.'

It seemed prudent to leave the metalled road and to take to byways and cart-tracks linking the isolated settlements of the cane country. But in doing this they were slowed down by broken road surfaces, dust drifts, and mud around wells and springs. Off the main road the plain proved to be less flat than supposed. First gear was used as often as second and the average speed dropped from fifteen to eight miles an hour.

They stopped to allow the engine to cool as the sun rose. 'How much further, Capitano?' Jerry asked.

'Plenty, my friend. Too far. We don't make any speed.'

'We still going to Rincón?'

'We hope. If the road is better, we can get there. But now already the time is late.'

'We'll make it somehow, Capitano.'

'What sort of a man is your buddy? You go to so much molestia for him.'

'He's a guy that puts up with things. You fellers call it resignado.'

'To be resignado is good. A man should be alegre, too.'

'Cheerful, huh? Yeah, I guess he's cheerful too. This kid is supposed to be a bit crazy but he never lets it beat him. His attitude is, OK, maybe I'm a nut-case. If I am, I reckon all I can do is string along with the situation and hope for the best.'

'We call that filosófico,' the Captain said.

'That's why he's a good guy to have around.'

They started again with the rising sun lifting the small hills, the windmills and the few palm-thatched huts out of

229

the blue sea of the cane at dawn. The Captain rarely changed up into second, and at this speed the plain seemed to have stretched out and widened its horizons, and the cane-cutters' hamlets drew further and further apart. Once a man on a mule overtook them, hat raised, and went cantering past.

The track led to, and over the edge of, a river bank. The Captain got out to study the rutted slope leading down into the water, where the farm carts had passed. He came back shaking his head. 'No is possible. Is too heavy to climb.' He told Jerry that it would be out of the question now to make Rincón before the prisoners were taken from the barracks and the only hope was to intercept them on the road to Batabanó, where they were to embark.

They turned down a track following the river bank to a point where the railroad joining Havana with the towns of the south coast bridged the river, and they bumped and crashed over the sleepers to cross the bridge. There were anguished noises again from the engine, and they stopped on the railway tracks on the far side to allow it to cool once more.

It was a moment of enforced relaxation in the cool morning air after the roasting confinement in the armoured car. The Captain, a cornflower stuck in his teeth, was inspecting the tyres. The lanky machine-gunner, like a scoutmaster on a picnic, had settled with an improving book, and the other soldier, who was small and festooned with weapons of all kinds and full of laughter, amused himself skimming stones across the surface of the river.

The Captain was the first to become aware of the helicopter chugging across the sky. It made a wide, cautious circle of them, and the Captain waved it to go away, and it went. 'Now soon will come the planes,' the Captain said.

He had finished his inspection of the car, and then he squatted on his heels at Jerry's side. 'Americano, my friend,' he asked, 'what makes you live on the wharf?'

'It's a big house without walls,' Jerry told him. 'The other house I used to live in was too small. Where I am, I'm looking out of a window all the time.'

The Captain nodded his agreement. 'I have been living in

230

a house with a big window too, since I joined the rebels. The revolution is our window.'

'Isn't it going to be over soon, Capitano?'

'We think so. Yes.'

'I hope it stays the same for you when it is. I mean the house and the window.'

'I hope so, too.'

'How old are you, Capitano?'

'Twenty-one.'

'You seen a lot of battles?'

'Oh yes. Plenty. We won them all.'

'Why do you win all your battles?'

'Because of our beliefs.'

'What do you believe in – Changó?'

'The Negro comrades believe in Changó. The rest of us believe in Marx. I guess he's a Changó for the Whites. This something I must study, but I have no time now. I cannot answer with certainty.'

'Can he stop bullets too? Marx, I mean.'

'No, he does not stop them. We win all our battles because the enemy does not shoot straight. They see we stand there. We don't run away. So they lose confidence that they kill us. You will see now if the planes come what will happen.'

Three minutes later they heard the throb of the B 26 bomber's engines. It was coming towards them, flying low, following the railway line strung from town to town across the yellow emptiness of the cane, and it was the largest plane Jerry had ever seen.

The Captain gave the order '*En pie*! They must all stand up together,' he explained to Jerry. 'It is better if you stand, too, and don't move.'

They stood together across the railtrack a dozen paces from the armoured car and the plane came at them, its nose wavering a little, swinging from side to side like a hound following a scent. Then the engines speeded up and it began to climb, leaving a curdling black trail from its exhausts at the bottom of the sky.

'OK, Americano?' the Captain said.

'Sure.'

'Something to tell your friends on the wharf, no?'

'They don't listen to me as it is, Capitano.'

'That cabrón is scared already,' the Captain said. 'No one is shooting at him. For why does he make like this?'

The B 26 had begun to roll and change direction as if to avoid flak. It banked away steeply, turned in towards them again, then went into a shallow dive that brought it suddenly overhead. Jerry had thrown his head back to watch these manœuvres. He recorded the little black oblong of the opened bomb-bays in the plane's shining, shark-like belly, saw the speckle of sunlight of the falling bombs, then the racing shadow of the B 26 dragged across them as it banked again to go into a climb. The bombs burst close together in a cracking staccato that pounded his ear-drums, leaving tufts of smoke over the cane, the nearest fifty yards away. Jerry burst out laughing.

'Nothing,' the Captain said. 'Absolutamente nada.' His body had fallen limp.

The plane disappeared in the distance and the men walked back to the armoured car. They were full of jokes and horseplay.

'You like that experiencia, my friend?' the Captain asked Jerry.

'It was great.'

'You see, we do not fire a shot. We just stand still and frighten them. Do you want to join the rebels now?'

'I'll wait and see.'

'Come with us to Pinar del Rio. In four days, five days maximo, we shall be in Pinar del Rio and the war is over.'

'Let me think about that, Capitano. Just now I'll settle for Rincón.'

They stayed on the track beside the railway line to reach quite soon the village of San Felipe, empty at that time of activity, except for peasants engaged in the somnolent process of buying and selling pineapples. At this village the surfaced road started again, carrying them into the country of the low hills holding back the great coastal marsh. Here the going was good, and they had just rattled round a bend at their maximum fifteen m.p.h. when they came into the

232

smoke, saw the prison van, the American lying face downwards in the road, the burning hillside, and the soldiers strung out along the roadside with handkerchiefs tied across their faces.

Chapter Fifteen

For the rebels the brief encounter that followed was almost a matter of routine. Surprise had always been the weapon of the ill-armed, and the vision of the rebel flag flying over the crude, iron-plated machine that trundled towards them on this lonely road twenty miles behind the lines, left the Government soldiers paralysed with astonishment. Only the deeply compromised prison officials had no option but to fight, the last of them dying when hand grenades were bowled under the prison van, and it exploded in flames.

Shocked by the fate of those who had preferred to resist, the soldiers and their corporal gave in instantly, stacked their weapons in an orderly fashion, and lined up, hands on heads, without even waiting for the word of command.

The problem of locating the missing prisoners proved far from easy. With the exception of Dick and the Negro, the direction of their escape and that of the wind made it impossible for the fire to reach them. They had split up quickly, spread themselves out, and gone to earth, understanding that salvation lay in absolute silence and abstention from even the smallest movement. The Captain called to them over a sea of gently waving fronds, and they listened, suspicious of trickery, and crouched even lower in their hiding-places. A loud-hailer was produced and he shouted into it with all the persuasiveness he could muster, explaining in simple words and short sentences what had happened, and begging the men in hiding not to waste his time. Finally the most adventurous of them made a stealthy

233

approach to the road, took in the scene, exchanged embraces with their liberators and went back to call to the others that their ordeal was at an end.

An attempted contact with Dick and the Negro, whose approximate position was indicated by the corporal, proved dangerous as well as difficult. Flashes of intuition, in which the Negro always put his trust, assured him that the hunt was on again and the unintelligible bawlings of the loud-hailer only strengthened this fear. The Captain bawled himself hoarse, then gave up his attempts. Then Jerry and three ex-prisoners began climbing the hillside in the missing men's direction. Alerted by the crackle of their footsteps and the distant murmur of voices, the Negro dragged Dick into a scrub-lined hollow. The fire had gone raging through a corner of this, leaving a low silhouette of branches blackened against the sky. Through this they glimpsed a movement of faces and limbs.

The Negro levelled his pistol at the whiteness in the geometry of black branches and fired, and the mutter of voices fell silent, and the white flash of skin disappeared. He grabbed Dick's arm and they began to run towards a tonsure of cane spared by the fire round the scalp of a smoking hillock. A bearded man carrying a loud-hailer suddenly appeared in their path. The Negro pointed the pistol at his chest, then lowered it and the bearded man laughed. '*Vivan los Rebeldes*,' he said. Then the Negro laughed too, cursed filthily, and went to put his arms round the Captain's neck.

The three stumbled back down the hillside. Jerry was waiting as they came into sight. His mood swung between euphoria and shock. He had experienced the nerve-pounding excitement of the brief battle when soft-nosed bullets fired ineffectively from Thompson sub-machine-guns had pinged and whined off sheet steel like pebbles on thick ice. Then he had climbed out of the armoured car to confront the sight and odours of violent death.

He grabbed Dick by the arms. 'For Chrissake, Frazer, where the hell you been all the time? How are you, man?'

Dick sat down in the road. He looked up, then rubbed his inflamed eyes. 'I'm OK, Jerry. What are you doing here?'

234

'Looking for you, Frazer. What else d'ya think? I been waiting for you to show up every day down on that wharf. Finally figured I'd come and look for you.'

Dick coughed up black spittle. He cleaned his lips with his fingers. 'Didn't you hear what happened?'

'I heard some rumours, but I don't pay attention to them.'

'I went hunting with Mr Stilson. There was an accident. He got shot.'

'Don't say *you* shot him, Frazer. Nobody would of convinced me you could hit anything using a gun.'

'They tried me for murder, and put me in prison. There was a mistake and I got put in with the political prisoners.'

Jerry could feel the vibration of his nerves. He wanted someone to join him in a joke. He turned to the Negro who squatted, naked to the waist, little black rivers of sweat trickling down his ash-greyed torso. 'What do you think of this story, Compañero?'

'What am I supposed to think, Mister? This guy is a friend of mine. When he says something I listen with respect.'

'He's a friend of mine, too. He used to be famous for his imagination.'

The Negro nodded towards the burnt-out prison van. 'Me and your friend were in that dog-wagon over there together. I took the chief hack's gun off him and stuck it in his neck. That's why we're here.'

'Well, looks like he couldn't of been imagining things this time. I take it back, Frazer. And a guy got killed, huh? That was a pity. How did that happen?'

'One of the hacks shot him,' Samson said. 'He was too sick to make the break, but I guess after what they'd done to him they couldn't let him live.'

Jerry looked again in the direction of the body, lying face down a dozen yards away. The bandaged arms had been flung out, and each clenched fist held dust.

'What did they do to him?'

'They gave him mazeppa.'

'I never heard of that.'

'They tie you up by the wrists to a car and drag you around. It pulls your arms out of joint. This guy couldn't use

235

his hands any more, even to wipe his ass. American feller. He was with the rebels and they caught him.'

'An American feller you said?'

'Sure. American.'

Jerry left them, to walk towards the splayed-out corpse, approaching it slowly, stealthily almost, with a great misgiving growing within him. He stopped, and bent over this effigy bundled in prison rags, contemplating the arms wrapped in dirty bandages and a boot kicked off in a final convulsion. He could see no wound. The head was turned slightly to one side to show a grey, waxen ear, the projection of a cheekbone over a caved-in cheek, and a nose flattened and turned at the tip, by contact with a stone.

Jerry forced himself to squat on his heels for a closer examination of the features, seeming to him to be formed from some dry, lime-washed substance, or even the *papier-mâché* from which masks are made. He put out a finger to close the lid over an eyeball coated with dust, then drew it back. Getting up, he found his mouth full of water. He swallowed, then went back to the others.

'Something wrong?' the Negro asked.

'I used to know the guy,' Jerry said. 'Buddy of mine. We used to go around together all the time. He was a great person.'

'Sure he was a great person,' the Negro said. 'It was great for anyone to be with him. He was in the can with us. He was a hero. Lemme tell you this, it was a nice thing for anyone to know that guy.'

The Captain came back holding out a bottle of rum. He was looking curiously at Jerry. 'Carta de Oro,' he said. 'If Capitalism has one good thing to offer, why refuse it?'

Jerry took the bottle and passed it to the others. 'Their need is greater than mine, Capitano.'

'My friend,' the Capitano said, 'you have a great need at this moment, too.' He waited until Dick and the Negro had swallowed a mouthful each, then gave the bottle back to Jerry.

'There's a dead guy over there,' Jerry said. 'He used to be a buddy of mine. What's going to happen to him?'

236

'We shall take him with us, and then when we stop maybe for an hour or two we shall bury him.'

Jerry unfastened the chain on his neck and put the silver bullet in the Captain's hand. 'Do me a favour, Capitano. I'd like him to be wearing this when you put him away.'

'That is understood,' the Captain said. 'Now we go to Rincón. I think we shall bury him there.'

He took the bottle and went back to the armoured car and the ex-prisoners gathered round the truck saw the Negro and waved and called to him to join them.

Dick and Jerry were alone, and at last Dick could ask the one vital question. 'Did my father come?'

'He sure did, like you said he would, and I got great news for you. He's going to be waiting for you at El Rincón. This was all set up. It didn't go the way we were planning on, that's all.'

Dick had turned to stare him in the face, as a terrible doubt possessed him for an immeasurably short instant. Is this real, or did I create everything out of nothing? – Jerry with his pale eyes and his flaking skin, the Captain's loud-hailer and the enthusiastic spittle on his beard, the Negro's rumble of laughter as he ran to his friends, the stench of caramelized sugar in the cane, the black phlegm in his lungs, the flies twitching their wings on the blood? The instant passed, never he knew to be repeated. Something like a vane in his head turned to fair weather. He had been released, gone free for ever, as he had from the prison cell.

'What's the matter?' Jerry said. 'Say something, huh?'

Dick laughed, and he could not remember the last time he had laughed before. 'You took me by surprise,' he said.

'I went for a ride with your old man yesterday. Some driver, huh?'

'He's good at most things,' Dick said. 'Were my father and mother in the car together?'

Jerry lied. 'Not then, but I seen them other times. Know something? I have a hunch that whatever problems they had, they got over them.'

'What makes you think that?' Dick asked.

'The way they act.'

'How do they act?'

'Well, they laugh a lot when they're together.'

'And that's a good sign?'

'For me, yes. It sure is.'

'And you said only my father came down to El Rincón?'

'Your mother wanted to but she couldn't. They're not giving out travel passes to women these days.'

'That's good,' Dick said.

'Why do you say that?'

'Because I want to talk to my father alone. If my mother was there, we'd all have to be kind and affectionate to each other. We wouldn't say what we mean.'

'No, you wouldn't, and the times come when you hafta. Because you're not a kid any more, Frazer, are you? You've been in the slam in Havana, and after that, man, nobody's ever going to call you a kid again.'

The engines of the armoured car and the truck had been started, and someone was shouting to them.

'Well, I guess it's time to go,' Jerry said. 'Rincón, here we come.'

Chapter Sixteen

The train through Rincón to the unimportant towns of the south-west left in the late afternoon. Only one third-class carriage had been attached to the engine, and in this Craker and Andrew Frazer settled themselves on a splintered bench. They were the only travellers. It was very hot. The windows, which could not open, were decorated with finger patterns traced in the grime, and all the corners of the carriage were plugged with cobwebs in which hung the shells of flies that the spiders had sucked dry.

Frazer, still unaware of the plot to massacre the prisoners, was implacably optimistic. He spoke of the future as if all the problems, the hazards and the uncertainties of the present, were already resolved. 'I've been in two minds,' he told Craker, 'whether or not to stay on and see this through.'

Craker was genuinely puzzled. There were pockets of innocence in this worldly-wise and efficient man that came close to foolishness. 'What do you mean by that?'

'I hate to run out,' Frazer said. 'I'd have been much happier to settle things on a proper legal basis.'

'But with whom?'

'The competent authorities, as they say.'

'There aren't any,' Craker said.

'But there will be eventually.'

'Eventually, yes. In the meanwhile there's going to be a long period of chaos. Don't be fooled by the fact this train left on time. The country's falling apart. Prieto's advice was to get out as fast as you can. You'd be wise to take it.'

'I'd be happy to give an undertaking to return.'

'There's no one to give it to. Don't complicate things. Whoever takes over will have far too much on their plates to bother about you. They won't want to know.'

'Yes, I suppose you're right,' Frazer sighed.

'Provided all goes well we'll be back in the capital tomorrow. If there's a plane still going anywhere, take it. The thing is to get out.'

'Lucky they're both on my passport.'

'It is indeed.'

The guard, wearing an American-style uniform and a peaked hat had been watching them from a chair in which he sat at the far end of the compartment. He had already come to clip their tickets, and now he unwrapped a package of food. A moment later he got up and came swaying unsteadily down the carriage towards them. He held a hard-boiled egg in each hand, and bared his teeth invitingly. '*Gusta?*' he said.

'*Gracias*,' Craker said, rejecting the offer with a polite smile and a shake of the head. He looked away.

The guard did not propose to be put off so easily. He came closer, to stand with his legs planted well apart, ingratiating but stubborn. 'My name is Puertas Miguel,' he said. 'H-what iss your name, blease?'

'I'm Pelham Craker. This is my friend, Andrew Frazer.'

The man dropped the eggs in his pocket and bowed slightly. '*Encantado*,' he said. He continued to study them scrupulously with an unblinking gaze that moved from face to face. A cluster of houses appearing suddenly among the cane provided a distraction in the juddering, bouncing landscape.

'Mazorra,' Craker said. 'We're more than half way.'

'Making good time, eh?'

'Very good.'

The guard was still there, smiling as firmly as ever, his lips moving silently as if committing details of the encounter to his memory. 'You go to Rincón, no?'

'That's what it says on the ticket,' Craker said.

'H-where you stay?'

'At the hotel, whatever it is.'

'El Hotel Comercio. Is good.' The guard came a short step closer, and Craker could smell the rank cooking-oil in his sweat. 'How long you stay this blace?' he asked.

'That I couldn't tell you. It all depends on this business we have to do.'

'Business, ha! In Rincón is no business,' the guard said. 'In Rincón is only comer batatas, make babies and sleeb.' He cackled startlingly, like a caged myna, pinched away the slobber left by his laughter on his chin, and left them to go and sit in his chair again.

'Rum sort of fellow,' Andrew Frazer said.

'Notice the expensive-looking shoes he was wearing?'

'I did indeed. Bought on a salary of about three pounds a week.'

'Perhaps he's a government informer, or something like that. I've always understood they do pretty well.'

'Just about what he is.'

It was early evening, with the bats in the sky, when the train pulled into El Rincón and a carriage drawn by a ruined horse rattled them through the sad streets to the Comercio

240

Hotel. The crisis had provided the town with an opportunity to indulge a natural propensity for inertia, and many citizens had taken to their beds, regarding the rebellion, in so far as it affected them, as something like a mild influenza epidemic, to be slept off if possible.

The two men checked in at the hotel, then took a stroll before going to bed. There was nothing whatever to see, nothing to do, nothing even to drink, as the town's only bar had closed for the night. The barracks was at the end of the main street. It was surrounded by a mud wall of the kind seen in films about the Mexican frontier; the silhouette of a guard holding a machine-gun showed in a tower against the darkening sky.

It was a sight that seemed to have a quietening effect on Frazer, and he soon excused himself and went off to bed. Craker, feeling in need of exercise walked on, shortly finding himself in an otherwise deserted side-street following a man stumping along on short legs, whose gait, and whose shape – in so far as it could be made out in the gathering gloom – were strangely familiar. The man stopped at a door, hammered on it with his fist and was let in, and in the moment that the light shone on him, Craker caught a glimpse of his face.

Craker and Frazer were both up shortly after dawn, drinking coffee-substitute in the dining-room.

'Did you actually notice whether the train left after we got off last night?' Craker asked.

'It did. We were just over the crossing when they closed the gates.'

'Of course. I remember.'

'Why do you ask?'

'The guard didn't leave with it.'

'Really? How do you know?'

'After you went off last night, I saw him.'

'Funny,' Frazer said.

'It is, isn't it? Queer sort of individual, wasn't he?'

'What made him so interested in us, do you suppose?'

'Heaven only knows,' Craker said. 'Natural inquisitiveness. Sheer boredom, perhaps. It was the shoes I couldn't get over. The tatty uniform and the splendid shoes. As you say, he was probably an informer.'

They went out on to the porch, and sat there talking for a while in a desultory way before lapsing into a burdened silence, while the sunshine filled the monotonous street. They were there when the prison wagon and its escort left for Batabanó, although they did not see this happen, and had hardly shifted their positions when a sudden, mysterious animal intimation that all was lost, touched the gaolers left in the barracks, and they fled into the sheltering wilderness of the cane.

'The waiting's the worst of it,' Craker said.

'Yes, it is a bit of a strain.'

The guard's absence from the tower was not lost on the watchful eyes of El Rincón, and conclusions were drawn. People went running to assemble the members of the town band, and rebel flags that had been stuffed away in crevices in walls and holes in trees were quickly recovered and left ready to hand. Nowhere in the world did the bush-telephone function more perfectly than in Cuba, and by the time the armoured car and the truck carrying the released prisoners was seen on the town's outskirts, the band had already crashed into the opening bars of the Triumphal March from *Aïda* – the favourite musical composition of the outgoing dictator, played whenever an excuse offered itself.

The two men were outdistanced, thrust aside, trampled on almost, in the enthusiastic stampede that followed, and it was minutes before Frazer was able to reach his son, tightly corralled with the rest of the ex-prisoners among their ecstatic welcomers. There had been an agonizing, heart-pounding moment when he had been convinced that Dick was not there, and then in a swirl of faces and bodies he caught sight of him, and fought his way through to drag him away. He tore Dick free from the hands tugging at them, mouthing jubilantly in response to Jerry's and Craker's gesticulations directed at them from a background of trombones and flags. A strong tide of citizens flowing towards them had to be struggled against to reach the hotel. They went up to Andrew's room and hugged in silence, but

242

there was a whiff of unreality, of the unexpected, almost of alienation about their reunion.

Frazer reassured himself with the familiar landmarks in the geography of Dick's face, that was somehow changed. He remembered Dick's long absence at Stoneyfields and the gap between them that had closed instantly when he returned so that nothing had been altered. The gap was there again and he sensed that this time when it closed their relationship would be on a different level.

'What happened?'

'We made a run for it. The rebels came along and shot them up. The police, I mean. An American got killed. I think he was a spy.'

The maid came with water and he drank two pints. 'The food's on its way,' Frazer told him. Dick smiled, closed his eyes, and opened them again.

'After that you'd better go to bed for a bit. We can talk later.'

Dick nodded.

There was a prison smell in the room. Frazer opened the window on a brassy cackle of Verdi and a voice trumpeting into a loud-hailer. He turned back to Dick, feeling he had to explain. 'Nothing,' he said. 'A warning about acts of sabotage and private vengeance, that's all.'

Dick pulled himself into a sitting position on the bed. A moment before Frazer had been reminded by his disjointed posture of a Christ taken from the cross. 'How's Mum?' Dick asked suddenly.

'She's well. Very well, and very happy.'

Dick had pulled in an arm to prop himself more securely on an elbow. Frazer would have liked to sit at his side and support him but he was prevented by a kind of shyness from doing so.

'Dad, may I ask you a question?' Dick said.

'Of course you can. Anything you like. I don't think you should talk too much just now, though.'

'What made you go off and leave us the way you did?'

Frazer had made a rule to deal with awkward questions by

243

replying to them unhesitatingly. 'My job entails a good bit of travelling,' he said. 'Men must work, etcetera. And your mother took rather a liking to Cuba.'

'Did you and Mum quarrel?'

Frazer took a quick breath, realizing that this was a nettle that had to be grasped sooner or later. 'We didn't quarrel but we both felt we might be growing apart. This was a trial separation. It's something you've heard of, I'm sure.'

Dick nodded. 'I think it's a good idea,' he said. 'Were you in love with someone else?'

'I wasn't in love with anybody else, but it so happened that I met someone with whom I shared a number of interests.'

'More than you do with Mum?'

'Yes, but when I think about it the interests were very unimportant. They weren't the things that matter a great deal in anybody's life.'

'And what happened?'

'We both thought better of it.'

'It was a mistake?'

'Yes, it was.'

'So nobody could blame Mum if she made a mistake, too.'

'No, they couldn't. I suppose you're thinking about Juan Stilson. That was another of my errors of judgement. He probably thought I was leaving the road open to him. Perhaps your mother thought so, too. It was the last thing I intended.'

'I'm sure she did think that,' Dick said.

He had gathered himself together now, and appeared to have shaken off his fatigue.

'Stilson telephoned me in Singapore. He told me you'd chosen to stay in Cuba, and he said he wanted to adopt you as his son. At that point I nearly gave up. Then I got your letter, and I was on a plane in a couple of hours.'

'I shot him. You know that, Dad?'

'I've been given all the details of the accident.'

'He's dead but I can't believe he's dead.'

'Your mother told me about these feelings you had. What you have to accept is that however you feel now, it's something that will pass. As soon as we leave Cuba things will seem very different. Now listen, why don't we put off this kind of discussion? What I suggest is that I leave you to sleep for an hour or two. You'll feel a different boy.'

'Dad, I want to talk about it now. He put something into my head, and I can't stop thinking about him. When we were in the hotel after the accident I started clapping and I didn't know why, but Mum said it was because they were playing a song he used to sing on the radio.'

'It's been a dreadful ordeal, but it will pass. All you need is a change of scene.'

A footstep creaked in the passage outside, and Dick turned his head quickly. 'I sometimes feel he's standing outside the door,' he said, 'and at any minute the handle is going to turn and he'll come in.'

'Well now, Dick, let's try to consider this in a rational manner. Supposing he *was* there, and supposing he did come in, what harm could he do?'

Dick shook his head. 'I can't explain how I feel. Knowing him, I suppose he'd just laugh and say something like, "Well, here I am, Dick. Weren't you expecting me?"'

'This is nothing more than a bad dream,' Frazer said. 'And like all bad dreams it will fade. You'll think less and less about it until in the end you'll put it out of your mind altogether.'

'Where did they bury him?'

'They buried him in his family vault in the Campo Santo and the Bishop officiated. We could arrange for a special service for him if you wanted. It's called an exorcism. Something a lot of people do here when they're troubled with memories of the dead.'

'It wouldn't do any good,' Dick said firmly.

'Unfortunately, guilt feelings may enter into this. It's something to be talked out calmly and quietly in different surroundings.'

'Please no more head-shrinkers, Dad. I don't want to see any more head-shrinkers.'

'And you won't. From now on it's going to be the two of us. You and me. And your mother, of course. Head-shrinkers are out. We'll settle our problems in our own way.'

'What's that noise?' Dick asked. He was alert again, physically taut, as he had been at the sound of the footsteps outside the door.

Frazer listened. He had been hardly aware that the crowd noises had stopped, and the band had packed up and gone away. Through the window he heard a thin, shrill piping that sounded a long way off, a sound that was almost an ingredient of the heat. 'Probably a beggar playing some kind of pipe,' he said.

'It's weird,' Dick said.

'It's hardly music, I agree.'

He went to look down into the street, realizing that the town had suddenly emptied. The rebels had gone and the crowd had gone, and for a moment he had a feeling that this was more than an ordinary exodus, and that now they were in some way isolated, and menaced and vulnerable.

Frazer scanned the bleak sun-ridden spaces beneath, then a small movement took his eye, and with the tiniest sensation of relief he saw Craker and Jerry a little way down the road, pressed into the shadow of a doorway. He called and waved, and Craker called back, 'Can we come up?'

He gestured to them to wait, then went back into the room. 'Your friend Jerry's down there with Mr Craker,' he said. 'I think I'll just pop down for a moment or two for a little chat about our plans. You stay there, and have a snooze if you can. Be back in a couple of shakes.'

Jerry was fanning himself with a ragged hat, his eyes clenched against the light. His smile contained a matter-of-fact, unemphatic irony. Frazer realized suddenly that reputation had clothed him with a stamina and physique that were largely illusory. On this second meeting he seemed almost frail.

Frazer succeeded in detaching Craker. 'Do run up and talk to Dick for a moment,' he said. 'He's fine. Tired, as you'd expect. He'd love to see you.'

He took Jerry's elbow and steered him into a side-street.

'Sorry,' he said, 'but I'm quite incapable of telling you how I feel about all this.'

Jerry waved away his protestations. 'It was a good experience,' he said. 'I wanted to be there. Also we had a lotta luck. Why don't we leave it at that?'

'I want to ask you something in confidence.'

'Go right ahead.'

'Do you find Dick much affected by what he's been through?'

'He's bound to be, isn't he? What do you expect?'

'But would you say he's been damaged in any way? I've hardly been able to speak to him yet.'

'I'd say his viewpoint's been changed. He was down on the wharf and that changes your viewpoint. Being in the slam does too.'

'Inevitably.'

'Maybe it needed to be changed. In which case you can't call it damage, can you?'

'We all need a second opinion. Perhaps as a father I've been too involved, too close to him. I suppose you know he was ill?'

'I know he was ill, and I know he was in the nut-house, but I guess the waterfront did more for him than any nut-house did. It was a nice change for a while to live in a big place with no doors.'

Frazer felt rebuked. The knowledge of his shortcomings itched like an allergy. 'Thank you,' he said. 'You've told me what I wanted to hear.'

They turned back. 'What's come over this town?' Frazer asked.

'I was just wondering about that. Kinda quiet, isn't it?'

'Why is everybody off the streets? There must be some reason. Did you hear that warning they were giving about acts of vengeance and sabotage?'

'This is something that always happens,' Jerry said. 'I was down in Santiago when they tried to start a revolution. Guys were being knocked off all over the place because they'd been laying someone else's wife.'

'Hear that?' Frazer said. 'Somebody's out and about, anyway. Hear that piping?'

'That doesn't count,' Jerry said. 'What you can hear is a voodoo flute. This is just the time when these guys come out. When you hear anyone playing one of those you get inside and lock the door.'

'Why?'

'Because they used to go in for sacrificing people. They probably do now.'

'I don't believe that.'

'I'm only telling you what they say.'

'Don't the police do anything about it?'

'They wait till the police aren't around. All the police here took off.'

'Yes, I was forgetting.'

They turned back. The flute squealed thinly and was silent again. 'Seems to be coming from a different direction now,' Frazer said. 'I thought it was someone playing over in those gardens we just passed. Now it's moved behind us.'

'I guess it's the way they play the goddam thing. It could be anywhere.'

They turned right, then left, and then right again, and found themselves in the main street, with a hundred yards to walk to the hotel, its tiers of wooden balconies already in sight leaning over a parade of shuttered shops.

'Must have walked about a mile without sighting a single soul. Amazing,' Frazer said. As he spoke they heard the flute again, but the sound was closer to them, louder. Frazer glanced back over his shoulder, but could see nothing.

They crossed the road to the hotel. Frazer glanced at his watch. 'One o'clock coming up,' he said. 'We've got a good hour, even supposing the train's on time.' He turned the door-handle and pushed, but the door would not open, so he rapped with his knuckles, and then rang the bell twice. 'Look at this, for Christ's sake,' he heard Jerry say. 'Look at what's here.'

He swung round and saw the train guard in his threadbare uniform with its braided cuffs, his peaked hat and his gleaming shoes. He was walking towards them slowly, almost painfully, as if troubled by his feet. In his left hand he held a flute, slashing with it at the air to clear the spittle before pushing it into an inside pocket. He stopped. The tip of his tongue showed between his lips and moved from one corner of his mouth to the other as if to refurbish his smile.

'Juan Stilson sent me,' the man said.

Frazer felt an instant of vertigo. Jerry had drawn close to him and he put an arm round his shoulder.

The tongue travelled back again and was withdrawn, and the man took his right hand from his pocket.

Frazer cried out 'No,' but the warning of his instincts had come too late, and he moved too slowly to their defence, all his reactions clogged by astonishment. He saw the outstretched arm, the small metallic projection over the fist, and he heard a snapping report hardly louder than that of a cap pistol.

A dog howled; a high window had been opened, then immediately closed. Jerry was on the ground, and Frazer, kneeling at his side, saw the train guard in his squeaking shoes walk on. He got up to hammer on the door, then went back to cradle Jerry's head in his arm. He heard the flute again, a savage, senseless little air soon extinguished by distance. Craker came clattering down the wooden staircase. 'Oh my God. Oh my God.'

'Where's Dick?' Frazer asked him.

'Asleep.'

'Don't let him come down here. It was a killer. One of Stilson's people. The guard on the train. Help me to get him into the shade.'

They dragged Jerry as gently as they could into the doorway, leaving the smallest of dark smudges on the pavement. His head had rolled sideways dislodging the sun's small white reflections in his eyes, and his clenched right hand opened slowly.

'He can't be dead,' Craker said.

'He must be,' Frazer told him.

But why *must* he? he asked himself, realizing that as he had never been present at the precise moment of death and could interpret none of the signs, his conviction was purely intuitive and illogical.

Craker had rushed into the building calling purposelessly on unheeding ears for aid.

'There was something to pay,' Frazer whispered. 'I always knew there was still something to be paid.'